ASHLEY'S SHADOW

CHARLIE CARLSON

LUTHERS
NEW SMYRNA BEACH
FLORIDA

Cover photo features Anna Annette Summa, circa 1935

ISBN: 1-877633-75-5

Published by
LUTHERS
1009 North Dixie Freeway
New Smyrna Beach, FL 32168-6221

INTRODUCTION

The following story, with a few exceptions, is pure fiction. It is based on a real murder of a young girl that occurred many years ago and on a lingering ghost legend of a real place known as *Ashley's Restaurant* in Rockledge, Florida.

The legend is well-known in American ghost lore and has been featured in numerous publications and television documentaries. Ashley's is known for its poltergeist activity, like dishes flying off shelves, electrical phenomena, customers being touched or shoved by unseen hands, and even apparitions seen in the ladies' room mirror. There are many stories about *what* causes these unexplainable shenanigans, but only one story seems to have any historical basis.

Several years ago, I participated in a paranormal documentary, directed by filmmaker Ryan Lewis, chronicling this ghostly legend. It was Ryan who created the title for this book and inspired me to search out the historical facts behind the Ashley haunting. Like with all legends, this one claims a few supporting facts, in particular the 1934 murder of a young girl, named *Ethel Allen*. Allegedly, her spirit still haunts Ashley's restaurant. I wanted to know if Ethel had ever existed as a real person and if she had, in fact, been the victim of murder. My research of old records proved it all to be true. *Ethel Allen* was a real girl who was brutally murdered in 1934. Her mutilated, nude body was found in the Indian River.

Whether driven by unknown spiritual forces, or simply my own curiosity as a folklore historian, I became somewhat obsessed with creating a fictional account about this popular haunting tale. I even joined the Spookhunters.com organization on their investigation of the establishment just to see if their spirit-detecting equipment would find anything. The results were mixed and vague, and for me, certainly produced no great revelations about any spirits in the place. Still, there was something very weird about this restaurant, sometimes writers can sense a good story, and even ghosts. It was like I was being urged to write something. Therefore, this book is dedicated to *Ethel Allen,* perhaps it will give her a legacy to replace the life that was tragically taken from her so long ago. In the course of my research and writing, I would frequently visit Ethel's simple grave on Merritt Island. She became my inspiration to keep writing. I even gave Ashley's and the Ethel Allen case a major spot in my popular hardback, *Weird Florida.* [Barnes and Noble 2005].

There are some curious things about this book which I would like to share with readers. Actually this book began as a screenplay, co-written with Dot Diehl-Carlson, for a proposed video production project. However, back-to-back hurricanes in 2004 put an end to that venture forcing me to rewrite the screenplay as a novel. This was a blessing in disguise as I discovered new information which contributed more to the story. Throughout the twists and turns in this story you will find many subtle clues, but beware, a few of these have been deliberately planted to send you wandering off into the twilight zone. What appears one way may actually be the other way—after all this is a ghost story and the paranormal works in mysterious ways. When you finish reading this story you may even think this book is *supernatural—or spiritually possessed.* I make no claims to such business, but it *sounds good* in this introduction.

There are real places in this story, such as streets, towns, stores, and geographical landmarks, but the characters are fictional. Well, not totally, since some have been given names derived from my fans, friends, relatives, and in some cases, even my pets.

While this is a fictional account, you can visit Cocoa, Florida, the backdrop for this story, and imagine that you are in this story. Just don't forget to stop at the real Ashley's for a good meal and spirits. In the meantime, I will let you figure out what is *real* and what is *unreal* in *Ashley's Shadow.* Of course, I may know *something* that you don't know. If I do, then it's secretly built into the story. I will just say that some things are best left alone. I hope I have stirred your curiosity a little. Lastly, I've tried to leave a little room in this story so you can exercise your own imagination—*you'll certainly need it in the end.*

—Charlie Carlson

CHAPTER 1

Eau Gallie, Florida, 1934

He was a lanky fellow in his mid-thirties and some folks said he resembled a scarecrow. Pete Thomas never wore any socks with his worn-out brogans and usually had the right leg of his bib overalls rolled up so it wouldn't get caught in his bicycle chain. Like so many folks on Florida's east coast, he had been hit hard by the Great Depression which is why he took a job making orange crates at the packinghouse. It was piece work and a good day's pay meant only four bucks but his cracker upbringing compelled him to refuse any semblance of charity even with six young'uns to feed. He once said, "I'll pick shit with the chickens before I'll stoop to taking handouts." So, every morning at six o'clock, on his way to work, he peddled nine miles on the dusty, shell road running along the Indian River.

Pete was used to seeing buzzards fussing over a possum carcass on the roadside, but on this morning he noticed a peculiar stench in the air and a half-dozen of the feathered scavengers circling low over the river's edge. Curious as to what might be attracting the birds; he leaned his bicycle against a palmetto tree and walked a few yards to the riverbank where he saw what looked like a dead manatee washed-up in the edge of the water. A second glance told him it was the wrong color for a manatee. Sometimes a person doesn't want to believe their eyes, what Pete Thomas was looking at was a naked dead person! He resisted any urge, if there was one, to go near the bloating corpse. His eyes nervously searched up and down the shore for another person, living or dead, but saw no one. Capping his hand over his mouth he made a frantic dash for his bicycle. Never had he expected anything like this, he had only wanted to get to work, now the only thing on his mind was reporting a dead person.

The nearest telephone was three miles back up the road at the Horse Creek Sinclair filling station. Sweating and out of breath it was seven-thirty by the time he reached the station. Dropping his bicycle between the gasoline pumps, he ran inside and asked to use the phone so he could call the sheriff. An hour later two deputies showed up in a sedan and he climbed in the backseat to direct them to the body.

With beads of sweat running down his neck, Pete stood by the car as the two deputies went down the slope of the riverbank to examine the body. After a few minutes the chief deputy returned to get a sheet from the car trunk. He slammed the trunk lid shut and shook his head at Pete, "It's a broad and from the smell...I'd say she's a bit ripe."

"A *woman...good god!...* Did somebody kill her?"

"Can't say yet," he replied, spitting a stream of tobacco juice on the ground. "Sheriff Jacobs should be along any minute." He wiped his mouth with the back of his hand. After slipping on a pair of rubber boots he went back down to the other deputy and began rolling the body onto the sheet.

Keeping his distance, Pete stretched his neck like a crane trying to see what the two deputies were doing. His eyes shifted down the road to a fast approaching pickup truck with a white cloud of dust trailing behind. He called to the deputies, "I think the sheriff's comin'... "

Jake Jacobs was in his second term as sheriff of Brevard County and drove a pickup truck that had a big star hand-painted on the door. He was a big burley man of fifty-five who usually chewed on a cigar stub. He always wore khaki-colored pants matched with a long-sleeved shirt that had a big, brass star pinned on the pocket. Slung low on his right hip was a holster cradling a long, six-shooter resembling a small artillery piece. He never went anywhere in his pickup without Bubba riding shotgun. Bubba was the sheriff's big dog of indiscriminate breed, and although he was not a bloodhound, he had tracked down five escaped convicts after a hurricane blew the roof off the county jail. That achievement had earned ol' Bubba an official position in the sheriff's department and the right to veterinarian care and rations at taxpayers' expense.

As the sheriff pulled to a sliding halt behind the deputies' sedan, a cloud of dust enveloped both vehicles. Pete fanned the dust from his face as the truck door swung open and the sheriff stepped out. Beating the dust off his sleeve with his wide-brimmed hat, he glanced over at Pete leaning against the deputies' sedan and nodded good morning. He then hooked a long, leather leash to Bubba and started off toward the river but noticed the door standing open on deputies' car. With dog in tow, he turned around and walked to the car and slammed the door. He took the cigar stub from his mouth and yelled to the chief deputy, "Frank, y'all left the blame door standing wide open on your car...some fool's goin' to come barreling down the road and knock the damn thing off...then the county will give me holy hell about that!"

With Bubba tugging his leash and sniffing every bush, the sheriff headed down the bank to the water's edge where the deputies had partially wrapped the body in the sheet.

"Alright, now let's see what you boys got for me," said the sheriff, bending over the swollen corpse. He pulled back the wet, blood-stained sheet for a closer examination as old Bubba strained to get a good sniff of the remains. "Get yore goddamn nose out of here, Bubba!" scolded the sheriff. "*Sweet Jesus*, somebody really had a fit on this poor girl! There's at least a half-dozen stab wounds...here...there...over here's one to the back of the head...and her face is busted-in here on the side. She's got a bunch of teeth knocked-out...and here's this nylon stocking wrapped around her neck. Hellfire, she could've been killed from damn near any of these things." He stood up, looking past his chief deputy at the mile-wide river. Hooking one thumb in his belt, he asked, "Frank, where was she when y'all got here? Was she in the water or on the shore?"

"We fished her out of the edge of the water." The deputy pointed to the shoreline. "She was washin' around right yonder in the shallows, naked as the day she was born...probably been in the water a day or two. She's a white Caucasian female."

The sheriff slid his hat back, and with an exasperating sigh, said, "Good grief, Frank, for your information, Caucasian is *white*, otherwise she would be colored, Chinese or whatever...and any damn fool can plainly see she's a female!"

The other deputy, thinking the sheriff's chiding was a bit funny, was trying to restrain a laugh building up inside only to have it burst out of his mouth like a braying jackass.

Frank gave him a dirty look. "What th' hell are you snortin' about Newt, you can't even spell Caucasian."

The chief deputy was Frank Turner, and his relationship with Sheriff Jacobs was shaky at best. It was because Turner was a close friend of the county judge, J.C. Baxter, and if you believe the local gossip, it was Baxter's influence that got Turner the job as chief deputy. It was no secret that Turner had a history of shady dealings, mainly bootlegging moonshine whiskey, which had landed a couple of his former associates in the state penitentiary at Raiford.

"Did y'all see this?" the sheriff called attention to the dead girl's hand. "Look at this here ring on her finger."

"I saw that," said Frank. "It looks like a ruby don't it?"

"It *is* a ruby," said the sheriff. "It means this weren't no robbery 'cause they left her ring. This is a case of pure meanness. Frank, get down here and smell, and tell me what you smell."

"I smell it from here...she's as ripe as a dead hog in the sun."

"Frank, get your nose down here and smell," ordered the sheriff. "I ain't talking about the stench, there's another odor...smell it?"

Frank took a quick whiff, "Kerosene...smells like kerosene."

"It is kerosene," said the sheriff, taking a draw on his cigar. "Look there in the water where you found her---see those iridescent colors flickering there in the sunlight?"

"The what...?"

"Iridescent colors, those rainbow-looking colors floatin' there," the sheriff gestured with his cigar along the shoreline. "Oil does that, it's from kerosene that washed off her. It's all in her hair. It looks to me like somebody doused her with kerosene. Did y'all poke around the bushes for anything?"

"I only saw some tire tracks on the road but that could've been from anybody," answered the second deputy. His name was Newton Simmons. At twenty-four, Newt was the sheriff's youngest deputy. He was a passionate reader of a new comic strip about a detective called *Dick Tracy* and had his mind set on becoming a private eye.

"Me and Newt looked around but didn't find anything," added Frank. "We didn't even see a cigarette butt, matchbook, or anything, except those tire tracks."

"No pieces of clothing?"

"No sir...nothing, except that stocking around her neck."

Sheriff Jacobs rubbed his chin, allowing his eyes to roam the river's edge. "Well, whoever did this, did it some place else and hauled her out here at night and threw her in the river."

"That means the killer has a car," responded Newt, who had taken charge of ol' Bubba's leash while the sheriff surveyed the situation.

"That's pure genius, Newt," the sheriff grinned, sarcastically. "Now all we got to do is find somebody with a car. Pretty soon you'll be as smart as ol' Frank here."

"I say she was dumped from a boat," remarked Frank.

"Not likely," said the sheriff. "She would've been weighted down and would be at the bottom of the channel, or would've floated in with a rope tied to her, plus that kerosene would have washed off her instead of being there in the water."

"I think it was two people who dumped her," suggested Newt.

The sheriff removed his cigar and spit. "Why two people?"

"Well, first thing, it would've been too much for one man to carry her down that steep bank from the road unless he dragged her and there ain't no sign of drag marks, and her heels ain't skinned up either...if she was dragged her heels would be skinned up."

"Maybe...who knows?" replied the sheriff, watching a passing fishing boat going up river. He took a drag on his cigar, then turned to the two deputies, and casually said, "I thought y'all boys were goin' fishing with us the other night."

"I would've gone but I had something else to do," said Frank.

"My father-in-law came by for supper," said Newt, scratching a mosquito bite on his neck. "He stayed to listen to *Amos and Andy* on the radio. He ain't got his own radio but he sure does like that *Amos and Andy* show."

"You should've brung him fishing with us, we got a dozen flounder." The sheriff turned his eyes to Pete up on the road still leaning against the car. "Is that the feller who found the body?"

"Yes sir," answered Frank, "...he's the one who called us."

"Well, guess I'd better see what he's got to say." The sheriff took hold of Bubba's leash and started back up the slope to the road. He glanced back at his chief deputy, "Frank, y'all take the Kodak and get us some pictures of this area and them tire tracks up here."

"Will do, sheriff."

Bubba pulled ahead as the sheriff walked up the slope to the rear of the deputies' car where Pete was standing. "Howdy...I hear you found that body down there."

"Yes sir...I did, I was riding by...and there was a bunch of buzzards flying around over there. I figured something was dead but never 'spected it'd be a human being."

"You said you were riding by?"

"Yes sir...on my bicycle. I rode on up yonder to the Sinclair fillin' station where I called y'all...and then waited there for them boys down there so I could show them where she was and then we..."

The sheriff cut him short. "Got a name? You live around here?"

"Pete...Well, my name is really *Ralph*, Ralph Thomas, folks just calls me Pete. I work up yonder at Ledbetter's packinghouse."

"Jimmy Ledbetter's place, huh?" The sheriff turned toward the deputies who were struggling up the riverbank with the body wrapped in the wet pink-stained sheet. "Frank, I'm heading back to town, y'all go ahead and finish up. I'll send Ed out to pick her up so we can get a report." He was talking about Edwin Collins, the county coroner and owner of the Golden Palms Funeral Home and Monument Company, which, after the last hurricane, doubled temporarily as the county morgue.

Having no desire to hang around waiting for a ride, Pete tagged along behind the sheriff as he walked toward his truck. "Can I hitch a lift, sheriff, up yonder to the fillin' station so I can get my bicycle?"

The sheriff opened the door for ol' Bubba who promptly jumped in and took his place in the passenger seat. "You'll have to get in the back, only ol' Bubba is authorized in the front seat."

Pete climbed in the back, and with Bubba's head hanging out the window, Sheriff Jacobs gave a short honk on his horn then wheeled the truck around and vanished down the road in a cloud of dust.

Sheriff Jacobs already had a pretty good idea as to the dead girl's identity. Just two days earlier, Mrs. Kimmel, proprietor of a boarding house in Rockledge, had come into his office to report a missing person. The subject of the report was one of her renters, a young girl named Ethel Allen who worked at a local tavern. On the previous

Saturday, Miss Allen informed her landlady that she was moving back home to Wauchula and asked to leave her suitcase at the boarding house until she could pick it up later that night. She said her boyfriend was going to drive her to Wauchula. The landlady was concerned because Miss Allen had not returned for her belongings. On the following Monday, Mrs. Kimmel called the missing girl's sister in Wauchula only to find she had never arrived home and her whereabouts were unknown.

Initially Sheriff Jacobs had paid little attention to the report and figured it was a case of a girl eloping with her boyfriend. Now that he had a dead girl on his hands he decided to drive by the boarding house for a talk with Mrs. Kimmel.

The Kimmel boarding house was on Fourth Street, about two blocks from the river in a residential section of town. It was a white, two-story, Victorian-style structure with a rust-stained tin roof. A wide porch stretched across the front on which sat a half-dozen straight-back rockers and wicker chairs for the guests. Its elegance was worn with age, yet it was no flop house. The yard was shaded from the warm morning sun by two large magnolias and one lone palmetto tree and out front, a hand-painted sign advertised, "Rooms for Rent, Week or Month."

The sheriff parked his truck next to the curb and as he walked up the sidewalk to the house, he could hear music from a radio drifting from a second story window. Just before he reached the steps, an elderly lady opened the screen door and came out on the porch. He politely took off his hat and removed his cigar. "Morning, Mrs. Kimmel."

"Hello sheriff...if you're here about that girl, I still ain't seen hide nor hair of her...and her suitcase is still inside."

"Well, ma'am, I don't know where she is either, but if you don't mind I'd like to ask you a few more questions about her."

"I don't know what more I can say...other than I ain't seen her boyfriend either. That car I saw that night might have been his, but I ain't sure."

"What car would that be?" asked the sheriff, knowing she had not mentioned it in the missing person report.

"The one that woke me up at two o'clock in the morning…the night Ethel was supposed to get her suitcase." Noticing beads of sweat on the sheriff's brow, she asked, "Sheriff, would you like a glass of ice tea?"

"Yes ma'am, if it ain't no trouble, that sure would be nice. Then I'd like you to tell me more about that car you saw."

"It's no bother, pull up that chair and I'll be right back."

She went inside and the screen door slammed behind her. On the door a little cotton ball tied to a string bounced against the screen whenever the door was opened or closed. It was a homemade invention meant to scare flies from entering the house. The sheriff took a seat in a big wicker chair and began fanning himself with his wide brim hat. A scrawny, grey-striped tomcat began meowing around the chair. The cat, wanting for attention, jumped up into the sheriff's lap and curled up. The sheriff began scratching its neck.

Mrs. Kimmel came out of the door and handed the sheriff a tall glass of tea with a lemon wedge floating between two big pieces of cracked ice. "I see you've done made friends with Skitty…he can be a nuisance sometimes. I call him my fish cat."

The sheriff took a gulp of tea, "Ahhhh, that sure hits the spot." He sat his tea glass down. "Fish cat? How'd you come by that name?"

She sat down in a chair facing the sheriff. "He was a stray that was hanging 'round Futch's fish market. He'd been eating fish scraps for so long that he smelled just like fish. I wanted me a cat to keep the rats away, so I brought him home and he's been here ever since…but he ain't caught nary a rat yet."

"He's probably spoiled like my big 'ol dog," chuckled the sheriff, as he leaned forward on the arm of his chair and laid his cigar stub in a tin ashtray on the table. "Now tell me about that car you saw."

"Well, like I said, it was about two in the morning…the car was sittin' right there in the side driveway with the motor running. I think it was a Ford coupe. I heard a woman's voice and thought it was Ethel…sounded like she was arguing with two men…but I can't swear to that."

"But you can't say for sure if it was her boyfriend's car?"

"Naw…I really couldn't tell much about what they was fussing about either…I'm near 'bout seventy-two and don't hear too good…but one of them men said, 'Shut your yap,' and the other one said something but I couldn't tell what it was. Then I heard the woman holler, 'Get your mitts off me!' When I heard the commotion I got up and turned on the porch light and about that time the car backed out and took off like a scalded dog down the street toward the river." She pointed toward the Indian River, about two blocks away.

"I don't imagine you know her boyfriend's name, do you?"

"Oh yes, indeed, it was Bill Kelly. He'd been up here a few times…they sat right here on the porch. He seemed like a real decent fellow, I mean he was always dressed nicely and had manners."

"Did you say…Bill Kelly? Are you sure about his name?" The sheriff knew more than he was willing to reveal at the moment, and he had a good reason for keeping some things to himself.

"Oh yes, I'm certain it was his name…Bill Kelly."

"Did you ever hear him talk about where he worked?"

"I don't know where he worked, he never said anything about that with me, but he must have had a job because he had that roadster coupe. Would you like to see the suitcase she left here?"

"Yes ma'am, I sure would."

She went inside and a moment later returned with the suitcase held closed by a clothesline cord wrapped around it. She sat it on the little table in front of the sheriff and untied the cord. She opened it, "Looks like it's mostly clothes, stockings…here's a cigar box with some things in it." She handed it to the sheriff. "Here you might want to look in this."

He paused to look at the colorful Tampa Kings trademark on the lid and then flipped it open with his thumb. "Here's an envelope with a two-dollar bill inside, a pack of Lucky Strikes, some pay stubs, and a matchbook from Jack's Tavern…and a couple of pictures." He held the two photographs, and with careful scrutiny, studied them for a moment, then passed them to Mrs. Kimmel. "Is this Ethel Allen?"

"Yes it is…that's her, and the boy is Bill Kelly. These pictures were taken right out there in the front yard."

"I was afraid of this," sighed the sheriff, slowly shaking his head as if he could change the unpleasant fate of his inquiry. "We found a young white girl's body in the Indian River early this morning near Eau Gallie…I'm pretty sure it's Ethel Allen."

Mrs. Kimmel sat still for a minute, her hands holding the photographs to her bosom. "Oh, mercy! Oh my Lord...that's terrible news...I can't believe it. I just felt there was something wrong when she didn't come back for her belongings. Please tell me it was a drowning or something...and that she didn't meet with a vile deed."

"I wish it was a drowning 'cause it would make my job easier, but it seems she was murdered," he said, looking down at the cat rubbing against his shoes. "My chief deputy, Frank Turner, has been assigned to the case and we'll do what we can to catch the thug who did this." The sheriff stood up and prepared to leave. "I'll need to take her belongings down to the office for evidence." He reached down and retrieved his cigar stub from the ashtray and stuck it in the corner of his mouth. He cradled the suitcase under his big arm. "And you say you haven't seen her boyfriend since last Saturday?"

"Bill Kelly? No sir, not since she went missing. Now I'm not one for eavesdropping, but one evening when they were sitting there in the swing next to the window, I overheard her ask how much longer Scarlet Biddy was going to keep him busy. I figured she was talking about his boss. I thought it was an odd name 'cause it sounded like they were talking about a baby chicken."

"Scarlet Biddy?" The sheriff raised one eyebrow. "Hmmm, I'll make a note of it, it's probably somebody's nickname. I'd appreciate it if you would be kind enough not to say anything about what we've talked about, we wouldn't want to mess up the investigation."

"Oh, I understand. I just wish I could be more help," replied Mrs. Kimmel, getting up from her chair. "I'm certain her boyfriend had nothing to do with something this awful. They were like love birds and were going to get married in December. I just can't imagine him doing anything this hateful."

"Maybe you're right, of course you can't never tell about these things." Sheriff Jacobs put on his hat and politely tipped it, "Ma'am, I sure appreciate you taking time to talk with me." He started down the steps from the porch with the suitcase under his arm and casually glanced up at the midmorning sky, "We could sure use some rain."

"We sure could," agreed Mrs. Kimmel. Still stunned by the news, she stood at the head of the steps with one hand gripping the banister and watched as the sheriff walked to his truck.

Thus began the forgotten case of Ethel Allen, an unsolved murder of a young girl that would linger silently in the shadows of Brevard County for over a half a century. It was written off long ago as a cold case, unsolved, and stashed away among dead files to gather dust in a records depository. Over the years it had gradually faded from the memories of old timers until it was brought back to life in a local legend. Sometimes there's more truth in legends than we would like to believe. Sometimes these things are best left alone; however, this was one forgotten murder mystery that refused to die. In its own strange way, it was begging to be solved.

CHAPTER 2

Brevard County, Florida, 2005

The old shell road that once ran alongside the Indian River, where Ethel Allen's body was found back in 1934, was later hard-surfaced as part of today's U.S. Highway 1, known as the *Dixie Highway*. For decades this was the main tourist path down Florida's east coast, until Interstate 95 offered a faster route. Of course, with less tourist traffic, the once busy motels, roadside attractions, and souvenir shops along the *Dixie Highway* began fading into vacation history.

A few motorists with time to spare still prefer the old route as a pleasant alternative to the rat race on the interstate. This is why Brad Kirby was driving northbound on U.S.1 when his small, four-door compact drifted into the passing lane nearly colliding with another car. The other driver reacted with an angry blast of his horn prompting Brad to jerk his steering wheel to the safety of the outside lane. He felt like an idiot for his reckless driving and attempted to apologize to the other driver by giving a shrug and offering a stupid-looking smile. In response, the irate driver mouthed a few cuss words and gave him the one-finger salute.

The close-call could have been avoided had he not been trying to drive while dialing his cell phone and reading a number scratched on a folded business card. He was a little shaken, so for the moment, he tossed his cell phone into the passenger seat and let it ride.

Ironically, in July 1999, Brad Kirby had published a two-page article in a magazine about the dangers of using a cell phone while operating a vehicle. Back then, he was a freelance writer fresh out of college. It was the first time he had ever made any money with words, and for him it was proof he could earn a living as a reporter.

Two years later he went to work for Trans-International Publications of Miami. It sounded like a big outfit, but was actually a publisher of two weekly supermarket tabloids, *Real World News* and

Strange Review, and a more legitimate slick page monthly titled, *Dead End Magazine*. Having reported for all three publications, he favored *Dead End Magazine* because it involved genuine investigative journalism with the fringe benefit of an expense account. The magazine focused on unsolved murders, especially any that were over fifty years old. The publisher generously offered a five-thousand dollar incentive to any staff writer who actually helped solve a case. After five years of cranking out intriguing murder mysteries, the publisher's five-grand bonus was yet to be claimed.

Brad Kirby's trip up Florida's east coast had started with a copy of a tattered 1934 newspaper clipping sent to his editor by a loyal reader. Although it was a little faded, the headline boldly read:

"BODY OF LOCAL GIRL FOUND ON RIVERBANK."

The clipping detailed the gruesome, unsolved murder of Ethel Allen and described how her mutilated body had been found in the Indian River. Brad saw it as an opportunity to grab a quick story about an old murder. He figured it would be an easy job, just drive up the coast to Cocoa and get a copy of the original police report along with any old newspaper articles, then simply rearrange the whole works into a feature story for *Dead End Magazine*.

Having recovered his nerves following the near collision, he reached for his cell phone and punched in a number. He was calling the chief clerk of the central records repository in Brevard County. In a previous telephone conversation he had arranged with the clerk to copy the Ethel Allen file for him, provided it still existed. He kept one hand on the steering wheel and listened as the phone rang several times before someone answered.

"Central Records, Mrs. Davis speaking, may I help you?"

"Hello, Mrs. Davis, this is Brad Kirby calling again."

"Mr. Kirby," she said, in a slight Southern tone, "you're the one who wanted me to do that impossible search for a 1934 murder case...the Allen case file...right?

"Yes ma'am, that would be me, I was wondering if you found it?"

"Well, I'll tell you it was no easy task; however, by some stroke of luck, I located it and will make a copy for you. There's a fee of ten cents for each page but you'll have to come by and pick it up."

"That's great, thank you so much. Can you please tell me how to get to your office? I'm in my car about a half hour south of Cocoa."

After she explained directions to her office in a county annex building where outdated records and surplus property were stored, he thanked her and tossed his cell phone into the passenger seat among his litter of empty fast food containers. The interior of his car was testimony to his environmental philosophy. As he would explain, "It's better to litter the inside of your car than to throw trash on the highway and be fined for littering the roadside." Therefore, he usually drove around in a car full of trash and when anyone would ask about it, he would respond with, "I'm planning to clean it when I get around to it."

To know the real Brad Kirby, you'd have to overlook his trashy car and focus on his personal appearance and mannerisms. Believe it or not, both were next to perfection, especially his attire. In public he always wore a necktie and a dress shirt tucked neatly into pleated slacks secured with a belt matching his shoes. As a matter of fact, for a twenty-eight year old, he was a very conservative guy. Although, he would never admit to any shortcomings, he was a bit awkward with women, even though his hazel eyes, chiseled features, neatly styled dark, brown hair and South Florida tan made him quite desirable. He seldom dated and wasn't exactly the party type, unless, it involved an intellectual discussion in which he could force his opinion. Oh, yes, he could be very opinionated. There was an inside and outside to Brad Kirby's personality and he did a good job at keeping most people on the outside begging to look in. He liked it that way.

———

In 1882, Cocoa was called Indian River City until the U.S. Postal Service said the name was too long to fit on a postmark. Even historians aren't sure why the town was renamed Cocoa. One account claims the name came from a box of baker's cocoa and another has Captain R.C. May suggesting the town be named for the Coco palm. For the moment, Brad wasn't interested in Cocoa's history; he was more concerned with trying to find his way to the county records repository. After driving up and down several streets, he soon figured out that the main part of town was trapped between U.S. 1 and the

Indian River. Situated in the center was Cocoa Village, the original downtown area, with its quaint sidewalk cafes and enchanting little shops selling everything from incense and crystals to trendy fashions. Officially designated as a historic district, the village is popular with eclectic shoppers, tourists, and antique collectors.

Brad finally located the building he was looking for on Florida Avenue in an old renovated city warehouse. He wheeled into the parking lot where the only vacant space was a handicap spot. A blue sign warned of a two-hundred dollar fine for anyone not having a handicap sticker. He continued circling the lot hunting for an open parking place. In the far corner of the lot an elderly African-American woman, wearing a floppy hat, stood next to a trash dumpster. She was clad in a colorful, long, sack-like dress with a pair of well-worn jogging shoes on her feet. With one hand on a shopping cart laden with plastic bags of old clothes, she curiously peered over a pair of colored sunglasses at him, like she knew he was a stranger in town. As he circled past, he acknowledged her with a friendly smile. She nodded her head and went back to scavenging for anything suitable enough to qualify for placement in her overburdened cart.

After finally finding a parking place, Brad grabbed his briefcase, locked his car, and walked down the sidewalk to the entrance of the building. Inside the door he was greeted by a short, pot-gutted, security guard in charge of a walk-through scanner.

"Empty your pockets of all metal items," the guard ordered, straining to sound official. "Put everything in the tray and walk through the scanner to my left, I mean my right...uh, I mean your right."

Brad compiled with guard's instructions and after walking through the scanner retrieved his personal items from the tray and shoved them into his pockets. Realizing he was wearing a metal belt buckle, he asked, "Hey, that thing didn't sound off and look...I'm still wearing my belt buckle, isn't it supposed to detect metal?"

"That's okay," replied the guard, "just take off your belt and walk back through again."

Brad removed his belt and handed it to the guard, then walked through the scanner again. This time it sounded off with a loud ringing alarm. "It's my keys…coins and stuff in my pockets," he exclaimed, "I hope you won't be doing a strip search!"

"Oh, no sir," chuckled the pudgy guard as he returned Brad's belt. "I know your keys set off the alarm. I already saw them when you went through the first time so you're good to go…Homeland Security you know; we just can't be too careful these days."

"Oh, right! Terrorism…Homeland Security," responded Brad, perplexed by the dubious security procedure. "Good to see it's working. Keep up the good work, I feel safer already."

"Thank you sir, and you have a nice day, sir," beamed the guard, watching as Brad threaded his belt through the loops on his trousers.

Holding his briefcase under one arm, Brad buckled his belt and headed down the hall to a sign above the last door which read "Central Records Repository." He entered and immediately came in contact with a long service counter. On the other side of the room was a line of grey-colored file cabinets. He could see the back of a woman sitting in a desk chair busy sorting files in a drawer. She was unaware of his presence. On the counter was a cardboard sign hand-lettered with "Ring Bell for Service." He hit the chrome, dome-shaped bell with his hand but instead of ringing, there was a muted "thud." He picked it up, looked under it, and sat it back down and called out, "Excuse me! I'm looking for Mrs. Davis, the chief clerk."

The woman wheeled around in her chair and scooted across the floor to the counter, "That's me and would you be Mr. Kirby?"

"Yes ma'am, Brad Kirby." He held up the dome-shaped bell, and said, "I, ah, rang your bell but your dingy thing must be broke."

"Yes, I know, it doesn't work; we're supposed to get a new one. Now if I recall, you're writing a book or something, right?"

He opened his briefcase and handed her a complimentary issue of *Dead End Magazine*. "Here's one of our magazines for you. I do stories about cold case homicides, mainly any unsolved murder mystery over fifty years old."

"Oh, I see, you're a magazine writer…"

Tapping his forefinger on the glossy cover, he boasted, "I wrote this feature story, it's about an unsolved mass murder that happened in Louisiana in 1924."

"How gruesome...I suppose some folks like that kind of reading," she replied, putting the magazine aside and placing a thin manila folder in front of him. "This is all there is to the Allen file...I'm surprised we still have it. I think the only reason these records were kept is because of the sensational nature of the crime. It should have been put on microfilm."

Brad opened the folder. "Not much here, only a few sheets of paper." He was a little disappointed since it meant he would have to do extra work to put together a story, if there was one.

"That's all I could find," she apologized. "Brevard County didn't have many murders back in the thirties; mostly bootleggers shooting each other. However, according to the older people who remember the murder, it was a horrible crime that shocked the whole town. So, I don't understand why the file is so slim."

"I can see one reason," he remarked, holding a letter from the file. "The murder was only investigated for thirty days. The case was terminated by order of Judge J.C. Baxter. Apparently, at least according to this, he thought the sheriff was chasing a wild goose...and wasting taxpayers' money on a perpetrator who had escaped the state. Why would a judge close a murder investigation? I mean it is not like they had a lot of murders to investigate. Who was Judge Baxter?"

"I've seen Baxter's name a lot in old records," said Mrs. Davis. "He was the county judge in the thirties. He was probably the most influential man in town. His son was Sonny Baxter, a lawyer who was elected to the state senate in the forties. I don't know if he is still alive or not. The old judge has been dead for generations. His son was a notorious character in politics...you've heard of Senator Sonny Baxter, haven't you? He's mentioned in a few local history books."

"Sonny Baxter? No ma'am, never heard of him. I'm from Miami," he answered, as his eyes scanned down one of the papers. "It says on this page that according to Chief Deputy Frank Turner, the victim's fiancé was the prime suspect...a Bill Kelly, twenty-six of Cocoa, Florida. It looks to me like he got away with murder." He flipped to another page.

Mrs. Davis directed his attention to a particular paragraph on the page. "Read this, it says the dead girl's landlady identified the body and provided two photographs of the victim and her boyfriend."

"I see that," said Brad, reading down the form. "Here's a whole list of evidence...a ruby ring, a stocking top, a cigar box containing letters, a two-dollar bill, and two photographs...and Kodak pictures of the crime scene. Would these things still be stored someplace?"

"That's a good question," said Mrs. Davis. "I really doubt it, since it was such a long time ago, but I'll be glad to check for you."

"Yes please, I would appreciate that."

"It may take me a day or so because it would be stored in the abandoned property warehouse. Everything used to be in a central location now the county has annexes scattered from pillar to post," she complained. "You owe me fifty-cents for the copies."

Brad put two quarters on the counter and placed the folder in his briefcase, "I appreciate your help...and see what you can find out about the evidence. Can I ask one more favor? Can you tell me where a good motel is? Not an expensive one, just a decent one."

Mrs. Davis pushed the copy of *Dead End Magazine* across the counter to him, "Sure, if you'll autograph this article you wrote. I've never had a writer autograph anything."

"That makes us even," he smiled, "because no one has asked for my autograph before. Okay, so what motel can you recommend?"

"Try the Sea Rest Motel on U.S. 1, about four blocks from here. You can't miss it. It's next to the big water tank with the American flag on it...on the right, just past the intersection."

———————

The Sea Rest Motel was certainly no tourist resort by any means and in spite of what the name implied, it was at least fifteen miles from the sea. It was a one-story survivor from the days when U.S. 1 bustled with tourist traffic. The gaudy blue and pink-trimmed motel owed its present existence to truck drivers and guests like Brad Kirby, looking for a cheap, clean room with cable television. After checking in, he found a parking spot in front of his room. He glanced at the plastic tag on the key just to make sure it was the right room. The number "1" was missing from the door, but its unpainted imprint left no mistake that it was Room 17. A trail of rusty water from the air conditioning unit trickled across the sidewalk into the hot asphalt parking lot. The day had been hot and humid, and the hum of the AC was a welcomed sound of relief.

Clenching a sack of fast food from the Burger Delite between his teeth, he unloaded his luggage and laptop computer, and then unlocked the door. It was cool inside even though the room smelled like cut-rate room deodorizer. For thirty-five dollars a night it had the basic comforts which included a bed, nightstand, dresser, television, phone, two chairs, and a small round table by the window. On the wall at the foot of the bed was a big rectangular mirror. He paused to make a silly face in it, then dropped his belongings on the bed and clicked on the television. He pulled a cheeseburger and medium soda from the fast food sack and sat down at the table to eat.

He was intrigued by the 1934 case and bothered by the way it was quickly terminated. His instincts told him there could be a good story here, although it would not be found in the case file he was holding. He picked up the remote control and began flipping through the channels on the television trying to decide whether or not to call his editor and ask for more time to research the story. He picked up the phone on the nightstand, then he put it down. He glanced at the TV, then picked up his cell phone and dialed it.

His boss answered, "Trans-International Publishing, editor."

"Hey Boss, Brad here, I may have a rather bizarre case."

"Oh, is that right? You're talking about the murder mentioned in that old clipping some reader sent to us?" his editor recalled.

"Yeah, that's the one. Remember, I called the clerk and she was to make me a copy of the old file?" he said, wiping his mouth between bites of his cheeseburger.

"Yeah, that's what you went up there for. So what's the deal?"

Brad was momentarily distracted by bikini-clad girls playing beach volley ball on television. "Well, I can't rightly put my finger on it...but, I see something odd about this case..."

"Okay, I don't have all day, tell me *what* you see?"

"Girls! Uh, ah, the *girl*, I mean the *dead girl*," he leaned closer to the television. "I mean there's not much in the file and on top of that, the whole investigation was stopped by a judge before it got off the ground. Basically, the whole murder was never investigated and that's why it was never solved. It seems very curious to me."

"That's a bit strange," agreed his editor. "So, what do you want to do? I don't want you up there in Cocoa wasting time and money if there's no story. There are other things you can be working on."

"I think I may have something here but I'll need time to look into it. Can you give me a week and let me see what I can dig up? I can hit the old newspaper files, maybe track down some people, or something. We may have a major feature with this one."

"Okay…you got a week to produce. Don't waste it."

"Thanks boss, I'll try to make it quick."

"…*And Kirby*…one more thing."

"What's that, boss?"

"The next time you call me, turn the damn TV off. Bye."

Brad held the phone out and gaped at it, "Well…bye to you too."

He planned to start his research by browsing the old newspaper files for an account of the murder. He grabbed the phone directory and began thumbing through the yellow pages searching for local newspapers. He ran his finger down the page through several newspapers but found only one listed for Cocoa. He looked at his watch. It was pushing five o'clock, but maybe someone would still be in the office. He dialed the number and waited for an answer.

"*Sun Coast Observer*, circulation department, this is Jan."

"Oh, good, you're still open…uh, can you tell me if you still have your old newspapers on file…like on microfilm or something?"

"Yes, but this is circulation, you'll have to call in the morning and ask for Matt. What year are you looking for?"

"1934, I'm looking for an article about a crime."

"Oh…that's before our time. The *Sun Coast Observer* didn't begin publication until 1955. You'll need the *Brevard Tribune*."

He pulled his ballpoint pen from his shirt pocket and prepared to jot down the number, "Do you have their number? I didn't see them listed in the phone book."

"That's because they went out of business in the forties…I think it was forty-seven. The county library should have most of their old papers on microfilm."

"Thanks, you've been a big help." He put down the phone and sat at the table. He flipped open the folder and shuffled through his copies of the case file to see if he had missed some tiny tidbit.

He began jotting down a few facts about the case on a legal pad. A ruby ring was found on the victim's finger, and her fiancé, Bill Kelly, was the only suspect and he disappeared at the time of her murder. Did he really kill her? Did he freak out in some kind of jealous rage? What happened to Kelly? He was still puzzled by the abrupt termination of the investigation. Something didn't add up.

As he shuffled through the report, he realized that at the time of her horrible demise, the victim was not much younger than him. Had she lived, she would be ninety years old. Yet the image in his mind was of a beautiful young girl and not someone old enough to be his great-grandmother. It had been a long day and his mind was getting tired. He laid his pencil on the writing pad and pushed it aside, then settled back and began clicking through the channels for something on television.

CHAPTER 3

The county library was only five blocks from the Sea Rest Motel at the intersection of Mulberry and Forrest avenues, not far from the downtown historic district. It had a reference room with several shelves of business directories, books pertaining to local demographics, history, maps and genealogy. What was not on the shelf could be found in the library's extensive microfilm collection which included almost every Florida census and several reels of defunct newspapers.

Brad was seated at a microfilm screen busy searching through a roll of film for old newspaper articles about the 1934 murder. On the far side of the room a man was studying a navigation map on the wall while a girl worked diligently on research at one of two long work tables. The reference librarian walked by and handed her a spiral bound book. "Have you seen this new census index for Florida?" She then crossed the room and placed two small microfilm reels next to Brad. "These are the *Brevard Tribune* rolls for 1933 if you'd like to look at them. Have you found anything yet?"

He momentarily turned away from the screen, "Thanks, and yes I found this article from 1934. It says the victim was employed at Jack's Tavern. Where was that?"

The librarian stooped to read the article, "Jack's? Oh, that was in Rockledge...on U.S. 1. It went out of business years ago...in the forties, I think. It had a bunch of names. It's called Ashley's now."

Brad pushed his chair back a little, "So, it was Jack's in thirty-four up to the forties...and then other names, Ashley's or whatever?"

"As far as I know, I just know Jack's was the same place as Ashley's." She gestured toward the girl at the table. "Erin over there can tell you more about Ashley's...she works there."

He glanced across the room as the girl looked up from her papers. "What was that *about* Ashley's?" she said, closing a book.

"Tell this gentleman about Ashley's," said the librarian, loading a cart with books. "He's working on a magazine thing about an old murder." She pushed the cart to the end of the room and began returning books to their proper places on the shelves.

The girl gathered her things and moved around the work table toward Brad. She wore a long sleeved white shirt with the cuffs turned back at the wrist and tucked neatly into a pair of tight jeans emphasizing her shapely figure. She was a little curious at what he was looking at on the microfilm screen. Although he would never admit it, Brad had an eye for good-looking girls, but not the bossy kind. Trying not to be distracted from his work, he quickly sized her up, early twenties, sexy, fair complexion, cat-like green eyes, and auburn hair which fell in soft waves down the sides of a pert face. Very nice, he thought, although a little too much of a tomboy type, which he equated to being bossy. "I hear you work at Ashley's," he said, slowly cranking the film reel and keeping his eye on the pages as they went past on the screen. "Then I guess it's still in business?" He stopped turning the crank, turned, and looked at her.

"It was still in business when I got off work last night," she replied with an impish smile. She leaned one hip on the table next to him. "Why, are you looking for information about it?"

He shifted his attention back to the screen. "I don't suppose anybody has ever mentioned a girl named Ethel Allen, she worked there in the thirties when the place was called Jack's Tavern?"

He was surprised when the girl answered, "Ethel...sure who hasn't heard of her...what kind of story you are doing?"

"I'm a writer...for *Dead End Magazine*. So you know about the girl named Ethel?

"Oh cool...a paranormal magazine," she replied. "So that's why you're looking for Ethel...you're doing a ghost story."

"Ghost story...*not hardly*," he laughed. "*Dead End Magazine* is about cold case homicides, unsolved cases from the past...I don't get into ghosts and goblins, that's for wacko types. There's no such thing as spooks." He grinned and continued studying the screen.

"Don't bet on it," she responded, sitting her books on the table. "Wacko types? I beg your pardon. I know a lot of people at work who would disagree with your closed-minded thinking."

"What do you mean they'd disagree?" He was silently thinking to himself, oh great, another wacko female in tune with the spirit world.

"That girl you're researching, Ethel, she still haunts Ashley's." She opened one of her library books and held it out so he could read it. "See here...Ashley's Tavern, there's her name, Ethel Allen. Ashley's has been in all kinds of books about haunted places. You mean you've never heard of Ashley's? Where are you from?

"Miami," he said, shifting around to look at the book she was holding. "Oh god, don't tell me you really believe in that stuff. It's a ghost story...it sells books to wacko people."

"Wacko people!" She slammed the book shut and put her hands on her hips. "I'll have you know it takes a wacko to write books about old murders. But, you don't hear me saying that murders are not real." There was a very soft Southern drawl in her voice.

"Well, this murder is real." He directed her eyes to the microfilm screen. "Here's your real Ethel in this 1934 newspaper article. Her body was found in the Indian River dumped there by her boyfriend." He began reading an excerpt, "Bill Kelly, her fiancé, is suspected as the killer and has not been seen since last Saturday night." Brad caught a faint hint of perfume as she leaned in close to look at the screen. "Has Ethel's ghost told you what happened to him?" He gave a slight snicker.

She drew back, folding her arms across her chest, "Of course not...but what if she came back to tell us about him or why he killed her. I guess you know she was killed in Ashley's storeroom."

"Give me a break!" He was getting a little perturbed. "There's nothing about her being killed there. I've read all the reports; the law never even investigated the killing. Nobody knows where she was murdered so how can you believe some nonsense about her being murdered at Jack's...or Ashley's...or *whatever* it's called?"

"It still doesn't mean she's not the ghost at Ashley's," she argued, picking up her books and holding them against her chest.

He turned completely around to face her. "So, let me guess, you're in here researching ghosts, right?"

"No, if it's any of your business, I was working on my genealogy. I was looking at the 1880 census index."

He turned back to the microfilm machine and started rewinding the reel, and in a sarcastic manner, with a laugh, said, "Find any skeletons in your closet?"

"Maybe...but since you're so smart why don't you check out Ashley's tonight just in case it was the scene of that crime? I dare you to come there tonight. Who knows, you might get lucky and see Ethel's ghost and she might solve your stupid old crime. Even if you don't see her spirit we've got plenty of other spirits to choose from."

"I guess they have names too?"

"Does who have names?"

"The other spirits at Ashley's."

"Of course they have names," she quipped. "Tom Collins, Johnnie Walker, Jack Daniels...and Bud Wiser."

"Oh, aren't you smart. Okay, touché, you got me," he smiled. "But really, I've got some things to do tonight."

"Like what? I thought you were serious about that story you're working on and Ashley's used to be Jack's where that girl worked."

"I appreciate the invitation but really, I need to go by the court records place then get back to my motel so I can sort out all the stuff I found today otherwise my editor will be on my case."

"Yeah, and call out for a greasy pizza and stay cooped-up working until you fall asleep. You need to rest your eyes, looking at microfilm all day isn't good for them." She struck a sassy pose and waited for him to respond.

"What'd you say your name was?" he asked.

"Me?...Erin."

"Erin what...?"

"Albright...Erin Albright. It's my Albright family genealogy that I'm researching," she explained. "Who are you?"

He stood up stretching and offered his hand. "Brad Kirby...a future Pulitzer Prize winning journalist."

She lightly shook his hand. "Yeah, dream on Mr. Smarty Britches. So come check out Ashley's tonight." She glanced at her watch. "Oops, I'm late again...I gotta run. Hey, I'll be looking for you at Ashley's tonight!"

"Maybe, but don't hold your breath...later." He watched as she strolled out of the research room toward the checkout desk. With a flick of her fingers she waved bye over her shoulder. For the first time he noticed her long painted nails and wondered if they were real.

———————

It was late afternoon and still warm outside when Brad left the library. He looked at his watch; he still had enough time to drop by the records repository before going to the motel. Maybe Mrs. Davis had found the old evidence box with the photographs then he could put a face on Ethel Allen. He could use a picture of the victim for his article too. As he drove the few blocks to the county annex, he wondered how close Ethel would match the image conjured up in his mind. Gawd, he thought, it would be really weird if she looked like the picture in his mind…that would be, like, psychic stuff. No, he thought, it would be coincidental. His thoughts drifted back to the girl he had met in the library. She would probably claim it was some kind of psychic communication from the spirit world. He let his thoughts ramble, hardly conscious of the sound of his tires on the brick street. Even if his mental image matched the photograph there was no way that he would ever tell that girl…Erika, or was it Erin? He tried to remember. It was Erin, yes Erin Aldridge or something…or was it Albright? He kept trying to remember as he turned on his blinker for a right turn into the annex parking lot. Albright, yeah…that was it, Erika Albright, or Erin. Oh, hell with it, he thought, it didn't make any difference, of course, if he did decide to pay a visit to Ashley's it might be nice to remember her name.

He parked his car and went inside the annex building and through the security scanning routine, then hurried down the hall to the Central Records Repository. The first thing he noticed was a new shiny bell sitting on the counter and Mrs. Davis locking a file cabinet. "I see you got a new bell," he smiled, tapping a ring from it.

She looked around, "Oh, Mr. Kirby, yes, and it works too. I'm glad you stopped by." She walked over and pulled an old brown-colored, cardboard container from beneath the counter. Placing the box in front of him, she removed the lid and said, "According to the archival inventory register, this is the evidence box for the Allen case. Unfortunately, it's empty…except for this paper. I think it's the medical examiner's report." She handed a single, yellowed sheet of paper to him. He took a moment to read it before replying.

"Yes ma'am, it's the coroner's report...signed by Edwin Collins. Wow, this girl really suffered some pretty bad trauma...beaten and multiple stabbings, facial trauma...burn marks, and a stocking around her neck. However, according to this, no sexual trauma was detected. I don't know what to make of it. There were no bullet wounds...it looks like her attacker used a knife and his fist."

"It's awful reading," grimaced Mrs. Davis. "I just can't imagine what would drive a human being to do such a thing."

"There were stab wounds to her front and back," observed Brad, as he began trying to decipher the report. "I think she knew her killer. She was close enough to him to be stabbed in the front. Evidently she tried to fend him off because she had cuts to her forearm...she held her arms up to protect herself...then tried to get away and that's when she got stabbed in the back...and in the back of her head. But that wasn't the cause of death...it was strangulation by ligature."

"By liga-what?" said Mrs. Davis, not familiar with the term.

"Oh...it just means strangling with a rope, or in her case a stocking," he explained. "It causes a constriction of the carotid artery cutting the oxygen off to the brain. She would have probably died from the stabbings but it was definitely the stocking around her neck that did it."

Mrs. Davis looked at the paragraph he was reading in the report. "How do you know that?"

"The hyoid bone," he explained, pointing to an entry made by the coroner. "It was fractured...that's a little U-shaped bone in the neck, and the coroner indicated bruising to her neck too."

"You sound like one of those homicide detectives on television," said Mrs. Davis, slipping on her reading glasses trying to read the upside down report. "Were you in law enforcement before you got into writing?"

"Nope, I've just picked up a lot of technical stuff from hanging around police departments...and from reading a lot of reports like this one." He turned the report around so she could read it and pointed to an entry. "Now here's a real good clue, see here where it says orange-colored clay was scraped from under the victim's finger nails? A detective would use such evidence to look for the murder scene. A young girl's nails would have been clean if she was out on Saturday night with her boyfriend. She was probably clawing at the ground during her attack. Here's another clue, according to the coroner, he found guava seeds stuck to folds in the stocking around her neck."

"Uh huh, so clay and guava seeds," she replied, trying to stay interested but ready to close the office for the day and go home.

"Yep, it's a safe bet that she was killed at a place where there was clay and guava trees," he said, opening his brief case and slipping the report inside. "I sure wish the evidence was still available...I was really hoping to see a photo of the girl, it would have been great for my story." He could tell Mrs. Davis was preparing to close the office for the day. He pulled his brief case off the counter and walked over and waited by the door.

After getting her purse from beneath the counter Mrs. Davis went over to a light switch and turned off all the fluorescent lights except for one row. "I'm sorry the box was empty, even the control card with the names and dates of who had access to the evidence is missing, which is a bit strange. Of course, after all these years it's a miracle that anything related to the case is still in storage. You said you wanted to write about a cold case, well this is about as cold as a case can get." She opened the door and they stepped into the hallway.

"Yeah, more like a frozen case," muttered Brad, as she locked the door. "But, something makes me think I can thaw it out."

CHAPTER 4

It was the edge of dark by the time Brad returned to the Sea Rest Motel. He locked his car, and then, with one hand holding his brief case, and another greasy sack from the Burger Delite, he opened the door to his room. He dropped the sack on the table and sat his briefcase on the bed, then pulled off his tie. He was disappointed about the empty evidence box and without a picture of the murdered girl, he was left with only a mental image of her. He removed his coat, turned on the TV, and sat down at the table to eat. He took a bite from his jumbo cheeseburger and began skimming through the copies of the old newspaper articles he had found at the library. On the television another homicide headlined the six o'clock news. With his jaw grinding away the last remnants of his fast food supper, he glanced up at the TV and thought about how murder had become a daily event in modern society, with so much of it never being solved. He clicked off the TV and wadded up his burger wrapper and stuffed it into the empty sack. His eyes burned from squinting at microfilm all day and he really didn't feel like reading tonight. He was bored. The thought of visiting Ashley's Tavern entered his mind, it would beat sitting in a motel room. He could at least see the place and have a beer, and maybe that girl from the library would be there. He slipped on his coat but left his tie on the bed. He tried to remember the girl's name, it was E-something, Erika…Erma, or was it Erin? Ellen? Oh, whatever, he thought, opening the door to go out.

———

Ashley's was a few miles south of the Sea Rest Motel on U.S. 1 in the small riverside community of Rockledge. As he pulled into the parking area he studied the Tudor-style architecture of the tavern thinking it looked like it belonged in an English countryside. The building was unique and seemed out of place for Florida but certainly looked like a place that should have a legend. He parked his car, locked it, and slipped the keys into his coat pocket. He started walking toward the entrance just as a southbound freight train rumbled through on the Florida East Coast tracks behind the building. He paused for second, feeling the heavy vibrations of the train in the pavement of the parking lot.

He opened the big wooden door of the tavern to the pleasant chatter of people and clinking glasses, and could immediately sense a nostalgic feeling in the place. Situated in the middle of the room was an island bar around which was seated a dozen talkative people. At each end of the downstairs, and on the second story, were several cozy dining rooms. He looked around for the girl he had met at the library, but did not see her. The hostess offered to seat him at a table. He politely thanked her, and said, "I think I'll sit at the bar." He sauntered casually around to the opposite side of the bar and found a vantage point on a stool so he could watch people coming and going through the entrance. Brad always claimed to be a people watcher, which was his way of explaining why he never liked to sit with his back to a door.

He began checking out the place. The area above the bar was open through the upstairs dining room. He glanced around, looking up at the polished wood railing around the opening of the upstairs dining area. Next to the railing he could see a couple dining at a table. Hanging baskets of green plants and sparkling drink glasses behind the bar made for a relaxing atmosphere. He liked the place; it had class with a casual mood. He reached for a menu, and there, on the back, was the ghost story! He glanced around the bar as if concerned someone would see him reading it. He had hardly finished scanning the legend when the girl he had met at the library, walked in behind the counter carrying a box of liquor bottles. She immediately saw him sitting there. "Motel get too boring for you?" she smiled, shoving the box under the counter and giving it a push with her foot.

He looked up, "Huh...Oh...You're a bartender?"

"I try to be," she joked, placing a coaster in front of him, "and in case you forgot my name...it's Erin. Now, can I experiment on you?"

"Okay, I feel like taking a risk, can you mix a draft beer?" He was glad she mentioned her name, because he really wasn't sure whether it was Erin or Erika. "Oh, by the way, I didn't forget your name either, I knew it was Erin."

"Well, if you did forget it, you won't have to worry about it," she quipped, drawing a beer from the tap for him. As she placed the glass in front of him another patron called from a nearby table, "Erin, darlin', we're getting a little dry over here. Bring us another pitcher."

She responded, "Hold your horses, Gilbert. I'll be right with y'all...give me a second." She drew a big, foaming pitcher of beer and placed it on a round tray. Handing Brad a menu, she said, "Here, read about our ghost...I'll be right back."

"I've *already* read it..." he replied, turning to watch her take the pitcher of beer to three people sitting at a table behind him.

After serving the patrons at the table, she climbed upon a stool next to him for a short break, "So...whatcha think about our ghost story? Did you see Ethel's name in it?"

"Yeah, I read it," he scoffed, sipping his beer. "It's just a crazy urban legend...nothing more. I don't buy it anymore than if you told me gargoyles were roosting in the attic of this place."

"What about the historical facts that back up the story and the other legends?" She was referring to several legends about Ashley's which have appeared in publications about the unexplained. "What about the fact this place is built on an old Indian burial mound? Or the girl who was killed in a traffic accident out front on the highway or...what about the boy run over by the train on the tracks out back? People say they all haunt this place."

Brad laughed with skepticism, "Yeah...sure they do. Show me a newspaper article about any of these things if they really happened. If any of this stuff was true there'd be so many ghosts in this place they'd be tripping over each other." He sat his glass down. "Listen, there's not one grain of truth to these urban legends. Show me the proof that any of these so-called ghosts ever existed as a real person. There's no way...you won't find one fact to support any of it."

"Ethel Allen... She's a fact, you said so yourself."

"Okay, she was a real person. I'll give you credit for that one... not as a ghost though!" He began changing the subject. "Speaking of Ethel, after you left the library I found another old newspaper article that mentions this place just before she was killed."

"Do tell…what'd you find?"

Brad reached inside his coat, pulled out a copy of the article and unfolded it. "It's from August 1934…two weeks before Ethel Allen was killed." He read the headline aloud, "LOCAL LAWYER INJURED IN FRAY AT JACK'S TAVERN."

She interrupted, "Jack's…that was this place, right?"

"Yes, Ashley's…back then it was Jack's place." His eyes scanned the article trying to find his place. "Anyway it goes on to say that Judge J.C. Baxter's son, *Sonny Baxter*, got into a fight over a girl. Sonny was a lawyer, in the forties he was elected to the state senate. It doesn't name the girl, but wouldn't it be something if the girl was Ethel. Of course, that'd be too far-fetched. However, Judge J.C. Baxter is the *same* one who terminated Ethel's murder investigation!"

She straightened up on her stool, "Awesome, maybe the girl was Ethel…and she was fooling around with this lawyer guy…and her boyfriend got jealous and killed her right here in this building!"

"No, there you go reading into it. Nothing says it was her or that she was killed here. All I know from what I've found is that her boyfriend was the only suspect listed in the investigation…and he either skipped town or something else happened to him."

"Well, if she was cheating…then he had a motive to kill her."

Brad put the paper back into his inside coat pocket. "Nothing says she was cheating on him…all we know is that he disappeared."

"So, it means without a murderer, you ain't got much of a story," she said, sliding off her stool to return to work behind the bar.

"No, it means I have an unsolved mystery which makes a good story for my readers. I just need to get enough stuff to write about. Of course, all people connected with the murder are long since dead… Oops, sorry about saying *dead* I don't want to get you started on ghosts again."

"Sounds like you're after a needle in a haystack to me," she replied, looking around at the bar manager. "Hey Roger…got a minute? Come over here, I want you to meet my friend, Brad. He's a writer from Miami. Tell him about Ashley's ghost."

Erin took over tending the bar as Roger shifted down to Brad and extended his hand over the counter, "Hey bud, how ya doin', the name's Roger." He was a tall guy, about fifty years old, with a receding hair line and jolly smile. He wore a black bow tie and a white dress shirt with the sleeves rolled up to the elbows exposing a blue and green tattoo of an alligator on his hairy forearm.

Brad gripped his hand with a firm shake, "Brad Kirby...good to meet you. Erin was just telling me about this place being haunted."

Roger wiped the counter with a towel, "The *famous* Ashley's ghost story. Yep, this place has been in all kinds of books, even a few television shows." He grabbed a menu and flipped it over, tapping his finger on it. "It's right here on the back of our menu."

"I know, I read it," said Brad, taking another sip of his beer. "I guess it's a good legend if you believe that sort of stuff."

"Oh it's more than that," explained Roger. "Crazy things have been going on here for years. Poltergeist type things...like the damn dishes flying off the shelf in the kitchen, lights going off and on, women seeing a ghost in the mirror in the ladies' room. Hell, I can't keep a night clean-up crew. You ought to hear their stories about what they've seen late at night."

"Sure, and there's probably a natural explanation," responded Brad, preparing to give his theory. "I mean, let's face it, this is a bar and if you drink too much you're liable to see space aliens riding pink elephants. The train runs right behind this building...it could shake dishes off the shelf. So, what have you personally seen?"

Roger leaned in close, propping his elbows on the bar, "Okay, try this on for size..." He paused, and looked around like he didn't want anyone to hear, then continued, "I've seen the lights go on and off, and all that shit...but I saw *something* one night when I was in here by myself doing inventory. I think it was about two in the morning. Anyway, I heard a bumping sound in the upstairs dining room so I went up there to check it out. The chairs were stacked on the tables. I looked around and didn't see anything...then about the time I started toward the stairs, I saw a chair float up in the air, *right off* the table, then...as gently as you please...it just settled down on the floor."

"And you saw it?" asked Brad, downing the rest of his beer.

"With my own eyes..." exclaimed Roger, demonstrating with his hands. "Just like this, that damn chair floated in the air."

"...And you believe a spirit did it?" grinned Brad, thumping his glass with his finger.

"Hell, I don't know what did it, but I damn sure saw it." He looked at Brad's glass. "How 'bout another beer?"

"No thanks, I gotta run," he replied, pushing his empty glass aside and getting down from his stool. "I guess the ghost story is good for business."

"Oh, yeah, we get all kinds of people coming in here hoping to see something unexplainable…Hey…I gotta get back to work. Good talking with you, buddy." He gave Brad a stiff pat on the arm and went back to the other end of the bar.

Erin saw Brad was about to leave and came over to remove a couple of empty bottles from the counter. "Calling it a night already? I hope Roger didn't scare you with our ghost story?"

"Nope, I already told you I don't believe in that stuff. I've got to get going early in the morning to find out if there's anybody still living in this town who remembers the murder. I also need to see Mrs. Davis at the records repository and see if she has any idea what happened to a ruby ring Ethel was wearing. The evidence box is empty, but maybe the ring was given to her next of kin. It may have had an inscription on it…or something that would give me a clue if I can find who has it."

"Ruby ring?" she said. "That's a birthstone for July."

"I didn't even think of that," he replied.

"Do you know what they say about rubies?" she asked.

"No, what do they say about rubies?"

"Rubies were once worn by royalty to protect against evil. They believed the stone would turn dark red when danger was near."

"Obviously the battery must have been dead in Ethel's ruby ring because it sure didn't help her," he snickered, trying to be funny.

She ignored his remark and continued with her story. "And in ancient times people thought the red color of rubies came from an internal flame inside the stone. That's why some people give it as a gift of everlasting love."

"So how come you know so much about rubies?"

"My birthstone is a ruby. I was born in July, that's how I know about rubies."

"Oh, your birthstone is a ruby. Oooooh!! You might be Ethel returned to haunt this place," he said, wiggling his fingers at her.

"Smart ass…but I bet she was born in July."

"There's only one problem," he replied, "in the police record her birth month was listed as February." He pulled out a ten dollar bill to pay his tab and handed it to her. "Are you going to the library tomorrow to work on your family history?"

"Not to the county library," she replied, counting out his change. "I'm going to the State Historical Society library."

"You're going all the way to the state capital…*Tallahassee?*"

"Of course not. Didn't you know the *State Historical Society* is located in Cocoa? It's right there at the intersection of Brevard and Orange. I do a lot of my genealogy research there. It's a real gold mine for old Florida records. Why'd you want to know if I'm going to the library?"

"I'll make you a deal," he said. "Check the 1934 census, it should be on microfilm, and see if you can find Ethel's birth date and if you find it, make me a copy and I'll buy lunch."

"Census records are for ten year intervals, so I would have to check the 1930 census."

"Okay, whatever…you find it and lunch is on me." He wasn't too sure if he was trying to find an excuse for a lunch date with her or just trying to get her to do some free research for him, or maybe both. Although he thought she was cute, he realized they had little in common, especially their differing opinions about the supernatural.

"It's a deal," she agreed. "I'll meet you at noon at the Harvest Moon Café…it's on Brevard Avenue in the old section of Cocoa. It's the sidewalk café with the green umbrellas, you can't miss it."

"You got it; Harvest Moon…sounds like a New Age joint to me."

"You'll like it, my friend Adele owns it. I'll see you there." She picked up a towel began drying glasses behind the bar, glancing from the corner of her eye as he put a couple of dollars in the tip jar and walked toward the entrance. He turned briefly and waved to her. She nodded, then smiled as he opened the door and left.

CHAPTER 5

The next day began with a light shower of rain and by noon had grown quite warm and sunny. After stopping by the records repository to see Mrs. Davis, Brad hurried on down to the historic part of town called Cocoa Village to meet Erin for lunch. He parked his car on a side street near Riverfront Park and walked a block to Brevard Avenue, a tree-lined avenue of enchanting boutiques and quaint cafes. As he wove his way in and out of strolling shoppers, he saw the same African-American woman he had seen in the parking lot on his first day in town. She was across the narrow street with her shopping cart and had just rescued a discarded purple shirt from a trash bin. Her eyes wandered across the street as he maneuvered down the sidewalk. He gave her a quick glance and nodded hello. She stuffed the shirt into a plastic bag and smiled back, as if she still remembered him from his first day.

When he got to the Harvest Moon Café, he found a vacant sidewalk table shaded from the noon sun by a large green umbrella and sat down to look over the menu.

Suddenly a woman's voice came from behind, "Hi, you'll never guess what I found." He put the menu down and turned, it was Erin. Looking feisty in her jeans and snug tank top, she laid some papers on the table and pulled a chair out to sit down.

"Oh, hi!" he said, getting up to help her with her chair.

Before she could tell him what she had found, a dark-haired woman, wearing a long, tie-dyed, linen dress, came out of the restaurant, "Erin! Erin...I thought that was you!"

"Adele! Oh, my gosh! How're you? Meet my friend Brad, he writes for a famous magazine." Erin turned to Brad, "This is my long time friend, Adele, she owns the Harvest Moon." He smiled and silently thought to himself; maybe she'll give us a discount.

Adele stretched her hand across the table to him and in a distinctive Bostonian accent, said, "Nice to meet ya." Her wrists dangled flamboyantly with more bracelets than any Gypsy fortune teller could ever hope to wear.

"My pleasure indeed," he said, slightly rising from his chair, noticing the sunlight sparkling on at least a dozen turquoise and silver rings adorning her fingers.

With her hands on her hips, she asked, "So…what's the famous magazine you write for?"

"Well it's not exactly famous," he replied, halfway cracking a smile. "It's *Dead End Magazine*…ever hear of it?"

"Wow! That's awesome!" she exclaimed. "Nope, never heard of it, but I just love anything about the supernatural, especially spiritualism. So, tell me, do you believe in ghosts?"

Here we go again, he thought. "No, I do not believe in ghosts, never did, and never will, and actually I write about unsolved homicide cases."

"Oh, well that's cool too, I guess," she smiled, removing a pencil from behind her ear ready to take their order. "So whatcha gonna have?"

"I'd like the garden salad with the tofu and soy nuts, and some unsweetened iced tea," said Erin, handing the menu to her.

Brad raised his eyes from his menu. "And I'll have a regular cheeseburger with a large order of fries, and iced tea with sugar and lemon in it…and no mayo on the burger."

As Adele headed inside with their order, Erin leaned forward and whispered sarcastically, "My, my, you *sure* do eat healthy…you're lucky she still has junk food on the menu."

"Hey, I get hungry," he retorted, adjusting his chair. "I've got to have more than twigs and leaves…or bland tea. Besides, I only had a donut for breakfast and that was nearly five hours ago."

"The ruby ring wasn't her birthstone," said Erin, getting back to what she wanted to tell him.

"What? Oh…Ethel's ring."

"I found Ethel on the 1930 census," she explained. "She was born in February 1916 just like the date on your police report. Now get this, I looked in an old business directory and found out that

Ashley's…well, Jack's or whatever it was called back then, was owned by a man named Jack Allen. He might have been kin to her, maybe that was the reason she was working there."

Adele returned with their order and slid Brad's cheeseburger in front of him. "If it wasn't for all the tourists, these greasy things wouldn't be on my menu," she frowned. "However, I always say each to his own. Enjoy, and let me know if you need anything."

"Thanks Adele," said Erin, getting back to her conversation with Brad who was already chomping into his burger. "…I found this too." She handed him a copy of an old newspaper article. "It's dated 1932. I don't know if it has anything to do with Ethel, but it mentions that young lawyer guy…Sonny Baxter."

He wiped the corner of his mouth with a napkin and started reading it aloud. "Charges were dismissed today against Felton Kennedy in Klan Burning. Who's Felton Kennedy?"

"I don't know, but read on down."

"Oh, I see it…Sonny Baxter testified for the defense. It was his testimony that got this Kennedy dude off the hook. Holy Smoke! Sonny's old man, Judge Baxter, was the judge! No wonder the charges were dismissed."

"Yes…the same one who terminated Ethel's murder investigation. I would think as the judge, he would've dismissed himself from the case if his son was testifying for the defendant."

"It would seem the ethical thing to do," he replied, continuing to read the old article. "It goes on to say Sonny Baxter and B.T. Marshal testified that Felton Kennedy was out of town on a hunting trip in the Ocala forest when two houses in the colored section known as the Washington Street Quarters were burned to the ground. Two black men identified Felton Kennedy as the white man they saw driving away from the fire. The prosecutor was Henry Moore…it doesn't appear he made much of an effort in prosecuting the case. I bet all those guys belonged to the same good old boys' club."

"Or more like a bad old boys' club," she added, taking a sip of tea.

"It makes me wonder about the article I found at the county library," he said, putting a French fry into his mouth, "the one I showed to you last night…about Sonny Baxter being in a fight at Jack's Tavern." He took a gulp of tea and sat the glass down.

"Remember, it was over a girl but stopped short of naming her? I still think there's a slight possibility the girl was Ethel. Obviously, Sonny Baxter must have been a ruthless character. I'm curious about Bill Kelly, her boyfriend, and what really happened to him. So far I don't see anything that would have suggested he killed her."

"Maybe this guy Sonny Baxter instigated the fight at Jack's with Ethel's boyfriend," She said. "Hey, maybe he didn't murder her; maybe somebody just stuck the blame on him." She sat her glass of tea on the table and dabbed her lips with a napkin leaving prints of her lipstick on it. "What if that judge stopped the investigation so nobody would find out who the real killer was?

"I don't know. Right now, I've got more questions than answers," said Brad, trying to put a few facts together in his head. "Now Kelly wasn't mentioned in that news article about the fight at Jack's place, so we really don't know if it was him, but two weeks later Ethel is found murdered and Kelly disappears…and now, from this newspaper account you found today, it looks like Sonny hung out with some unsavory characters. I think all of this stuff is somehow connected."

"I can't see Bill Kelly killing Ethel," she said. "I mean, like the murder article said, he was her fiancé. If they loved each other enough to plan on getting married why would he kill her? Unless he did it out of jealously. Okay, I've changed my mind; I don't think she was cheating on him. I get the feeling she loved him too much."

"Who knows? People can be motivated to do almost anything," he said, stuffing the last morsel of his cheeseburger in his mouth. He licked his fingers and continued, "Sure, it's very possible Kelly could have killed her, then again, he may have been totally innocent. What happened to him is part of the big mystery. It will make a great story, if I can get enough facts to write about."

Erin suddenly looked across the street and waved, "Oh my Lord, there goes Toogers Babbit…Gawd, I ain't seen him in a coon's age."

Brad turned see what she was talking about. "Who?"

"Toogers Babbit…"

"Toogers? Is that his real name?"

"I guess so…he was my 12th grade algebra teacher and a football coach. I learned more about football in his class than I did algebra."

"Then you went to school around here?"

"All the way from the first grade."

"Were you born here?"

"No, I was three when we moved here from Tampa after daddy went to work at the Space Center."

"Don't tell me you're the daughter of an astronaut," he joked.

"Gawd no," she laughed, shaking the ice in her tea glass. "Although, he does work for NASA. He supervises a crew that installs those heat tile thingamajigs on the space shuttles."

"Did you ever go to the University of Florida?" he asked.

"Lord no, I was lucky just to get two years at Brevard Community College. Why? Do I look like I went to a university?"

"You really remind me of someone I once met somewhere. I just thought I might have met you when I was in college."

"So, you graduated from the University of Florida?" she inquired, sitting her glass down on the table. "Then I suppose you're a *Seminole* fan..."

"Nope, you're thinking of Florida State," he answered, laughingly. "The University of Florida's football team is the *Gators*."

"I always get those two mixed-up," she said. So what'd you study in college?"

He sat his tea down. "I started out as a music major. I figured there wasn't much future for a sousaphone player...so I switched courses and ended up with a degree in journalism. Now I'm an investigative writer for what you'd call a supermarket magazine."

"And paying off a student loan," she added.

"Yep, now you know why I have to keep digging up good stories, even if it's about a dead girl with a ruby ring," he said, "...and that's another thing that bothers me about Ethel."

"What? Her ghost?"

"No...forget ghosts...the ruby ring. It was on her finger when she was found. It wasn't her birthstone, and it's listed as evidence but it's missing with all the pictures of Bill and Ethel...and all the other stuff that was supposed to be in the evidence box."

"Can you tell who had access to the evidence?"

"No…and Mrs. Davis is puzzled about that too. She said the card is missing that had the record of anyone handling the evidence…but the card and everything is missing!"

"What do you reckon happened to the evidence?

"Maybe Ethel's spirit has the stuff," he smiled, finishing off a stray French fry left on his plate. "It may have been given to her next of kin, but Mrs. Davis couldn't find any record of that either."

"Or maybe her killer took the things," speculated Erin, opening her purse to pay the check.

"I don't think so, because he would have taken the ring when he killed her." He saw Erin pulling out her money. "Put that away…I told you lunch is on me for confirming Ethel's birth date."

"Hey…that's right, you owe me!" She closed her purse.

He paid the check and asked if she would like to walk with him down to Riverfront Park where his car was parked. "Sure," she replied. "I'm parked down there too."

Riverfront Park sat on the Indian River, neatly landscaped with play areas for children and crisscrossed with sidewalks of red brick laid in a herringbone fashion. As they strolled along, Erin returned to the topic of the ruby ring.

"What if that ring didn't even belong to Ethel?" she said.

"You mean like she stole it or something?"

"No, like the killer put it on her…maybe he had some kind of crazy perverted obsession. Like some kind of ritual thing."

"You mean a killer who puts rings on the fingers of his victims? I doubt that's the case. What's really curious is that the ring was left on her finger…it definitely was not a case of robbery."

Erin slowed her walking pace, "Okay, wouldn't you think she'd have an engagement ring if she was getting married?"

"I guess so…of course no engagement ring was found on her unless the ruby ring was her engagement ring."

"What hand was it on?"

"It was on her left hand."

"Then it could have been an engagement ring," she said. "Remember what I told you last night about how the ruby is a symbol of everlasting love?"

"Yes, however, some people don't wear engagement rings," he replied "I know a bunch of people who don't wear rings...but that don't mean they're not married or engaged."

Erin saw an opening to discreetly probe through his facade. "You mean like you? I don't see any rings on your hand...so what does that mean about you?

He looked at his hand, "No, I'm not married. I'm flying solo and I like it that way." He slipped his hand into his trousers' pocket and jangled his keys as he walked.

It worked, she thought. She had skillfully slipped behind his persona and stole a bit of information and he didn't even realize it. Then a second thought entered her mind, now he would probably turn the question on her. She knew what was coming next.

"Are you attached or married?" he asked. "Ever been married?"

That's just like a man, she thought. No discretion at all. Just plow right in with a load of questions. She returned a slim answer, "No."

"No what? You're not married...or you're not attached?"

He's not giving up, she thought. She decided to dump her full load of answers on him. "Not married, never been married and I'm not attached because every time I find a guy I think has the right chemistry, it turns out to be nothing but baking soda and vinegar."

"Baking soda...and vinegar?"

"Yeah, like those chemistry experiments in grade school," she said, "when we mixed baking soda with vinegar and it fizzed up, that's what always happens to my relationships, they just fizzle out."

"I suppose that's a good way to put it," he laughed.

"Like they say, all the good ones are taken. Of course, I could change my mind if the right one came along." She began steering the conversation in another direction. He was getting too nosy and she wasn't about to give him the controls. She looked up ahead on the sidewalk at an elderly black gentleman coming toward them. "Oh look...there's Herbert Hoover!"

Brad's eyes glanced around, "The ex-president? He's dead!"

"No, silly! That guy coming up the sidewalk?" She waved to the man. "His name is Herbert Hoover...he's old as the hills...but is a kind soul. Everybody knows him. He used to be a fireman."

"For the fire department?"

"No, for the Florida East Coast railroad…he was a locomotive fireman, you know…on those old steam engines…sorta like an engineer, they kept the fire going in the boiler or whatever."

"He looks like an interesting character," remarked Brad, studying the elderly fellow as he came closer. A Panama hat covered his graying cotton-like hair and shaded the lines of age etched in his leathery, brown face. Sitting on his shoulder was a large bushy tailed squirrel wearing a tiny harness with a small leash leading to the man's hand.

Brad leaned close to Erin's ear, "Does he know there's a squirrel sitting on his shoulder?"

"That's Sweet Baby, his pet squirrel!"

She greeted the man with, "Hi Herbert, how's Sweet Baby?" The big squirrel scampered across the man's chest and perched on his other shoulder to seriously study the two humans.

"Sweet Baby's doin' just fine Miss Erin, how 'bout yourself?" A big friendly grin ran across the man's face. His eyes smiled as he nodded hello to Brad.

Erin reached to pet the squirrel. "Sweet Baby sure looks fat and sassy." Brad just stood there quietly taking everything in, feeling like the stranger in town. Erin seemed to know everybody.

"Sweet Baby's sassy 'cause he's too doggone fat," chuckled the man. "I got him on a diet…no peanuts for awhile…just vegetables and sunflower seeds. Those peanuts was junk food, you know what I'm saying?"

"I sure do, Herbert, just like that junk some people eat," she said, giving Brad a gentle nudge in the ribs with her elbow. "It was good seeing you, Herbert. Take care of Sweet Baby, I'll see you later."

"Yes ma'am…Sweet Baby is goin' to be much skinnier next time you see him," he said, tipping his hat before ambling on his way.

As Erin and Brad continued on down the sidewalk toward the river they passed by some kids playing in a fountain pool. Brad glanced back at the man walking away. Sweet Baby was still riding on his shoulder, still looking back at Brad. "I think that squirrel is sneering at me," said Brad, almost walking into a street sign.

"Sweet Baby's not sneering at you, *not* that you don't deserve to be sneered at. My car is over there," said Erin, pointing to a small burgundy-colored Toyota parked facing the end of the boardwalk that ran along the river. "Thanks for lunch. I'll be working tonight if you would like to come by." Gads, she quietly thought, he'll get the idea I'm making a play for him. She quickly rephrased her words, "I...ah, mean, like, if you're looking for a place to eat supper. Ashley's is really, really good, and I could show you some good things on the menu."

"Only if you promise not to force me to read that ghost story on the back of it again," he replied, standing there with both hands shoved in his pockets. "I can't be distracted by weird fiction when I'm searching for facts." His fingers fidgeted with his keys in his pocket. "I might drop by this evening, it depends on how I feel later."

She put the key in her car door. She opened the door and slid behind the steering wheel. She rolled down the window and with an impish smile, turned to Brad, and said, "Okay, I promise...if you decide to drop by tonight, I will make sure nobody tells you any ghost stories. Bye!"

CHAPTER 6

It was the middle of the dinner hour by the time Brad arrived at Ashley's. Every bar stool was occupied. Around the bar a dozen subdued conversations had fused into an indistinguishable babble of tongues. Erin was too busy keeping up with never-ending drink orders and had no time to chat. She saw him come in and sent a smile with her eyes while motioning to the end of the bar where a patron was paying his tab. Brad knew she was signaling that a stool was being vacated. He moved around the bar in time to claim the seat across from where Roger was drying glasses with a towel.

"Hey, Roger, how's it going?" He asked, opening a menu.

"Busy as a damn bee hive this evening," he answered, stacking glasses on a tray. "You still chasing after that old murder mystery?"

"Yeah...still working on it...so what's good on the menu tonight? Roger tapped his wet finger on a special clipped to the menu. "Try the broiled scallop special. It's a good deal for six bucks, and you get a dozen big scallops...guaranteed fresh off the boat at Canaveral."

Roger's menu suggestion was good, especially with a beer followed by another beer and another. Not being the party type, Brad wasn't used alcohol, one beer was okay, he could feel it with two, but after three he would always switch to a soda. After three beers, he had a habit of talking too much. When Erin finally had time to chat, he ordered a coke. She sat the coke in front of him, "Didn't you say Jacobs was the sheriff in 1934?"

"That's right, Jake Jacobs...why?"

"Because I was talking with this guy tonight from the historical society and asked him if he knew anything about the Ethel Allen murder. He said he only had heard about it. Then he said that the sheriff in the thirties was named Jacobs and some of his personal papers are stored at the Palmer House."

"What's the Palmer House?" he asked, starting to feel his beers.

"It's like a museum. It's an old house in Cocoa, one of those restored houses that's open to the public. It's over a hundred years old. I think it's listed on the National Register of Historic Places."

"You mean that big ol' mansion on Delannoy, with the pillars?"

"No, no, that's the Porcher House; the Palmer House is on Riverside Drive, a few blocks south of Riverfront Park. It's a neat place with antique furnishings, oh yeah, and they have an unusual exhibit there too. Anyway I just thought you'd like to know about the sheriff's papers being there. I'm sure the two old ladies who run it will let you look at the papers if you give them a call."

"Yes...I'd like to check them out," he said, writing the name of the place on a napkin. "You said they have an unusual exhibit there...like what kind of exhibit?" His speech had a very slight but detectable slur from the three beers, but he was feeling good.

"You wouldn't believe me if I told you," chuckled Erin. "You'll just have to find that out for yourself."

"Now you've got my curiosity riled up," he replied. "It better not be some kind of paranormal stuff...is that what it is?"

"No...It's something else, and it's historical."

The bar crowd was beginning to thin out. Brad continued small talk with Erin as a parade of twelve people led by a man in a bright orange jumpsuit came through the front door. They trouped around the end of the bar and down behind where he was sitting, then headed up the narrow stairs to the second story. When the guy in the orange jumpsuit went past, Brad turned around and noticed a 'Ghost Busters' patch on his sleeve. "What the hell's that about?" he asked Erin.

"That's the Spook Hunters. It's a ghost hunting group from Orlando and the guy in the orange suit is Owen, he's their leader."

Brad sat his coke down on the bar. "You've got to be kidding me! Now I've heard it all. A ghost hunting group...so what do they do?"

"They're here to test the place."

"Test it for what?"

"Ghosts!"

"There are no ghosts!" he responded. "Are you telling me all those people believe in spirits?"

"Heck no, Owen is more of a skeptic than you are," she said.

"Now I am really mixed up, you mean he doesn't believe in spirits and he's in here hunting for something he doesn't believe in?"

"Well, at least he is not as closed minded as you," she said, wiping the bar. "He's out to prove his theory that ghosts do not exist. You on the other hand just talk and never offer any proof that you are right. You should join that group if you want to prove there's no such thing as a ghost."

"I've got to see this," he said, climbing off his stool. "I'm going up there and see what kind of crazy stuff these people are up to." He headed upstairs leaving Erin at the bar laughing. Roger saw him going up the stairs and looked over at Erin with a big grin, "Now you've got him goin'."

When Brad reached the second story dining room he saw the group had split up and were walking around with electro-magnetic field detectors and digital cameras. Sitting at one of the tables were two women working an Ouija Board watched over by the guy in the orange jumpsuit. Brad went up to him, "I hear you're Owen, the honcho ghost hunter...is that right?"

"You got it, dude...that's me."

"I'm Brad. So, what're you guys doing?"

"We're the Spook Hunters...we're looking for ghosts. This place has a legend about a murdered girl haunting it."

"Yeah, I know all about that legend stuff," injected Brad. "But I hear you don't believe in ghosts...so how do you fit into this spook hunting thing...and this orange ghost buster suit you're wearing...It just seems like a contradiction to me 'cause I don't believe in ghost either."

"The suit is just something I came up with for the fun of it. The Spook Hunters have a wide range of beliefs, from skeptics to middle of the road types...to those on the extreme fringe, like these two trying to conjure up a spirit with that Ouija Board." Brad glanced at the Ouija Board.

"But you, yourself, you don't really believe this spook stuff do you?" Brad was trying to gain an ally in his skepticism about the paranormal."

"Let me say this," started Owen. "I believe in an afterlife, just not sure about ghosts or using a toy like that Ouija Board to contact spirits."

"Oh, I agree, definitely," said Brad, "perhaps an afterlife, but not ghosts, not like the legend about this place. So, why do people believe this stuff?"

"It's overactive imaginations at work," exclaimed Owen. "It's a lot of fun, but I'm out to find evidence of ghosts. I'll keep an open mind, so if they really exist then I want to see one. I'm not one for believing in things I can't see, I need proof."

"So, you haven't seen one?"

"Nope, and we use all kinds of equipment as you can see. EMF detectors, infra-red equipment, you name it. I'll even give that Ouija Board the benefit of the doubt. It's all a lot of fun, but so far, I haven't seen anything that changes my mind."

"I guess you've read all about the murdered girl that supposedly haunts this place," said Brad, with a cynical smile, thinking he had found someone who agreed with his skepticism.

"That's the most popular tale," replied Owen. "There are other tales too, like this place was built on an Indian burial mound and another about how it was the train station that burned down killing some people...then there's the yarns about a girl killed on the highway out front and she's allegedly haunting the place...oh yeah, and a boy killed on the railroad tracks out back. The only story with historical credibility is Ethel Allen, the one you're talking about, because we know she was a real person. Of course, it only means she was real and was murdered...not that she's haunting this place, or any other place for that matter."

"That's what I've been saying," exclaimed Brad. "But some of the employees really believe she's a ghost...but not me."

Brad couldn't wait to get back down stairs to tell Erin about his discussion. This will pop her supernatural bubble, he thought. As he reached the bottom floor he saw that someone had taken his seat at the bar. He motioned for Erin to come over to the end of the counter. "I'll see you later, I'm fixing to leave," he said, hoping she would ask him what he thought about the Spook Hunters.

"So did you learn anything from the Spook Hunters?" she smiled.

48

"Yeah, I learned it's all a bunch of baloney just like I've been telling you. Even that Owen dude doesn't believe in ghosts."

"I told you he didn't, but what about the others?"

"With the Ouija Board? Ha...*Get real*, it's a crock," he laughed, before changing the subject. "Hey, I'm going to that Palmer House in the morning, I'll call down there first to see if they really have the sheriff's old papers. Where is that place anyway?"

"It's not far from Riverfront Park. Just park on Harrison Street and go across the park and walk about three blocks south on Riverside Drive, there's a sign out front. Maybe I'll see you downtown tomorrow; I'm going to the State Historical Society in the morning to work on my genealogy. I'll look for your car on Harrison Street. I'd like to hear about what you find at the Palmer House."

"Okay, but don't count on it, 'cause I'm not hanging around after I go to that house, I'll drop by tomorrow night." In reality he was really planning to look for her, even if he had to cut his research short and hang around the park like a vagrant until he saw her leave the library. He would just make it look like an accidental meeting.

He said good night and headed out the door. Erin went back to work, as the Spook Hunters came down the steps and started working the downstairs dining room with their EMF detectors.

The next morning Brad parked his car at Riverfront Park. About five spaces down, he recognized Erin's car and figured she was at the Historical Society. If his timing was right, he could finish up his research at the Palmer House and be back at the park in time to see her. He then walked across the park and followed the sidewalk past St. Marks Church along Riverside Drive, which was separated from the river by a thin line of Palmetto trees and a few coquina rocks. It was exactly three blocks to the Palmer House, a beautiful, white Victorian-era house with front and side gables. Its wide porch was trimmed with ornate spindle work. For years, it had overlooked the Indian River until recently when the view was blocked by a new high rise condominium. This part of town had changed many times since 1896 when Dr. Cyrus Palmer built the house.

Brad walked up the brick path to the porch and opened the screen door. Stepping into the foyer, he was greeted by a woman in her late sixties attired in period costume. "Welcome to the Palmer House," she said, in a gracious Southern tone. "Have you been here before? Her manner and appearance reminded him of his grandmother, except for the purplish hairdo piled on her head which resembled a big fluffy cloud. Before he had a chance to respond, another lady, also dressed in old fashion attire, grabbed his arm and pulled him over to a guest register on a small table. "Would you please sign our guest book?" He picked up a pen attached by a string to the book, and signed his name while the two ladies hovered over him.

"Here's a folder on the Palmer House," offered one of the women.

"And here's one about Cocoa's history," said the other woman.

"Thanks. Actually, I'm here about the sheriff's papers," He explained, as one of the ladies interrupted him.

"Oh, you're the young man who called this morning."

"Yes ma'am, Brad Kirby."

"Oh, I do beg your pardon, Mr. Kirby...I'm Alicia, Palmer House historian," she said, turning to introduce the other lady. "And this is our administrator, Mrs. Karen Howard."

"I'm pleased to meet you. What I'm doing is a little research on an old murder that happened back in 1934; when Jake Jacobs was the sheriff, and I'd just like to take a look at his papers."

"That's no problem," said Mrs. Howard.

"No problem at all," repeated Alicia.

"It's only a small amount of papers," explained Mrs. Howard.

"It's not much, just a small number of papers," echoed Alicia.

"Well, I'd appreciate seeing what you have," he said, thinking the two ladies seemed to be in some kind of contest by constantly repeating each other's remarks.

"But first, you must see our special exhibit," insisted Alicia.

"Indeed," said Mrs. Howard, "you *have* to see it!"

Brad had little choice, as they quickly ushered him into what had originally been the large dining room. He stood there for a moment in total awe, as his eyes beheld a curious exhibit that was obviously very out of place in the Palmer house.

"This is our machine gun collection!!" Alicia proudly announced. Brad was momentarily lost for words. He was looking at a room full of machine guns, some on the wall and others in glass fronted display cases. Just about every type of *machine gun* that was ever built was in the historic Palmer House.

"Machine guns? This is awesome!" he exclaimed, with his eyes glancing around the room and focusing on a big fifty-caliber machine gun mounted on a tripod in the middle of the floor. Its muzzle was aimed right directly at him. "You...you must have hundreds!"

"One hundred and sixty-three to be exact," boasted Mrs. Howard.

"We have one of the largest private collections in America," said Alicia, as she unlatched the glass door to an exhibit case and removed a *Thompson* sub-machine gun for Brad to examine. "Baby Face Nelson..." she said. "Ever hear of him? This weapon belonged to one of his gangster buddies."

Brad held the gun with both hands...feeling its weight. "So...ah, what're you doing with so many machine guns?"

Mrs. Howard took the gun from him and began swinging it around the room like she was firing it, "*Tat-tat-tat-tat-tat...*can you imagine how fast this thing could eat up ammo?"

Brad ducked back as she whirled the gun past his face, "Ah, yes ma'am, ah...I guess it could eat a lot of bullets."

"This beautiful collection belonged to Colonel Earl Palmer," explained Alicia, as if referring to fine china. "He was the great grandson of Dr. Palmer who built this house. When the Colonel passed away a few years ago, we learned he had willed his entire collection to us provided it would be placed on permanent public display."

Brad, still in a state of wonder, was impressed with the unusual collection, but he wanted to get to the papers. Mrs. Howard escorted him to the rear of the house to the former pantry, which now served as a storage room. She opened a tall wooden cabinet and removed a box placing it on a table in the center of the room. "The papers are in this box...you can sit right here and look to your heart's content."

"How did you acquire these old papers?"

"The sheriff's niece used to be on our board of trustees...she donated them to us because she did not want them to get lost."

"I'd sure like to talk with her," said Brad, beginning to read some of the papers. "Would that be possible?"

"Well, that would be a little difficult," replied Mrs. Howard, putting her hands on her hips, "because she left us a few years ago."

"Do you know where she went to?"

"She's in Palm Gardens."

"Is that in Florida?"

"It's a *cemetery* darlin'...*she's dead!*"

He looked up, "Oh...I didn't realize she was dead. I'm sorry."

"Well, it's not your fault," she smiled. "It was that hose she hooked up to the exhaust pipe on her car that did it. She just sat in the car and went to sleep. After losing her fourth husband she just went down hill, if you know what I mean. She was a very *sophisticated* lady." She hesitated, and then cackled like a hen, "Of course after she got a dose of carbon monoxide, she was like an *asphyxiated* lady!"

Brad reacted to her odd sense of humor with a surprised grin, and then went back to sorting through the box of letters and papers. "These look like personal letters," he said, opening an old yellowed envelope.

"They are," she answered. "It's mostly a few old notes...and his personal correspondence while he was sheriff. I really don't think you're going to find any thing important in there."

He spent the next hour looking through the sheriff's old papers and letters, mostly general stuff yielding no clues. Then he found a folded handwritten memo. He carefully unfolded it. It was dated July 7, 1933 and was from Judge J.C. Baxter. He flattened it out and read down to the last paragraph:

"The boys tell me that you don't like to play ball the way I do. I find that unfortunate for you because it is better to be a player than the water boy. We both know the 21st. Amendment is going to repeal Prohibition and all this wasted policing of speakeasies is going to stop. We can take care of our own without Washington outsiders meddling in our county's private matters, so think about which side you want your bread buttered on. I'm sending Frank Turner over to see you on Tuesday. I want you to hire him as your chief deputy. Let him and Sonny deal with the Feds for you. J.C. Baxter."

The memo sounded like the judge was threatening the sheriff in some kind of subtle way by using baseball lingo. He had no idea what it meant, but it smelled crooked. One thing was clear; it was Judge Baxter who got Frank Turner the job as chief deputy. Brad began connecting dots in his head, Turner was the investigator in the Allen case, Baxter closed the investigation, Turner and Baxter were connected and obviously Baxter didn't like outsiders. Maybe since the judge mentioned Prohibition he was referring to federal revenue agents, but why should that bother a judge? And who were "the boys" mentioned in the note? Was the judge involved in some kind of illegal business? Brad was trying to read between the lines, it all sounded very suspicious. His discovery had cast a little more light on the mystery, but not without more questions.

He dug through the old letters to the bottom of the box looking for more notes from the judge. He found nothing. Then he pulled out an envelope addressed to the sheriff from the U.S. Bureau of Internal Revenue in Washington D.C. Inside was a short one page letter dated June 8, 1934, signed by J.W. Stiles, Special Agent, Alcohol Tax Unit. As he began reading it he knew from the first sentence that he had struck pay dirt, quite possibly the biggest clue he had found so far and it practically jumped off the page as he read it.

Dear Sheriff Jacobs,   *June 8, 1934*
Please convey my gratitude to Mr. Kelly for his confidential efforts in Scarlet Biddy which greatly aided our agents in confiscating forty cases of non-taxed whiskey at Canaveral. The ATU is now focused on the two speakeasies and their suppliers. I am certain Bill's work will ultimately lead to shutting down these criminal enterprises. Until these operators are in federal custody, we must remain prudent and not jeopardize our sources. I appreciate the assistance rendered to Scarlet Biddy by your office and will wire Kelly's money through your home address at the end of this month.

                              J. W. Stiles
                              Special Agent in Charge
                              Alcohol Tax Unit

"Eureka!" said Brad, to himself, as he read the names *Kelly and Bill!* This had to be Bill Kelly, Ethel's fiancé. Was Bill an informant for the sheriff or a federal agent? Was Scarlet Biddy a code name for someone? He made some quick notes on his writing pad. He looked at his watch. It was almost time for Erin to leave the library and he needed to get back to Riverfront Park. He placed the lid on the box and headed out of the room down the hall to the front of the house.

"Finished?" asked Mrs. Howard. She was on a short step ladder trying to hang a painting on the wall. "Did you find anything useful?"

"Yes, I did," he replied, pausing to thank her for letting him search through the sheriff's papers. He started forward, then turned to her, "Whatever happened to Sheriff Jake Jacobs? Was he elected for another term as sheriff?"

She stepped down from the ladder, "Oh, then you don't know about him being shot?"

Brad was stunned, "…Shot?"

"Oh yes, he was shot," Mrs. Howard began explaining. "It didn't kill him. Somebody shot him one night on his way home. They never caught whoever did it…everybody said it was a bootlegger. That's when Sheriff Turner took over. Sheriff Jacobs moved to Blackshear, Georgia…he ever returned, not even to visit his sister and niece."

"Sheriff Turner? You mean…*Frank Turner?*

"Yes, it was…he was the sheriff until sometime about 1940."

"That's *interesting,* I didn't know that." He thanked her again and headed for the front door. He had not expected to find so much information in a small box at the Palmer House, now the case was getting deep. It was turning out to be a much better story than he had ever expected, although with all the people now dead, it would not be easy digging up the past. He needed more time. On the short walk back to Riverfront Park he used his cell phone to call his editor and managed to get an extra week to work on the old mystery.

CHAPTER 7

Brad was eager to tell Erin what he had discovered at the Palmer House. As he crossed the street to Riverfront Park he could see her car still parked in the same spot. Great, he thought, she hasn't left yet. He walked past some kids playing in a fountain pool to the shade of a big white gazebo in the center of the park. He looked at his watch; it was already 12:30 and no sign of Erin. Maybe she decided to eat lunch. He could use some lunch too, but did not want to take the chance of missing her by leaving his post.

The sun was directly overhead and warm. Beads of perspiration trickled down his temple and he wondered why he had worn a coat and tie. Occasionally, a slight breeze would blow in from the east bringing with it a peculiar salty-sulfide odor common to the Indian River. He loosened his tie, then opened one side of his sport coat and took a discreet sniff of the inside to make sure his deodorant was still working. After about fifteen minutes in the shade of the gazebo, he saw Erin coming down the sidewalk on the far side of the park. He straightened his tie, and hurried across the grass toward her. She saw him coming and waved. "Hey," he waved back, acting as if it was a chance encounter. "What a surprise to see you."

She was carrying a large, straw beach bag stuffed with books. "I just left the library…did you go to the Palmer house?"

He got in step with her, "Sure did. Can I carry that bag for you?"

"No thanks…I'm used to toting this thing. Did you see the special exhibit?"

"The machine guns?" he shook his head. "Whoa, man, that was one awesome exhibit for a place like that…but you'll never guess what I found there in those letters."

"Like what?" She answered, switching the bag to her other hand.

"You're not going to believe it. It's my biggest discovery yet." He acted anxious. "Sure is humid today. Hey, I have an idea! Since I know you'll want to hear about what I found, let's go over to my room where it's cool and we can have a Coke and I can tell you all about it."

"Your room?"

"Yeah, Room 17, Sea Rest Motel, you can follow me in your car…it's only a few blocks from here."

"I'm not going to your room!"

"Why not?"

"Well for one thing, I've got to go to the grocery store and then go home and feed my cat and get ready for work." She stopped in the middle of the sidewalk and stared at him. "Besides, you're crazy if you think I'm going to fall for some old come-to-my-room trick." She started walking again as he hurried to catch up. He thought he had a cool plan, but could tell it was rapidly falling apart.

"Okay, be that way," he said. "Alright, forget my room. I'll tell you what I found. Listen to this…it's going to spin your head around."

As they continued on the sidewalk, past where their cars were parked, toward the boardwalk that ran along the Indian River, Brad went through everything he had read in the sheriff's letters at the Palmer House. She listened intently, trying to sort out what he was telling her. She stopped, "So, you think Ethel's boyfriend…Bill Kelly, was like an undercover guy for the sheriff who was helping some federal agents."

"It sure looks that way," he said. "I think the name Scarlet Biddy was the code name for whatever it was. The sheriff probably knew everything, but he couldn't let anyone else know about Kelly or it would've blown the lid on some kind of federal investigation."

"So this stuff about Kelly being the suspect in Ethel's murder…was that just a cover thing the sheriff came up with?"

"No, it was Frank Turner, the investigator, who listed Bill Kelly as the suspect," he explained. "I think Turner was one of Judge Baxter's good old boys. I don't know what Baxter was up to, but I have a sneaking suspicion that whatever it was, it was under federal investigation and somebody fingered Bill Kelly as an informant."

"So, are you saying they killed Ethel because Bill was a spy?"

"She probably got in the way," he surmised. "I think they bumped Bill off, and she was with him, so they did her too." They had reached the railing of the boardwalk where a flock of sea gulls were fighting over some bait left by a fisherman. To their left could be seen the two high rise bridges connecting the mainland to the Merritt Island causeway.

Erin leaned on the railing watching the gulls. "Why wasn't Bill's body found in the river with Ethel's?"

"Simple," said Brad, "I think they wanted to make it look like he murdered her in a jealous rage then skipped town. They couldn't have both bodies being found at the same place."

"I guess it makes sense...it's still wild speculation though. Okay, then what do you reckon happened to Bill's body?"

"I've got to work on that," he said, scratching his head. "Hey, get *this*, I called my editor and he gave me another week to work on it."

"That's *great*," she replied. "Then maybe you'll take me out to a movie or something" Brad was caught off guard. He couldn't believe what he heard. "Did...did you say you wanted to go to a movie?"

Before she could answer, her attention was drawn a few yards down the boardwalk to a blonde woman painting at an easel. "There's Christine, come on you gotta meet her." She took his arm and jerked him in the direction of the woman. "Hi, Christine..."

The woman, wearing a floppy straw hat and cover-alls, with the legs rolled up to her knees, waved her brush at Erin, "Oh Erin dear, how're you?" Erin went around to the front side of the easel. "I'm fine Christine, oh what a nice painting." Brad paid no attention to the painting; instead he went over to the railing to look at the boats anchored in the river. Erin pointed to him, "That's my friend Brad; he's a writer from Miami." He gave a quick wave, "Hi."

While Erin and the woman chattered about how the sunlight was sparkling on the water, Brad was content just standing at the railing looking at the boats. It was a great scene for an artist to paint. He began counting the boats. He counted twenty-three boats...and a man on a raft! Shading his eyes with his hand, he focused on the curious sight. Just off shore was a man sitting in a lawn chair on a floating wooden platform under which were four large oil drums. It's like Huckleberry Finn's raft he thought, except Huck didn't have oil drums. He decided to go around to the front side of the canvas to see Christine's painting. He took one more quick glance at the man on the oil drum raft, then remarked, "Nice day for painting."

"Yes it is...the light is just right," smiled Christine, working a brush of white paint into the clouds of a picture of...*Mount Everest!*

"Mount Everest!!" he gaped at the painting, then at the river. "I thought you were painting those boats out there..."

"Heavens no, sugar, I hate boats," she said. "But I love mountains and the light is just perfect for painting today."

"You could paint that man on that crazy contraption out there," he snickered, noticing a slight grimace on Erin's face.

Christine peeked around the corner of her canvas at the floating platform. "Paint him? Ha...that's Vincent...my husband, why would I want to paint him?"

Brad's eyes darted from Christine to the raft. "That's your husband floating around out there?"

"Yes, he started building a houseboat for us...that raft is as far as he got with it. Now he just sits on it...feeding the gulls."

"How in the world did he get out there?" asked Brad.

"Don't ask me, sugar, I've been busy painting," she replied, cleaning her brush. "He can stay out there if he wants; it keeps him from pestering me while I'm painting."

Erin decided it was about time to go. "Christine, it was good seeing you. I'd love to chat but I've got to do some shopping." She pulled Brad along by the elbow and in a low tone, said, "Come on art critic, you need to get to your car and remove your foot from your mouth."

"She's painting a mountain and looking at boats," he said, glancing back at Christine. "And her husband is floating around on oil drums. Don't you find that just a little odd?"

"Christine is a psychic," said Erin. "She paints what she visualizes in her mind. Today she is seeing Mount Everest."

"No wonder her old man was floating on that raft...I would be too. I bet she believes in ghosts like you."

"Of course she does," answered Erin. "Speaking of ghosts, are you coming by Ashley's tonight to eat?"

"Maybe," he said, trying to be vague as they reached Erin's car. "Looks like a thunderstorm coming up." He gestured toward the south at a formation of heavy grey clouds. "I bet it will rain tonight."

"Oh, I hope so," she said, searching through her bag for her keys. "I love to sleep to the sound of rain at night." She got in her car, started the motor, and rolled down the window. "I'll look for you tonight if you decide to come out." She was interested in him and was throwing hints his way hoping he would catch one. So far he had fumbled. He started toward his car as she backed out of the parking space. He waved to her as she sped off toward Delannoy Avenue.

———————

That night, just as Brad had forecasted, it was pouring rain when he opened the door to Ashley's Tavern letting in the sound of rolling thunder. He shook off the rain and said hello to Roger behind the bar. Instead of sitting at the bar, he went into one of the small dining rooms and sat down at a table. There was plenty of room at the bar, but just in case Erin had a time to chat, he wanted a little more privacy. He had brought with him an excuse to talk with her too. After leaving the park, he had gone to the local historical museum to look at the old city police blotters from 1929 through 1936. Actually, the blotters were in pieces with many pages either blurred by stains or completely missing. Fortunately most of the 1934 blotter was intact, and it was in this one that he had found an entry where Ethel had filed a complaint against Judge Baxter's son, Sonny Baxter, for "harassment of a female." He made a copy of the page and this was what he wanted to show Erin.

It wasn't long before Erin showed up at his table. "Is it still raining outside?" she asked, brushing her hands on her apron.

"I told you it was going to rain," he replied, looking around the bar. "Looks like it's keeping your customers home tonight."

"Yeah, it's a slow night…wanna to order something to eat?"

"Bring me a club sandwich…and a cup of coffee…then if you get a chance I want to show you something I found at the museum this afternoon after I saw you in the park."

"Okay…let me take care of your order and I'll be right back."

She scurried off to the kitchen. While Brad waited for his food, he pulled the copy of the old blotter page from his coat pocket and looked it over. He sensed something. His eyes peered over the top of the paper at the dining area…then down at the table. He thought the salt shaker had moved. He lowered the paper and stared at the salt shaker…it was no illusion, it really did move! It's probably caused by a vibration, he thought. Then the shaker slid all the way across the table stopping at the very edge. He glanced around to see if anyone was watching then rolled up the paper and lightly pushed the salt shaker. It zipped back across the table to the other side. Cautiously, he picked it up with his finger tips and examined the bottom thinking it could be a prank. He looked under the table. There were no strings and no logical reason for this thing to move. He sat the shaker back on the table and it immediately took off to the edge of the table again. This is nuts, he thought, not too sure about what he was witnessing. There had to be a reason for the shaker moving on its own, but he could not figure out what it was. He got up and moved to another table that had no salt and pepper shakers. He kept his eye on the other table until Erin brought his order.

"What'd you do, switch tables?" she asked. "Here…let me get you some salt and pepper." She started for the other table.

"NO! NO!, that's okay…I don't need any," he said. "I'm cutting back on salt. I might even cut it out all together." He wasn't about to mention the moving salt shaker and get her started on psychic stuff.

"Hot dang!" she exclaimed with a laugh, "…all of a sudden you're *Mr. Healthy* concerned about salt…"

"I just got to thinking about what you said the other day at lunch, about healthy eating. Never mind that, look at this copy of the old police blotter. Read the third line." She sat down at the table and began reading the copy as he took a big bite from his sandwich.

"Oh yeah, I see it, Ethel filed a police complaint against Sonny Baxter. Wonder what that was all about?"

Brad took a sip of his coffee and sat the cup down. "It looks to me like she was being harassed by him. Three weeks later she was dead. I also noticed that she went to the city police and not the sheriff's office. Maybe she didn't trust the sheriff's office for some reason."

"Or maybe it had something to do with her boyfriend being an informant for the sheriff," said Erin. "Something is crooked as a dog's hind leg. So what do you make of it?"

"I really don't know, but it adds more suspicion to this Baxter dude. My guess is that Sonny Baxter was involved in whatever his old man was doing, and so was Frank Turner. By the time Ethel filed this complaint, it's my bet they already knew her boyfriend was spying on them for the Feds." Erin handed the copy back to Brad. He put it in his pocket and said, "Well I need to get back to the motel and see if I can figure out this mystery." The bar had thinned down to only two customers and Roger, who was busy with his clipboard figuring the liquor inventory.

"You're leaving so soon? It's still raining cats and dogs outside," said Erin. "It's going to be one of those boring slow nights."

That was what Brad wanted to hear. In his perception, she was begging him to stay and talk. He would test her by acting uninterested. Every scheme he had come up with seemed to fizzle leaving her in control. He would like a date with her, but couldn't stand the thought of possible rejection. He had to be sure first. He walked out of the tavern thinking, she's cute but shrewd as a fox.

———

After Brad left Ashley's, Erin went into the ladies' room to check her lipstick. Originally, in the 1930s, the ladies' room had been a storeroom. On the end was a swing out window with a latch, and down the left side were several stalls, and on the right side a long mirror above the sinks. She leaned close to the mirror and was about to freshen her lips when all of a sudden she was startled by a loud slamming noise. She placed her hand on her chest and tried to get her breath. The window had blown open and she could see the rain coming down in the outside darkness. She could hear the thunder outside as she shut the window and tightly latched it. There was no wind outside and she wondered what caused it to blow open. One thing for sure, she wasn't going to allow her imagination to conjure up any scary stuff. She returned to the mirror and finished putting on her lipstick. A small sign on the wall reminded employees to wash their hands before returning to work. She turned on the faucet and began washing her hands but was overcome by a strange feeling. Slowly her eyes drifted up to the mirror into the eyes of the *ghostly face* of a girl with long reddish hair. She gasped, "Oh...*Oh, God!*" Frozen in fright, she stood there unable to move as blood began trickling down the girl's face and dripping into the sink where it swirled around before vanishing down the drain. Erin, scared and shaking, pushed away from the sink pressing her back against the stall door opposite the mirror. She made a start for the door, and then paused to glance at the image. It was *gone* and so was the blood. In the mirror she saw only her own reflection. Warily, she reached out and touched the mirror, running her trembling fingers over the glassy surface and then around the sink basin. She knew it wasn't her imagination; she had really seen *something* in the mirror.

She rushed out of the restroom toward the bar where Roger was still working on his inventory. "Roger...I'm not feeling so well. Since it is a slow night can I take off?"

He laid his clipboard on the counter. "Sure babe...are you okay? You look kinda washed out."

She grabbed a shot glass and filled it with straight bourbon. "I need something to settle my nerves." She slugged the whiskey down and in a raspy tone, said, "I'll be alright...just need to go home and lie down. I just feel a little woozy."

———

In the brief moments of Erin's unexplained encounter at Ashley's, Brad was driving through the downpour on U.S. 1 headed back to the Sea Rest motel. Visibility was almost zero even with his windshield wipers beating at full speed. He strained to see the lines on the wet, black road while going no more than ten miles per hour. It was well after nine by the time he turned into the flooded motel parking lot. He parked his car and made a splashing dash through lightening flashes to his room.

He fumbled with his key and finally opened the door. He was soaked by the time he got inside. He took off his wet coat and shirt and threw them in a pile in the bathroom. Grabbing a fresh towel he began drying his hair and looking at some notes he had taped to the big mirror on the wall at the foot of the bed. He was using the mirror like a big bulletin board. Whenever he found a clue to the Ethel Allen murder, he would write it on a piece of paper and tape it to the mirror. He could then move his clues around to do what he referred to as "connecting the dots." He thought of it as an easy way to see the big picture. By now over thirty little notes were taped to the mirror and he was fixing to add three more. On the first one he wrote in capital letters, "BILL KELLY-INFORMANT," on the second note he printed, "SONNY BAXTER," and on the last note he wrote down Ethel's complaint to the police about being harassed by Sonny Baxter. The clues were adding up, but not quite coming together yet.

He was about to tape the last note to the mirror when he noticed a reflection of the bed behind him. Sitting on the bed, was a *nude girl* with her back to him. She was wearing nothing but a white, bridal veil. One hand was outstretched and on her finger he could clearly see a ruby ring. He quickly snapped around at the bed…but there was *no one* there. He looked back at the mirror and again saw the clear image of a young girl. There were several red puncture wounds on her naked back, maybe three or four, he didn't take time to count, instead his eyes switched back to the bed again. There was no girl on the bed. Twice in the mirror, he had seen the reflection of a girl sitting on his bed. He thought, maybe it's my eyes playing tricks, but he was sure of what he had seen.

He eased over to the bed, rubbing his hand through his hair. The bed was not disturbed; it was just like the maid had left it. Thinking out loud, he said, "What the hell is going on?" Maybe it was a prank. He thought of all kinds of possibilities for the strange phenomenon. He called out, "Erin…is that you?" No such luck, he thought. "Is anybody in here?" There was no answer. He looked in the mirror again but only saw the bed. He went over to the window and peered through a crack in the curtains. The parking lot was dark and the rain was still coming down. The lights flickered. Probably the storm, he thought. He jerked the curtain closed and moved over to make sure the door was locked. As his hand gripped the knob, he felt a sudden heavy pounding on the door, like somebody, or some thing, was trying to get in. The lights flickered again. His imagination began taking over as he let go of the door knob and jumped back, fearful of what might be on the other side.

CHAPTER 8

Brad stood there, wide-eyed, barefoot, in his trousers and tee-shirt, and listened with his ear to the door. He quickly recognized the sound, it was someone's fist pounding against the door. "Brad, let me in!" It was a muffled voice. "Brad...open the damn door!" He quickly unlocked the door and opened it to see Erin standing there with her pretty auburn hair hanging wet down the sides of her face. She pushed her way into his room clinging to his shoulders as she pressed her body close to him.

"Erin...what...what're you doing here?" he said, thinking his imagination was really working overtime, first a girl on his bed and now Erin standing in his room hugging him. "What's going on?"

"I saw her!" she exclaimed, holding on to him. "In the restroom, it was *Ethel's* ghost!" He caught a whiff of her damp hair and perfume as he held her close and kicked the door shut with his foot.

"I think I saw her too," he said, "she was sitting on my bed."

Erin pushed back slightly, "NO, I'm not kidding!! I saw her in the restroom mirror. It was her...*she's real!*"

He held her steady by her shoulders. "Erin, listen to me, I'm not making fun! I saw her in that big mirror sitting on my bed...with blood on her back and...and she had on a wedding thing on her head...and a *ruby ring* on her finger! A ruby ring! I turned and she was gone. I saw her *twice*...but only in the mirror."

"Brad...what's going on...?? This is too weird. It's freaking me out. What does she want? She knows what you're doing...she's trying to tell us something!"

"Look...you know I don't put much stock in this ghost stuff...but really I can't explain this one. I know what I saw...and it was like she wanted me to see that ring..."

"Because the ring was her way of letting you know who she was!"

"Gawd...now I'm not only believing in ghosts...I'm *seeing* them too! He exclaimed. "This is as freaky as it gets! Okay, I accept it. I've gone totally insane, send me to the nut house on the next bus."

"It's not your imagination!! Brad, think about it. Both of us saw her image in a mirror. Two different people, two different mirrors in two different places! For some reason she can only be seen in a mirror...just like the story at Ashley's. She's always seen in the mirror. Call it my woman's intuition, but I really get the feeling that she wants us to find Bill. She still loves him."

"Maybe your intuition is right...and I would really love to solve this mystery...but with a ghost? That's getting a little far out." He had hardly finished his words when a deafening crack of thunder knocked out the lights leaving the room in total darkness.

Erin jumped and grabbed hold of him. "Oh great! Now what?? The lights...Brad I'm scared."

"Shhh...calm down," he said, going over to peek through the curtains at the wet dark parking lot. "It's just the storm. Lightening must have struck an electric pole, the lights are out all over. Hey, you're shaking like a leaf, are you okay? You're upset."

"Of course I'm upset! First I come face to face with a ghost...it's raining cats and dogs...and now the blame lights go out. God...I won't be able to sleep tonight..."

"You can stay here tonight...if you like."

"Oh yeah, and now you want to take advantage of the situation..." Erin was standing at the foot of the bed but couldn't see him in the dark. "I can't see you, where'd you go? What're you doing...?"

"I'm sitting on the bed." He reached out in the darkness toward her voice and took her hand. "Here, sit down for a minute. Seriously, you can stay here...I promise to be good."

She sat down beside him on the bed. "I just don't feel like being by myself," she said, as he pulled her close in a comforting hug.

"Look, don't worry about it," he said. "We'll figure it out in the morning. Wrap up in this blanket and take those wet clothes off. I'll get you a towel for your hair."

As he made his way through the dark toward the bathroom, Erin removed her damp clothes and wrapped up in the blanket. "I still love rainy nights," she said, watching flashes of lightening through the curtain. She heard Brad bump into the dresser, "Ouch…dammit!" he moaned. "I stubbed my toe! Pull that curtain back and get some light in here." He tossed a bath towel to her and she began drying her hair in dark.

"It's just as dark outside," she said, placing the damp towel on the back of a chair. "Besides, I need privacy. I don't want to wake up in the morning with every pervert and his brother looking through the window at me in bed with you." Lying down on the bed, she turned over facing the window as he climbed in on the other side. She felt his arm pull her close in a secure snuggle. "Make sure you stay on your own side," she mumbled, with a smile he could not see in the darkness. She felt safe with him. The room was black, except for intermittent lightening flashing through the window curtains. He gave her a secure hug, and said, "Just listen to the rain."

———

The next morning came fresh with bright sunbeams piercing through fluffy cumulous clouds floating against a blue sky. The rain had vanished with the night, leaving behind little crystals of water sparkling in the sunlight as they fell in slow motion from the tips of green leaves. Millions of tiny droplets covered the cars parked in front of the motel rooms. At eight o'clock, Erin came out of Room 17, with her shoes in her hand and left to go home. For Brad it had been the strangest night of his life. He had seen a salt shaker move by itself, saw a ghost in the mirror, and Erin had spent the night with him. He went to the sink and turned on the water and began shaving. As he looked in the mirror he kept looking beyond his reflection just in case something unexplainable decided to make a morning manifestation.

At nine o'clock, he left the motel and drove down to the old section of town to a small barbershop on a side street. He really didn't need a haircut, but barbershops can be good places to pickup local gossip. He parked his car and walked across the brick street toward a short, red, white, and blue striped barber pole attached to the front of a building. He opened the door and was told to have a seat by the barber who was busy with a customer in the first chair. The narrow shop had two barber chairs, but only one barber. Down the left side were seven chairs, patched with duct tape, for waiting customers. Above the chairs was a long mirror that could hardly be seen for a collage of old photographs and newspaper clippings pasted on it. There were no other customers, so he took a seat next to a small table stacked with out-dated magazines and newspapers. He picked up a newspaper and flipped it open to the sports page.

From behind the newspaper, he could see the sign painted on the large window facing the street. The painted letters read, "Barber Shop," but from inside the letters were reversed. He thought about how two people can see the same thing differently. He was still trying to figure out his weird experience last night. Then he noticed someone standing outside looking in. It was the old African-American bag lady he had seen on his first day in town. She stood there for a few seconds, smiled, and then proceeded down the street with her grocery cart.

"Next!" called the barber, as he finished sweeping up hair from around the base of the chair. Brad laid the newspaper down and climbed into the chair. The barber draped a cover around him and snapped it together in the back. "Okey, dokey...trim or full cut?"

"Just an outline on the sides...and taper the back," he replied, turning his head from side to side as he looked in the mirror.

The barber picked up a pair of scissors and a comb, and with hand movements reminiscent of a surgeon, began working around Brad's ears. "That was a genuine toad strangler last night," remarked the barber, raking a comb through a layer of Brad's hair. He pointed his scissors toward the window. "Water was still running down the street out there when I opened the shop this morning."

"Yeah, it was a pretty wet night," Brad replied, eyeing all the pictures and news clippings covering the long mirror above the chairs. "Looks like you've got quite a collection of old photographs there. Are they pictures of local people?"

The barber paused, "Most of that stuff was put up there by my dad. He opened this shop after he came home from the Second World War. Most of them things are sixty years old; I just never took it down. There's pictures of fish caught by Dad's customers, I suppose most of them are dead now." He pointed his comb to a picture of several men with a large catch of fish. "As far as I know, that fellow on the end was the last one still living. That was the Baxter Pack, or that's what everybody called them. A real influential bunch, they practically ran the county at one time. I dare say, they were a notorious group too."

Brad's eye brows raised, "Baxter Pack? Like in *Judge Baxter?*"

"No, not the judge, he was already dead by then, that's his son and his buddies. They all had ties to under-handed dealings in town. Two of them were lawyers, and a couple dabbled in politics."

"You mean Sonny Baxter? The one that was a state senator?"

"Yeah, old Sonny. That's him holding the fish in the picture."

"Who are the others?"

The barber walked over for a closer look, "Well...that's Felton Kennedy next to Sonny...that one is Frank Turner...and Henry Moore, and this one wearing the captain's hat is Billy Marshall, he owned a big boat. Folks say he used to run rum from the Bahamas with that boat. Felton Kennedy managed Sonny Baxter's campaign for the state senate and Frank Turner was a tight buddy of both Judge Baxter and Sonny. Turner was the sheriff for awhile. Henry Moore was the county prosecutor. I can't remember what Marshall did, other than being a rum runner. Hell, every last one of them was involved in the numbers racket."

"The numbers racket?"

"Bolita and Cuba, it was like the lotto today. It was illegal but made a lot of money for those in the business. Sonny was getting kickbacks from all this stuff but nobody could touch him because he had the law in his pocket. Like I say, playing the numbers was illegal back then. Now the Florida Lottery is doing the same thing...there ain't no difference...except it's legal for the state to sell numbers."

"I read somewhere that Felton Kennedy was charged with burning down some houses," said Brad, referring to the old newspaper article he had found at the library.

"Hell, he was involved in more than that," said the barber, as he edged around Brad's ears with a straight razor. "Son, you're looking at the local Klan leaders in that photograph. Everybody knew it and nobody did anything about it. Not one of them ever went to jail."

"Ever hear of anybody named Bill Kelly or Ethel Allen?" asked Brad. "She worked at Jack's Tavern and was murdered in 1934 and Kelly got blamed for it."

"Nope, can't say that I have, but that was before my time. I've heard my dad speak of Jack's Tavern. It was on U.S.1 in Rockledge."

"Yeah, that's the place. It's called Ashley's now."

"That's right. I know it's been under several names." The barber removed the cover from Brad, handed him a mirror, and began brushing off his shirt. "Okey dokey, how's it look?"

"Looks good to me," he answered, reaching in his hip pocket for his wallet. He gave the barber a ten dollar bill. "Keep the change, and thanks for the interesting conversation."

His visit to the barber shop had confirmed that almost every name he had found in the Ethel Allen case was connected to either Judge Baxter or his son, Sonny Baxter. There were only two exceptions, Sheriff Jacobs and Ethel's boyfriend, Bill Kelly. Both Jacobs and Kelly, according to the letter found at the Palmer house, were assisting in a federal investigation. For the first time he was starting to untangle this mystery and the motive behind Ethel's murder.

On the way to his car after leaving the barber shop he saw the old bag lady down the street going through a trash bin. Once again she paused and looked his way. He ignored her and kept walking.

It was impossible for him to think about the murder without thinking about his strange encounters. The threads of his skepticism were unraveling; he could not deny his strange experiences with moving salt shakers and an apparition in his mirror. He was beginning to understand why people never talk about such things. His editor would call him crazy. Perhaps such things are best left alone he thought, of course, Erin would never allow that to happen.

Brad spent the afternoon in his motel room taking a nap until he was awakened by the phone ringing. He looked at the clock on the nightstand beside the bed, it was five o'clock. He sat up and almost knocked the phone off the nightstand trying to answer it.

"Ah...Yeah...Hello?"

"Hey Brad...it's Erin. Where have you been?"

He was still drowsy from his nap. "Uh…Oh Erin, I must have slept all afternoon. I got a haircut this morning…then came back here and fooled around with some research notes. I guess I was just catching up on sleep that I missed last night. So, what's going on?"

"Oh nothing, I hadn't heard from you today and was just thinking about last night."

"About what part of it?" He sat there rubbing his hand through his hair. "You're not mad about spending the night are you?"

"Of course not, that was like an emergency situation. I'm talking about Ethel. Do you think she will appear again?"

"Gosh, I don't know, I don't know what to think of any of it. I'm still trying to figure out what I saw in the mirror…part of me wants to say it was a ghost and the other part of me…well it's confusing. Where are you?"

"I'm in my apartment…getting ready to go to work. I'd like to see you. Are you coming by tonight?"

"Ah…Sure. I'd like to see you too. I did pick up more information about Baxter and those other guys mentioned in the old newspaper articles. Let me shower and get my head straight and I'll drop in around seven…okay?"

"Then I'll see you tonight." Her voice was almost mesmerizing to his ear. Then in a sensuous tone, she whispered, "Bye, bye."

He said "Good bye," and hung up the phone. Down deep inside of him, she had aroused a primeval urge, which since prehistoric times has often caused the male species to act like fools. It was a funny sensation and hard to explain, but so was being haunted by two women, one dead and the other alive. In a strange way he loved it.

———

That evening Brad walked through the door of Ashley's at seven-thirty. There was a talkative crowd at the bar, at least more people than the previous night. Erin was setting up drinks for a waitress and saw him come in. She gave him a sultry smile as her green eyes followed him to a vacant stool. He still preferred to sit on the opposite side of the bar so he could watch people coming and going through the front door. He had become a regular customer at Ashley's. Roger shoved a draft beer in front of him and commented about the storm last night and how Erin had gone home early. Obviously, Erin had not told Roger about her encounter in the ladies' room, thought Brad, or about where she had spent the night. He was not about to tell anyone either. It wasn't long before Erin came out from behind the bar to take a ten minute break. She climbed upon a stool next to him, and said, "So, what's new?"

"Hi, are you feeling okay after last night?"

"Sure, I'm fine. Just a little confused by you-know-what," she replied, trying to be discreet.

"You mean the mirror or..." he looked around, then jokingly whispered, "...or spending the night with a strange man?"

She gave him a soft jab on the shoulder, "Will you shut up about *that*...you know *what* I mean...the *mirror*...and by the way, you snore!"

"I've never heard myself snore."

"Well you do...and it sounds like an old boar hog too."

They laughed and for a fleeting moment their eyes locked. Brad broke the spell by telling her about his visit to the barbershop and the pictures he had seen. "They were all in cahoots with Sonny Baxter," he said, explaining what the barber had told him. "Remember Felton Kennedy, and Henry Moore, the county prosecutor, and Frank Turner, the chief deputy...and remember that guy mentioned in the old newspaper article about the house burning, B.T. Marshall?"

"Oh, yeah," she recalled, "that was in the 1932 article I found at the library...about the Klan burning the houses."

"Right, that's the one. Well, it turns out Marshall owned a big boat and was known for hauling illegal booze from the Bahamas...his name was Billy Marshall and he was in the picture standing next to Sonny Baxter and the rest of the Baxter gang." Before he could continue, they heard an argument going on near the ladies' restroom. Brad turned to look, "What's going on over there?"

It appeared that Roger, the bar manager, was trying to keep a woman from entering the ladies' room. The woman hauled off and swung her purse at Roger and told him to keep his hands off her.

"Oh lord. Not again!" exclaimed Erin. "I better see if Roger needs a hand..." She slid off the stool but before she could reach the argument, it had ceased and Roger was returning to his work behind the bar. Erin followed him and went back to tending bar. The woman, wearing a low cut black dress and lavender bolero jacket, sashayed over and took the stool next to Brad. She crossed her long, fishnet covered legs, patted her blonde curly wig, and winked at Brad, "Buy me a drink, Honey." Brad looked down at her fishnet hose and stiletto heels, but before he could respond, Roger was leaning across the counter saying, "Listen Robert, this is the last time that I'm..." The woman interrupted, shaking her finger at him.

"No! You listen to me, Roger!" she said, sliding her dress up slightly, exposing her knee. "My name is R O B E R T A...Not Robert!!!"

Roger acted a little perturbed, "Roberta, Robert...whoever the hell you are tonight...you're not going in the women's room, and you're not going in the men's room dressed like that either!" She stuck her tongue out and wagged it at him as she gave Brad another wink. "Honey, you ain't hard to look at. I wanted you to buy me a drink but thanks to Roger I've done changed my mind."

"Why is that?" asked Brad, noticing out of the corner of his eye that Erin was about to bust out laughing.

"Because alcohol goes right through me and Roger won't let me use the restrooms in this place!"

Brad was beginning to sense that behind the red lips and make-up was a cross-dresser, in other words, Roberta was a man. "So, let me guess why he won't let you go to the restroom. Is it because of the way you're dressed?"

"No, it's because I've complained about the spiritual energy in the ladies' room. We women are especially sensitive to it."

"I think it's because you're dressed like a woman," Brad replied.

"Whatever, sweetie, but I'm always a lady when I come in here and expect to be treated like a one too. Now let me buy you a drink."

"Ah...No thanks, I've had my limit. I have to keep my head straight." Erin moved down the inside of the bar to Brad and tried to rescue him by changing the subject. "So, is Sonny Baxter still living?"

"I don't know," said Brad. "If he is, I'd sure like to talk with him." Roberta overheard and butted in, "Old man Baxter? Honey the last time I saw that old man he had old timers' disease or whatever they call it. He couldn't even put his drawers on without help. Hell, he couldn't even find his drawers..."

Erin interjected, "Roberta, you *don't* know Sonny Baxter."

"Oh yes I do! Back when I was an in-home care nurse I had to make calls at his place. I guess he's still living but if you want to know about anybody in this town you need to talk to Indigo Blue."

"Indigo Blue," exclaimed Erin. "She's a bag lady!"

Brad was listening, "Bag lady? Is she that black woman who pushes a grocery cart around town?"

"Yeah, *that's* her," said Erin. "I know you've seen her downtown in the Village. She is a friendly soul, almost a landmark in town."

"She's more than that," added Roberta. "Indigo Blue is a root doctor. She knows all about mojo, hexes, herb remedies...and she can read your mind...she's a psychic."

"So, what does she know about Sonny Baxter?" asked Brad, taking another sip from his draft beer.

"Does she talk with the dead, like the spirit in this place?" Erin asked. "Or can she tell us about the ghost Brad saw in his motel last night?" Her slip of the tongue caused Brad to choke on his beer. "Oops!" she said, capping her hand over her mouth. "Sorry..."

"GOOD GOD!! *YOU SAW A GHOST* in your room??" shouted Roberta, loud enough to turn every head at the bar.

Brad wiped his mouth and sat his glass down. He reached for a napkin to dry his shirt, "*Never mind that!* I don't want to talk about *ghosts*. I want to talk about *Sonny Baxter*. Now what about this Indigo Blue woman, can she tell me anything about Baxter?"

"It'll cost you a pint bottle of gin if you want to talk to Indigo," Roberta replied. "I'll guarantee you that old woman can tell you more about folks in this town than you ever thought to ask."

Brad glanced at Erin. "Whatta you think?"

"Let's try it. It's worth a chance."

"Listen, sweet cakes," said Roberta, getting up from the bar stool. "I've got to go pee, even if I have to find myself a tree to get behind. So, if you want to visit Indigo Blue, be out front of this place in the morning at nine, with a bottle of gin."

"What kind of gin?" asked Brad.

"It don't make no difference, the cheap kind will do."

"Okay, we'll meet you in the morning at nine, out front, with a bottle of cheap gin." Erin sketched something on a napkin and stuffed it in Brad's shirt pocket.

"What's that?"

"Directions to Spanish Oaks Apartments, where I live, pick me up at eight-thirty…I'll be waiting at the curb."

"Okay, but if you're not there, I'm not going to wait."

"Don't worry, I'll be there…just don't forget the gin."

Brad said goodnight to Erin and headed back to the Sea Rest Motel. Along the way he pulled into Bud's Discount Liquors and bought a pint of cheap gin and a lotto ticket.

CHAPTER 9

The next morning, after driving up and down several side streets, Brad found Spanish Oaks Apartments where Erin lived. It was right on the line where the twin towns of Cocoa and Rockledge meet. As he wheeled into the parking lot, he spotted her sitting on the curb with a bottle of water. She was wearing a white cotton blouse tucked neatly into a pair of tight jeans. After throwing some empty food containers into the backseat to make room, he leaned over and opened the passenger side door. She got in and immediately noticed the floor and the backseat, "Good grief, when was the last time you cleaned this car?"

"Good morning to you too," he said, pulling out of the parking lot.

"Oh, I'm sorry, good morning," she smiled. "Really, how do you drive with so much junk in this thing?"

"I've been planning to clean it out, but you know…running here and there…I just haven't got around to it." He drove straight up the street to U.S.1 and turned south. Five minutes later they pulled into Ashley's where Roberta was waiting. Instead of wearing a dress and blonde wig, he had short brown hair and was dressed in tight fitting jeans topped with a Hawaiian shirt with a bright, floral pattern. "He looks a little more like a man this morning," said Brad. "I'm damn glad you're riding in the front seat." Erin laughed and rolled down the window, "Morning, Roberta."

Roberta climbed into the backseat, "Did you get the gin?"

Brad looked in the rear view mirror and held up a brown paper sack, "Right here, one pint of the finest, cheapest gin. Now which way do we go to get to Indigo Blue's place?"

Roberta leaned over the back of the seat and pointed, "Make a left here and go back up U.S.1 toward Cocoa and make a right on Mango Trail, it's only about three or four miles."

He followed Roberta's directions. Half way down Mango Trail they turned down a narrow dirt alley that led to a small clapboard house with a porch and an unpainted picket fence across the front of the yard. It was a well-kept little dwelling nestled in the shade of several live oaks dripping with Spanish moss. In the yard were a dozen rusty grocery carts parked in a row. "This place looks like a storage lot for used shopping carts," Brad mused. "She must have half the grocery carts in town in her yard."

"Except the ones from the drugstore..." added Roberta, as Brad pulled the car up next to the fence and turned off the motor. They got out and walked through a little gate toward the house. The old woman was sitting on the porch with a large round pan in her lap, snapping and shelling green beans. She leaned forward and squinted through her wire-rimmed glasses to study the three visitors. She recognized Roberta who was in front of the other two, and with a broad grin, she said, "Robbie! Child you be a sight for sore eyes. I sees you done brung me some company."

"Miss Blue, this is Brad and Erin..." Roberta stepped up on the porch where there were four straight back chairs. Several cats scattered from the porch and disappeared under the house.

Indigo Blue eyed her two guests as if looking into their souls. "I know who they be..." She fixed her eyes on Brad, "Boy, I figured sooner or later you'd pay me a visit." She switched to Erin, "...*And you, girl*, I *knows* you too...I knows both y'all and you gots a lot of questions and you thinks I gots all the answers."

Roberta had already taken a seat while Brad and Erin remained standing in front of the old woman as if in court before a judge. Indigo looked at Brad, "You got me some gin, boy?"

He handed the sack, concealing the bottle, to her, "Yes ma'am."

She pulled the bottle from the sack and inspected it. "Sit down...- and let me take care of this here gin." Brad and Erin pulled up a couple of chairs and sat down while the old woman unscrewed the cap and poured the gin into a jelly jar sitting on a small table. She picked up a stick resembling a homemade feather duster. She waved it across the jar and recited a few inaudible words of magic.

"What's that for?" asked Brad, observing the strange ritual.

"Keeps the spirits busy," she answered. "It'll keep them from pestering me so can I think. They'll smell that liquor and here they'll come. They'll start lapping it up and won't bother me. You gots to know how to deal with spirits."

"Is that really true," Erin asked, eager to hear anything related to the paranormal, especially after her personal encounter in the mirror.

Indigo squinted one eye at her, "Girl...anytime a ghost bothers you, just pour him some liquor and he'll leave you alone. You knows all 'bout haints, I can see it all in you." The old woman snapped a quick look at both Brad and Erin, and went back to shelling beans. "Now git on with it, what y'all want from Indigo?"

Erin focused on Indigo's fingers as they shelled out the beans. She was wearing a ruby ring. With her eyes, Erin silently directed Brad's attention to the ring. He returned a smile with a subtle nod to let her know he had seen it.

"Senator Baxter..." began Brad, "have you ever heard of him?"

Indigo stopped shelling beans and sat still for a moment like she was going into a trance, then with eyes wide open, said, "Mister Sonny? Sure, I knows 'bout Mister Sonny and 'bout all his doings."

"You mean his politics?" he asked.

"I ain't talkin' 'bout politicking. I knows 'bout his devilish friends. I knows their secrets...I can still see them now...drunk, and dancing 'round in sheets with eye holes. Oh, they was bad medicine for anybody who messed with them."

"You ever heard of a girl named Ethel Allen?" inquired Brad. "She was murdered in 1934 and had a boyfriend named Bill Kelly and he disappeared at the same time."

"I was little when that happened," she answered, as she put the pan of beans on the floor and settled back in her chair. "Everybody knew 'bout her being kilt. But that was another place in time."

Erin chimed in, "Miss Blue, I really believe in psychics. In your visions can you tell me what Ethel looked like?" Erin was hoping to find out if Ethel matched the image she had seen in the mirror.

"Girl, you *knows* what she looked like. These ain't visions I'm talking 'bout." Indigo picked up a pipe and began packing tobacco into the bowl. She struck a match on the side of her chair and lit the pipe. Tiny puffs of bluish smoke came from her lips.

"If you're not having visions or whatever," said Brad, "then how do you know about Sonny Baxter?" He sensed the old woman was leaving something out of the conversation.

Indigo took a long drag on her pipe and with a straightforward reply, said, "I was Mr. Sonny's housekeeper for fifteen years and my momma worked for Judge Baxter at the old place. Me and my momma lived out there when I was little."

"The old place?" Brad had found a trail that could very well lead him right into the Baxter family.

"The Baxter farm…" answered Indigo. "We lived in a little shack, nothing much out there now. Mr. Sonny was a lawyer then, and him and them boys used to raise the devil out there. We knew to keep our mouth shut. I wuz little, but I seen a lot going on there."

"Like what?" Brad was eager to keep the discussion moving.

"Mr. Sonny was a young feller, they all wuz. They'd get drunker than skunks and put on sheets with eye holes. They'd burn a big ol' cross down there in the clay pit and whoop and holler all night long. They'd be gone by morning. The Judge and his wife was living in town but they kept the old farm 'cause they had cows out there. The old house is gone now, but back then they used it for a hunting camp. Sometimes me and momma would be the only ones out there for weeks at a time when they needed momma to cook for them. I remember seeing those crosses they burned. I would go down there to the clay pit and take that clay and mix water with it to make little pots. It was about the only plaything I had."

"You made clay pots?" Brad asked. "You said there was a clay pit there. Do you mean clay…like red clay?"

"Don't you know what a clay pit is?" she said. "It was where they dug clay out of a pit. Judge Baxter sold clay to the county for putting on the roads. There weren't many paved roads back then; most roads were either covered with shell or clay. Oh yes, it was red clay 'cause my momma would give me the dickens for getting' it on my clothes 'cause it was hard to wash out."

"Was Sonny Baxter married?" asked Erin.

"He was, but him and her fought like bearcats. He hit on her all the time. He was hard on women…meaner than a snake, but you never would've know'd it if you saw him. He knew how to act in front of folks…you know what I'm saying?"

"I know the type," remarked Brad. "So, what happened to Miz Baxter, is she still living?"

"Dead…she drove her car off the Coconut Canal bridge. They found her drowned, still sitting in her car. Everybody said she had a little help."

"You mean *somebody* killed her?"

"That was the gossip. But the police said it was an accident."

"You ever hear of Jack's Tavern?"

"It was a juke joint up yonder on the highway," replied Indigo, pointing with the stem of her pipe. "Mr. Sonny and them boys used to hang 'round there on Saturday night till midnight and then most times would come out to the old place and wake us up."

"Wake you up?"

"With their noise, they'd be drinking and driving 'round in circles. I remember one night they came out there and knocked on our door wanting some kerosene. I was real little then."

"Kerosene?"

"For starting a fire down there in the clay pit," she explained. "Momma kept a can of kerosene for the stove. We were always scared they'd burn down the place. One time Mr. Frank caught his sheet on fire from one of those crosses. I was peaking out the window." Indigo slapped her knee, and laughed, "Me and momma almost died laughing about that."

"Mr. Frank? Would that be *Frank Turner?*" Brad inquired.

"That's him, he was a sheriff or something. He was like part of the Baxter family, always hanging 'round Mr. Sonny or the Judge."

"Was Frank Turner with Sonny Baxter the night they wanted some kerosene to build a fire?

"I don't really remember, it's been a long time ago, there were two other folks, I know there was a woman 'cause I could hear her talking. And there was some men but I don't know how many. I just know they wanted to build a fire. They was down in the woods shooting guns 'cause I remember hearing the noise. I know one of them left their car there. It must have been broke down 'cause it sat there nearly a week. Then one day it was gone."

"What year was that?" he asked, taking a wild chance that he could be uncovering something of relative importance.

"Oh lordy, I don't know. I was about nine or ten. I'm 79 now."

Brad did some quick figuring in his head. "So you were born in, ah, 1925. That would have made you nine...or ten in 1934."

"I imagine that's about right."

"Do you remember going down to the clay pit the next morning?" He was curious about the gun fire she had heard as a child.

"No, momma wouldn't let me. The Judge moved us to town a week or two later to work in his house."

"So what happened to Sonny Baxter?"

"That old polecat...ha, the devil took his mind a long time ago."

Brad stood up from his chair, ready to leave. "Miss Blue...you've been very interesting. Thank you so much for your time."

Erin reached out and shook the old woman's hand, the one with the ring on it. "Thank you, I've always wanted to meet you, I heard that you're a real psychic. I wish I was one too."

Indigo's eyes gave a penetrating stare at her, "Girl, you know more than you think." Indigo then switched to Brad, "And you, boy, you gonna know too when the time is right...*You hear me, boy?*"

"Yes ma'am," he answered, watching Roberta stepping off the porch like something was going to happen.

Indigo stood up for the first time and walked to a post that held up the porch roof. "You *listen* to me. Both of you done been through the looking glass, I knows it, I can see it. Time ain't what it seems to be. You're talking to the old timekeeper." She turned to Brad, "Boy, you got a watch?"

"Yes ma'am, I sure do," he said, pulling back his sleeve to show her a digital watch on his wrist.

"That watch is the only way you can show time, if you didn't have it, you couldn't show time to anybody, 'cause time ain't what it seems to be. Folks in China and France gots clocks too, but it ain't got the same time as that one on your arm. A real timekeeper doesn't use that kind of time, so don't let that watch make a fool out of you. Mark my words, boy, I knows you'll be back, and be sure to bring me some gin, now y'all *git on out of here!*"

Roberta said goodbye to Indigo, but was well ahead of Brad and Erin as they walked toward the car. "That's one strange lady," Brad whispered to Erin. "Did you hear what she said about the clay on the Baxter farm? I almost flipped...Remember in the coroner's report where traces of clay was found under Ethel's finger nails? And they found a guava seed...damn, I should have asked her if she remembered any guavas trees at the old Baxter farm. I think she was talking about the night Ethel was murdered...I think we're onto something."

He opened the car door for Erin. "And when you saw that ring on her finger, wow, I almost fell out of the chair when I saw it." He went around and got in behind the steering wheel and buckled his seat belt.

"Do you think it could be the same ring?" asked Erin.

"I was afraid to ask her about it, but it was a ruby. Of course, anybody could have a ruby ring..." he replied, starting the motor. As Brad turned the car around Erin looked back at the house and saw Indigo pick up the jelly jar and down the gin in one swallow.

Roberta leaned over the back of the seat, "She probably found that ring in the trash. It's probably an imitation ruby."

"Who knows, but I'm going to find out," said Brad, driving down the bumpy alley toward Mango Trail.

"What was she talking about with all that time stuff? About being a timekeeper?" Roberta wondered aloud. "She talks a little weird sometimes."

"And when she mentioned going through the looking glass," said Erin. "I thought she meant a mirror, like she knew about our experiences...like us seeing images in mirrors."

"Yeah, I did too, but don't jump to conclusions," Brad cautioned, "it could just be the way she talks and she really didn't say much about Ethel. I mean, she wouldn't even tell you what Ethel looked like, she seemed to change the subject."

"She said I knew what Ethel looked like," added Erin. "I felt like she was talking about what I saw in the mirror."

"I don't think so, it seemed like she avoided the question when you asked her what Ethel looked like." He slowed down for the stop sign at the intersection of U.S. 1 and Mango Trail, and then abruptly said, "Let's go find Ethel's grave!!" He made a quick right on U.S.1 and headed north to the intersection with State Road 520.

"Are you serious? You don't even know where she is buried," said Erin. "She might even be buried in some other part of the state."

"Mrs. Davis at the records place said she is buried over on Merritt Island in a small cemetery on Crooked Mile Road."

"What if her grave is unmarked?" asked Erin. "I mean...like in searching for my genealogy in old cemeteries I found some of my ancestor's had wooden markers that have totally rotted away."

"This one is supposed to have a cement marker," he replied. "I just feel like we should find it. I don't know why...but since we are dealing with this girl, it would be nice to know where she is buried."

Roberta leaned over the back of the front seat, "Whoa...this queen don't like the bone yard scene...are you two crazy? You're messing with the dead. Brad, honey, you're one weird dude."

"Roberta, I can't believe you're calling *me* weird," he chuckled. "You were the one wearing a dress and high heel shoes last night. So, just sit back and enjoy the ride."

———

Brad turned east on State Road 520 and crossed the high bridge over the Indian River to Merritt Island where he turned south on Crooked Mile Road, which winds through a historic part of the island called the *Old Settlement*. The cemetery, one of the oldest in the county, was right beside the road just past a little white church. It was well-kept and shaped like a long rectangle surrounded with a vine covered chain-link fence. Stretched across the entrance was a heavy iron chain. Brad pulled to the side of the road and got out to unhook the chain. He drove in and parked on the narrow, grassy road separating the right and left sides of the cemetery. There were at least a couple hundred graves markers of varying shapes and sizes shaded by numerous live oaks, four or five tall palmettos, and other trees. The older graves were up front near the entrance with more recent burials on the back side.

"I thought it would be a little run down graveyard with wooden markers," said Erin, opening her door to get out. A slight breeze was causing the moss to sway in the trees. "It's much bigger than I expected."

"Hey, Erin," said Brad, walking over to a tall ornate monument, "I can tell you how many dead people are buried in this cemetery just by standing here looking around at the graves."

"How many?"

"*All of them!* Get it? They're *all* dead...or they wouldn't be buried!" he teased, as Roberta snickered at his witty joke.

"Smart ass, that ain't funny," she replied, hurrying to catch up with him. "This place gives me the creeps, like somebody is watching us...and you start out by making a stupid joke."

"We're trying to find a needle in a haystack," complained Roberta. "There's got to be two hundred graves in this place."

"We'll split up," suggested Brad. "Mrs. Davis told me that Ethel's marker is a very small, flat one. Erin, you start on the left about halfway down this road, Roberta, you check the right side and I'll search the front part. We're looking for a small, homemade marker."

They began searching through the grave markers which dated anywhere from 1905 up to recent times. Many of the graves were those of early settlers who had lived on Merritt Island. It wasn't long before Erin called out and waved her arms, "Hey...I found it! It's over here!!" Brad and Roberta ceased their search and cut across the cemetery to where she was standing next to a small flat marker.

"It sure is a simple marker," said Erin, standing over the grave with her hands stuck in her hip pockets. Next to the marker was a glass jar holding a small bouquet of faded, plastic flowers. Brad knelt beside the grave and brushed away the dead leaves revealing the dates "1916-1934." It was a homemade cement marker without an epitaph to commemorate her short life on earth. He gently traced the letters of her name with his finger tips as if trying to make a connection with her.

Roberta glanced around at the granite tombstones, and then down at Ethel's simple marker. "That's a gravestone of a poor girl. There wasn't even enough money for a nice marker."

"I think you're right," said Brad, looking up, "but somebody made her one by hand and that might mean more than having a fancy expensive one." He had hardly finished talking when Erin began feeling dizzy. Almost losing her balance, she tried to balance herself by grabbing his shoulder.

"OH..." she mumbled. "Brad...I feel funny...oh, my gawd, Brad..." She started to tremble and her legs felt weak. She felt like she was going to pass out.

He stood up and held her steady, "What's the matter, Erin?"

"I feel faint...I just saw a flash of a..." she didn't quite finish.

"A flash of *what? A vision?* Are you okay?"

"It was a like a dream...no, more like a string of quick flashes," she said, trying to describe a strange mental illusion. "It was like frames in a movie film...*it was a girl*...she was like, transparent, and she was walking away from this grave...*then she just vanished*...it was like I was hallucinating. Then all of a sudden I got real dizzy...oh, man, do I have a pounding headache." She held the back of her hand against her forehead.

"Okay, *that's* it for me folks!!" exclaimed Roberta, starting to head for the car. "You two can do what you want but I'm out of here. This is getting a little too weird for me."

"I think it's time for all of us to leave," agreed Brad, putting his arm around Erin's waist. "Come on, I need to get you home."

CHAPTER 10

It was a little past noon when Brad and Erin dropped off Roberta at Ashley's Tavern. By the time they arrived at Erin's apartment, she was feeling better after her strange experience in the cemetery. Brad wheeled into a vacant space and turned off the ignition. For a second he just sat there, then, he got out and walked around to open her door.

"Are you going to be okay?" he asked, still concerned about her unexplained dizzy spell. "How's your headache?"

"Oh, I'm okay now," she said, getting out of the car. "Would you like to come in? I can fix some lunch." He had never been inside her place, so he was eager to accept her invitation and perhaps, he might find enough courage to ask her out for a date.

Erin lived in a second story one bedroom apartment in a complex of twelve Spanish-style units. As they started up the stairs, she paused to check her mailbox, pulling out five pieces of junk mail. As she shuffled through her mail, she made small talk by pointing out her neighbors. A policeman lived in one of the bottom floor apartments and an elderly lady in the other. "And my friend Diana lives across from me, she has two little boys. We sort of watch out for each other, you know, being females living alone." She continued to chatter as she unlocked the door to her place, "Of course, we do have a cop living downstairs."

"It looks like a safe place to me," remarked Brad, noticing a pair of snow skis leaning next to the door of the other apartment. "Snow skis in Florida?"

"Oh, those belong to Diana, she loves to ski," replied Erin, unlocking the door. As she opened it a large, fuzzy grey cat ran out. "That's Dingy, my cat. I found him in the Walmart parking lot about a year ago when he was just a kitten, it was raining and he was soaked...now he's a big bum," she laughed. "I hope you're not allergic to cats."

"Not that I know of," he replied, shutting the door and following her into the living room. He immediately sensed a feminine touch to the room, with sweet scented candles, straw flowers creatively arranged on a glass topped coffee table and matching throw pillows on a sofa. He stood there looking around, as if waiting for instructions on what to do next. "So...ah, are you saying your neighbor friend snow skis in Florida?"

"No silly, she takes trips to Colorado. Come on in to the kitchen and sit down. The kitchen and dining area was separated from the small living room by a wide archway. She laid her purse on the table and opened the refrigerator. "Want something to drink?"

"Do you have a Coke?"

"Sorry, I don't have any sodas."

"How about a beer, I don't suppose you have a beer?"

"I have water, green tea, milk, and...oh, yes, I do have a beer," she smiled, pulling an amber-colored bottle from the fridge. "But it's organic ginger beer. It's good, you'll like it."

"Okay, it'll do," he said, wondering what she intended to fix for lunch. "What do you have to eat? Maybe a bean sprout sandwich?"

She laughed, "I can make one if you want it. Don't worry I can make something you will eat. What about a peanut butter and jelly sandwich? It's organic but you can't tell the difference...or I can open a can of tuna fish."

"Tuna fish? Is it organic too?"

"No, it's in a can; I buy it for my cat."

"Then, I'll take a peanut butter and jelly sandwich. I don't want to eat your cat's food."

She made two sandwiches and neatly sliced them into triangles and started to sit down at the table when the door bell rang. "Let me see who that is." She left him at the table and went to answer the door. He could hear her talking with someone. The door closed and she came back into the kitchen, "Brad, I want you to meet someone." He put down his bottle of ginger beer and turned to see an attractive young woman with long, dark hair and fingers loaded with rings. "This is Diana, my best friend..." she said. "Diana, this is Brad, he's a writer from Miami."

He politely stood up, "Hi, nice to meet you..."

"Brad's investigating Ashley's ghost," said Erin, shoving a paper plate with the sandwiches in front of him. "Here, eat."

Diana pulled out a chair and sat down at the table. "That's awesome, Ashley's ghost, how neat. So, you're doing a ghost story?"

"Well, not exactly," he replied. He always had to clarify Erin's introduction of him. "Actually, I'm researching a 1934 murder of a girl who just happens to be the same one in the Ashley legend. I write about old unsolved homicide cases."

Erin sat down, "Oh, Brad, you can tell Diana about our spiritual experiences, she used to be a waitress at Ashley's before she went to work at the sheriff's department."

"Sure, I can keep a secret," Diana smiled, giving Erin a wink and eager to hear about encounters with the unknown. "Erin and I have been friends for years, and besides, I know all about Ashley's shadow. I've seen it myself, it's a girl named Ethel."

"Ashley's shadow? That's the first time I've heard it called that," he remarked. "I thought people always saw the ghost in the mirror."

"That's what I call my own sighting of her," explained Diana. "When I worked there I used to feel something tug at my hair, or brush the side of my face, but the really eerie experience happened to me twice. Both times in the ladies' room, late at night when we were cleaning up, it was scary!"

"What kind of experience?" he asked, as Erin sat smiling, listening with intrigue, as Diana described her supernatural encounter.

"It was a shadow of a woman on the wall. It moved all about the room but there was no one else in the women's room but me. It had a perfect outline, I could even see her arms moving…but it was a perfect shadow just like a living person would make on the wall."

"See, Brad! I told you we weren't crazy," said Erin, reaching across the table to playfully slap his arm. "Other people have seen her too." Against Brad's desire for discreetness, Erin proceeded to tell Diana all about them seeing an apparition in the mirrors. He cringed as she began telling about the girl he had seen sitting on his bed. He was now up to his neck in the paranormal and trapped between two women engaged in a discussion about ghosts. His skepticism had completely jumped the track, and as difficult as it was for him to believe, he was becoming a true believer of the supernatural.

"That's awesome!" said Diana, sitting back in her chair with both of her ring studded hands on the table.

"Not only that," said Erin, "but, today we went to the cemetery and found the girl's grave and I had this dizzy spell come over me...and saw a strange vision of a girl walking away from the grave. I think it was her. It was weird."

"Look," said Brad, "I know both of you really believe in this stuff, but there could be some other explanation too." He was trying to regain some of his skepticism. "Although I'll admit that I can't explain what I saw in the motel mirror."

"There's no other explanation..." said Erin. "How could we all be hallucinating about the same thing? I mean all three of us sitting at this table have had experiences with the same thing. Diana saw the shadow...and we saw a girl in the mirrors...and then my dizzy spell in the cemetery today."

"Sounds like we're all dizzy to me," remarked Brad, taking a sip from his ginger beer.

"I guess you realize nobody is going to believe any of it," said Diana. "That's why I've never told anyone but Erin about the shadow I saw. I don't have any doubt that Ashley's is haunted. Heck the place has been in all kinds of books. Erin, show Brad that book you have."

Erin went into the living room and returned with a large hardback book and opened it, "See, right here, there's a story about Ashley's"

He took the book and gave a quick glance at the article, then looked at the cover, "*Weird Florida*...who wrote this, some weirdo?"

No, the author is *not* a weirdo, perhaps he's a *little* strange, maybe even a tad insane, but he's *real* nice, he even autographed it for me."

"I guess he did, you *bought* his book," said Brad, closing the book and pushing it aside. "I'll sign my book too...if I ever write one."

"Well," said Diana, drumming her long nails on the table, "what we have seen is not in any books...and now that I've heard what you guys have seen, well, that's *downright eerie* if you ask me. Hey, your secret is safe with me. So, what are you going to do about it?"

"I'll tell you *what* I'm going to do," stated Brad. "I'm going to solve a 1934 murder mystery and if, by some remote chance a ghost gets in my way, I might include it in my story...but my main focus is trying to find out what happened to Ethel Allen and her boyfriend."

He briefly described the information he had uncovered which strongly suggested the Baxters may have been engaged in a criminal enterprise that was under a federal investigation. "What I can't understand," he continued, "is why no one ever pursued this case. They just shoved it away to gather dust and now most of the evidence is lost. Just the clues I've dug up should be enough to reopen it. Of course, it's such an old case that I doubt that will ever happen."

"Don't be so sure," replied Diana. "I'm a dispatcher with the sheriff's department and know a couple of the detectives. I think you should take the information to them and see if they would be interested in it. It's good for them anytime they can solve a case, keeps their numbers up, if you know what I mean. Even if it's an old case, they still get the credit if they solve it. You'd be surprised at the number of murder cases that are never solved. In this case you've already done a lot of the foot work too. I'll tell you what, go down to the sheriff's office in Titusville…to the criminal investigations division, and talk with Jessie Sims, she's a friend of mine…she's a super good detective, too."

"You really think she'd be interested in a murder that's over a half century old, and one in which all the key players are dead?" he said, thinking to himself about the unclaimed five thousand dollar bonus his publisher was offering to any journalist who helped solve a cold case homicide. "On second thought," he continued, somewhat inspired by the prospects of the publisher's bonus, "I forgot about Sonny Baxter, I think he's still living. Diana might be right. I think it's time to take this case to the authorities."

"Ask for Jessie Sims," said Diana, getting up from the table. "I've got to run, I've got clothes in the dryer and the boys will be home from school pretty soon; anyway, let me know what happens." She showed herself to the door. As she went out the door, Erin's big cat ran in and headed into the kitchen to check its food bowl.

Erin removed Brad's plate and empty bottle from the table. "Are you really going to the sheriff's office?"

"I think I will, just as soon as I leave here," he replied, getting up from his chair. "But, first, what about me and you?"

"What do you mean?" she asked, putting the paper plate in the garbage receptacle beneath the sink. "You mean about our weird experiences with the images in the mirrors?"

"No, I'm talking about what you said, about wanting me to take you to a movie." Maybe she doesn't remember he thought, or maybe she's changed her mind, or maybe she's being difficult. He stood there as she opened a cabinet and took out a small bag of dry cat food. "Don't you remember saying that?"

"I said *that?*" she grinned, playing with his mind as she put some food in the cat's bowl. "When did I say *that?*"

"The other day in the park...I swear you said something about wanting me to take you to a movie, remember?"

"Oh, that! Okay, I'm off tonight...so let's go out."

That was almost too easy, he thought. "Cool, then I'll pick you up around five...we can get something to eat first."

"Okay," she said, as he walked to the front door. "I know a nice little Chinese place you'll like...and I'll call the theater and find out what's playing."

"Great, and in the meantime, I'm going to see if I can get a detective interested in turning this old murder mystery into an official investigation. I'll see you at five."

CHAPTER 11

After leaving Erin's place, Brad stopped by his motel room and gathered up his research notes and copies of old newspaper articles. He made a fast change of his shirt and tie, combed his hair, and then jumped in his car for the trip to the Sheriff Department.

The Sheriff Department now covered several precincts and is a much larger organization than it was back in 1934 when Sheriff Jacobs worked out of a two room office in Titusville with less than a dozen fulltime deputies and two jailers. Over the years, Brevard County's increasing population had attracted an increase in crime. The present day homicide unit has ten times more personnel than Sheriff Jacobs' entire force. It was another sign of how things had changed since Ethel's murder.

After waiting about thirty minutes, Brad got in to talk with Lieutenant Jessie Sims, a short, attractive blonde in her mid-forties, who dressed in fashionable civilian attire. She hardly looked like a homicide detective who had been featured in the national press for discovering a new technique in examining skeletal remains of homicide victims. Her office wall was graced with a collection of awards reflecting fifteen years of excellence in Florida law enforcement. She sat on the corner of her desk next to a potted plant with her arms folded, listening intently as Brad flipped through his note pad and went over the details of his research. When he was finished, she walked over to a coffee pot on a table beneath the window. She held up a cup and asked, "Can I get you a cup of coffee?"

"No thanks," said Brad, crossing his leg. "So, what do you think?"

She poured a cup of coffee, then walked back over to her desk and leaned against it. For a moment she starred into her cup as if reading tea leaves, then took a sip, and said, "I guess you know you're dealing with something that's over seventy years old."

"I know that…however, it was never really investigated…and that's very unusual for a violent crime like this, not to mention it might have involved a hit on a federal informant."

"Don't get me wrong, I'm not disputing any of that," she said, sitting her cup down on the desk. "But you realize you're also implying a state senator had something to do with a murder. Even if it happened seventy years ago, that's still heavy business, especially if the man is still living."

"I get what you're saying, but Senator Baxter's name pops up everywhere…and his father was the judge who mysteriously shut down the investigation before it got off the ground."

"Mr. Kelly, I can't…"

Brad interrupted, "*Kirby…Brad Kirby*, Kelly was the victim's fiancé who disappeared at the time of the murder."

"Kirby, I'm sorry, Mister Kirby," she apologized, "I just can't waste time on a seventy year old case based on the information you have. In the first place I doubt I could get authorization to reopen it. We have enough to do with protecting the present citizens of the county. I'm sure you can understand my position."

"I understand," he replied. "But what about the way all of these people are connected…I mean like, Frank Turner for instance. He was the deputy assigned to the case, and he was a personal friend of Judge Baxter, who got him the job. And the Judge terminated the investigation after Turner fingered Bill Kelly as the killer…and I found out that Kelly was an informant for a federal investigation that was looking into what appears to have been a crime ring run by the judge and his son. Then Kelly vanishes without a trace, and his girl friend is found dead…doesn't this raise a lot of suspicion?"

"Yes, to me and you, but for a case this ancient, you need a real smoking gun to justify spending taxpayers' money. Based on what you've found, developing a suspect might be the easy part; however, getting evidence to support it is another thing."

"What about something called Scarlet Biddy? It was mentioned in a letter to the sheriff from a federal agent."

"Scarlet Biddy? Doesn't ring a bell for me. I've never heard of it. It may have been some kind of code name." She sat her coffee cup down on the desk, and said, "Let me ask you this, how would reopening an outdated case like this serve any purpose for the taxpaying public who are more concerned with present day crime?"

"It would serve the victims to find their killer," he answered.

"I agree with your point, but I can tell you now that my bosses will want more than speculation, they'll want good physical evidence in order to pull me away from a current case."

"Then what would it take?" he asked, with his eyes following the detective as she paced back and forth in front of her desk.

She went over to the window and looked out. She crossed her arms then turned toward Brad, "We could start with Bill Kelly's remains, or his vehicle, but that's not going to happen...or good forensic evidence which after all these years would be impossible. And we can forget about finding any living witnesses."

Brad rose from his seat and prepared to leave. In a last ditch effort to interest her in the case, he said, "Baxter's former housekeeper is a lady named Indigo Blue and she is wearing a ruby ring like the one that disappeared from the evidence...what about that?"

"*Indigo Blue?*" exclaimed the detective, "Good lord, everybody in Brevard County knows Indigo...she probably found that ring in a junk pile. Look, I know you want a good story to write about, but you've got to have more to offer me."

She walked him to the door and opened it. He shook her hand, and asked, "What if I find a smoking gun?"

"Then you'll have my full attention. It has been interesting talking with you, Mr. Kirby, you have a nice day."

She followed Brad as he stepped into the hallway. "Ah, Mr. Kirby...you've done a good job with your research."

He nodded okay, and then walked down the hall to the entrance. He was now bound and determined to find physical proof to back up his research. Somehow he felt Indigo Blue was the key to finding something. Maybe that's why she said he would be back to see her.

Brad drove back to the Sea Rest Motel and spent the remainder of the afternoon trying to figure out the best way to find a "smoking gun" in the Ethel Allen case. It would take more than old newspaper articles to inspire Detective Sims to take a serious look at it. He really didn't have much more to go on, except for Indigo Blue. She may have overheard or saw something while working in the Baxter house. He still had the impression Indigo had not told him everything she knew. For now, he had to put his mind on hold because the clock was pushing four-thirty and he had to get ready to pick up Erin at five.

———

The theater was on Merritt Island, in a shopping center on the causeway halfway between the mainland and Cocoa Beach. It was about nine-forty-five and the evening was still warm when Brad and Erin left the movie. He had told her about his visit with Detective Sims and how he needed to find hard evidence to prove his theory about the murder. Driving along the causeway toward the mainland, their talk centered on the supernatural aspects of the mystery.

"I don't suppose you said anything about what we saw in the mirrors?" Erin asked, looking at the lights of Cocoa as they crossed the high rise bridge over the Indian River. She glanced to the right at all the little white lights on pleasure boats sitting in the marina. In the distance a red and green light flashed on a navigation beacon.

"You've got to be kidding, Sims would've thrown me out of her office," he answered, making a left on Forrest Avenue which would take them to Florida Avenue and in the direction of the Spanish Oaks apartment complex. "She liked my research. She even agreed with me. The main reason she didn't want to reopen the case had to do with spending time and money on such an old case. If I had said anything about a ghost she would've called the men in white coats to haul me off to a rubber room."

"Yeah, I know what you mean," she smiled. "I think there has to be a clue in all that research you've done." She seemed to have something else on her mind. "I mean you've really gotten to know everybody who was involved in this mystery, even more than what we know about each other."

"I think we know each other pretty good," he replied, slowing down for a stop sign. "I've told you all about me…and I think we've both confessed or confided things to each other, don't you think so?"

"I suppose…"

"You suppose?" He glanced at her. "I've told you all about me. Hey, if there's something more you want to know just ask me."

"No, not really. It's not you, it's me." She acted a little nervous.

"You? What do you mean? Is there some great revelation that you're concealing about your past?" He watched the street ahead, afraid of what was coming next. He wondered if she was hiding something that would change his opinion of her.

She looked out her side of the car as they passed the Elks Lodge, and then turned her eyes toward him. "I need to say something…and I'm not sure how to say it. I'm not even sure I should say it."

"What? Tell me, if it's a secret it's safe with me." He was becoming anxious. "Are you a serial killer or something? Gads, you're not going to tell me you're really a man, are you?"

She usually laughed when he joked, but this time she seemed serious. "No, trust me, it's nothing like that. Just promise me that regardless of what I say…that you won't get upset or make fun."

He pulled into the parking lot of the Spanish Oaks apartments and turned off the engine. For a moment he sat there, and then said, "Okay, I won't get upset, I won't get mad…so tell me what it is."

"Oh, gawd…I don't know how to say this…" She hesitated, then went on, "…it's just something that has me confused. Brad…I…uh, well…I'm really *attracted* to you and I'm not sure how to deal with it." She clasped her hands in her lap and waited for his answer.

"Attracted to me? Like *how much* attracted?" He always tried to analyze everything. "Like on a scale of one to ten, how much?"

"I don't know, like *real* attracted…I mean like *deeply* attracted." She looked away briefly, unsure if he understood her feelings.

He wasn't too sure about how to respond. "Like sexually? Like you're in love with me…or something like that?"

"Yes, I think so…Oh hell, I'm really not sure…yes I'm *sure*, it's just that I'm not sure about the way you feel."

He looked at her, and in a serious tone, said, "That's strange…because I feel the same way about you. I guess I've just been afraid to say anything…I'm attracted to you too."

"God, that's a relief to hear you say that, I was afraid to say anything because I didn't know how you'd take it."

"Well, I'm glad you told me...I guess we will just have to figure out where we go from here. We'll manage it." He looked at the clock on the dash, "It's almost ten-thirty, come on, I'll walk you up to your door." He got out of the car and went around to open the passenger door for her. He took her hand and without saying a word, they walked up the stairs to her apartment. They reached the door and for a moment stood silent, each waiting for the other to say something.

"I'm glad you told me what you told me," he said.

She looked at him with a smile, "I'm happy you told me what you told me too," she said with a shy smile, while opening her purse.

"Well, did you enjoy the movie?" he asked, as she searched her purse for her keys. She unlocked the door, but did not go in. She turned to face him with her back to the door frame.

"Yes, I *really* had fun," she said, as a gentle night breeze teased her hair. "I'm glad we finally went out."

"Yeah, me too. I really enjoy your company," he said, caressing her shoulders with his hands. He reached his right hand up and stroked a strand of her pretty auburn hair. "I like the way you fixed your hair tonight."

"It's the same way I wear it all the time."

"Oh...well, it just looked different tonight. Maybe it's the light or something," he said, thinking how stupid his comment must have sounded to her. He was lost for words, searching nervously for something to say to round off the evening. "So, ah, I guess you'll sleep tonight."

"I usually do..." she giggled. He was stumbling around trying to find the right time to steal a kiss. As her green eyes locked silently with his, she could sense his desires, "Is this the part where we kiss?"

"I think so," he smiled, drawing her close with his arms. He gently lifted her chin with his hand and kissed her. As she held her breath, he could feel her melting into him. It was a fleeting moment of passion which ended much too soon. She pulled back slightly from his embrace and gazed into his eyes, then softly whispered, "That was nice. Good night...I'll see you tomorrow." She gave him a quick kiss on the cheek then went into her apartment. He stood there for a few seconds facing the closed door as if mesmerized by her kiss. He raked his hand through his hair, smiled, and then went down the steps to his car. He looked up at the light in her window as he got in his car and drove out of the parking lot.

————————

As Brad drove up the highway to the Sea Rest motel his mind kept replaying what Erin had said about being attracted to him and the sensation he felt when he kissed her. He could no longer deny the strange tingling feelings he had held inside for her. She was still on his mind when he unlocked the door to his motel room.

After taking a quick shower, he slipped into his pajama bottoms, and with a towel draped around his neck, walked over to the mirror to study all the clue notes taped to it. It was a puzzle of information and somewhere in all the bits and pieces was the key he needed to unlock the mystery, something that would lead to the hard evidence he needed for Detective Sims. Recalling his previous strange encounter, he snapped his eyes around at the bed, in case a spirit was sitting on it. "Good, no ghosts tonight," he mumbled out loud to himself.

Picking up his note pad, he went over to the bed and pulled the covers back. He climbed in and stacked a couple of pillows against the headboard, punching out a dent for his head. He settled back with the intention of reading through his research notes, which lasted only about ten minutes before his eyes began growing heavy. He put his note pad on the nightstand beside the bed and glanced at the clock, it was eleven-thirty. He turned out the light and in a matter of minutes fell sound asleep. At first, it was a restless sleep; he mumbled, tossed, turned, and twisted in the sheets until a little after midnight when he finally drifted off into what began as a peaceful dream.

It was unlike any dream he had ever experienced. It was a hazy vision of a circle of sunlight in a grassy meadow and in the distance there was an old wooden barn. It was like an early American painting and he was standing in it, all alone, as if waiting for someone. A light green mist encircled the spot where he was standing. Everything felt fresh and pure like after a summer rain. All around him, from every direction, the faint sound of music fell upon his ears. The sound began very low, gradually increasing until he could hear a romantic melody. It was enchanting, almost magical, and more like reality than any dream. He sensed a presence and turned to see a beautiful girl materialize in the mist. She seemed to float slightly above the ground and as she came closer he could see she was wearing a long, flowing, wedding gown with a sheer, white veil covering her head and face. At first, he thought it was a vision of Erin. Her hand was reaching out as she came near. He took her hand, slowly pulling her close, and began waltzing around the meadow with her, gracefully swaying and turning with the music.

Although her face was obscured by the veil, he had a strong feeling that he was dancing with Erin. He gently lifted her hand to his lips and kissed it. His eyes were drawn to a large ruby ring on her finger. Its huge red stone seemed to pulsate and glow, as if full of fire and ready to burst. It looked hot, but when he touched it to his mouth it was as cold as ice. She slowly moved her hands to his shoulders as he parted the veil hiding her face, and softly kissed her lips. Her mouth seemed sweet with passion, then, all of a sudden he realized he was kissing the bony face of an *ugly skeleton!!* He pulled back in horror! *"Aaaahhg!"* he yelled out, waking up in a soaking sweat. His heart was racing as he untangled himself from the covers. He sat up on the edge of the bed trying to return his mind to reality.

In the dark he could see the glowing numbers on the clock beside the bed; it was almost two in the morning. His hands searched blindly for the light switch. He clicked on the light and for a couple of seconds just sat on the side of the bed holding his head in his hands trying to make sense out of his unusual dream. It had certainly stirred mixed emotions inside him, he loved it, and yet he hated it, but it had seemed so real. The girl in the dream seemed like Erin, yet she seemed like someone else...*like Ethel*. Yes, it had to be Ethel, he thought, knocking his writing pad off the night stand as he fumbled for the telephone. He rubbed the sleep from his eyes, then picked up the phone and dialed Erin's number.

Erin's phone rang several times before she answered. "Uh, Hello," she mumbled, still half asleep and hugging a pillow.

"Erin, this is Brad, it's about two o'clock..."

"Brad, you *woke me up* to tell me the time?" she yawned, pulling the sheet up under her chin. "I *know it's two o'clock*, what in the world are you calling me for at this time of night?"

"Listen, I just had the craziest dream and I didn't want to take a chance on forgetting it in the morning. I think it was about Ethel. At first it seemed like you, but then it seemed like Ethel. I was dancing with her in this grassy field...she had on a wedding dress and this thing covering her face...*a bridal veil*...and when I went to kiss her hand I saw a ruby ring and it was super big...I mean, the stone was like really huge."

"What'd you do, eat a bad pizza before going to bed?"

"No, nothing like that...I was in a good sleep...it wasn't really like a nightmare, it was more like...well, *like it was real*. It wasn't like any normal kind of dream." He rubbed his hand through his hair.

"It's probably because she's been on your mind," she yawned, still half asleep with the phone between her ear and the pillow.

"I don't know, but it seemed so real, and when I parted the veil and went to kiss her...she...her face, it was like a skeleton's face. It really freaked me out! That's when I woke up."

"Weird. Are you okay?"

"I guess so, but listen; I believe the place in my dream was the Baxter farm. I mean that's the feeling I get."

"Okay, so what makes you think that? I mean dreams are really crazy to figure out sometimes."

"It's just a real strong feeling and there was a barn or some kind of old wooden shack and what looked like a grassy field. Maybe it's just a hunch, but I think we need to see the old Baxter place even if my dream don't have nothing to do with it. "

"Then you'll need Indigo Blue to show you where it is. You'll have to get her another bottle of gin too..."

"Hell, I'll get her two bottles. Listen, we're going to get Indigo in the morning and go to that farm. I'll pick you up at eight-thirty; we need to get to her place before she starts making her rounds to the dumpsters."

"Sure, whatever," she yawned, "but if you're bent on doing this we'd better get some sleep. I'll set my clock for seven and I'll see you in the morning. Now go to bed." She hung up the phone, rolled over, hugged her pillow, and went back to sleep.

CHAPTER 12

By eight o'clock the next morning Brad and Erin were knocking on Indigo Blue's door. At first she refused to go with them to the old Baxter place because Brad had violated her sacred rule, he had failed to bring a pint of gin with him. It may not seem like much to the average person, but to Indigo it was a big deal. She compared it to crossing the palm of a gypsy fortune teller with silver. "Boy, a gypsy won't do business till you lay silver in their hand. I be the same way," she said. "I don't need no silver, I just needs my gin for them spirits…you know what I'm saying?"

He explained that it was too early in the morning and all the liquor stores were closed. "Listen, I promise I will buy you two bottles of gin," he said, trying to strike a deal with her. "It will make up for not having one bottle this morning." With that, Indigo agreed to take them out to the old Baxter place. She took a moment to lock her door and put some food in a bowl for her cats, then followed Brad and Erin to the car.

Erin got into the front seat while Brad held the rear door open for Indigo. She climbed in the backseat and noticed the litter in his car, "Boy, this car gots more junk in it than one of them dumpsters downtown."

Erin snickered, "I told him the same thing, Indigo."

He got in behind the wheel and started the motor, "I tell ya what, Indigo, anything you find in my junk you can keep." She quickly looked around.

Following Indigo's directions, Brad drove south on U.S. 1 toward Eau Gallie and after fifteen minutes he turned right on a road that crossed the railroad tracks and headed west into the country.

"How far is it?" Erin asked, turning around to Indigo.

"About nine or ten miles straight out this road, past the interstate," she answered, pointing over the back of the seat with her finger. "I guess you know the old place belongs to the state now."

"I didn't know that," said Brad. "But, all I want to do is see it."

Erin couldn't help noticing the ring on Indigo's finger. "I was looking at your pretty ring the other day, Indigo. Is it a ruby?"

Indigo looked at the ring and replied, "Girl, this is a *genuine* ruby. Miz Baxter gave it to me just before she died. It was the only decent thing Mr. Sonny ever gave her."

"Why'd she give it to you?" asked Erin, glancing out of the corner of her eye at Brad, as they passed a pasture full of cows.

"I think she wanted to spite Mr. Sonny by giving it away. They wuzn't gettin' along too good at that time. Miz Baxter wuz a fine woman, much too good for that old coot. I guess she wanted me to have it for working for her all those years…besides she hated Mr. Frank…and that's where it really came from."

Brad was driving along and listening to her telling about the ring. "Why'd Frank Turner give a ring to Sonny Baxter's wife?" He kept both hands on the steering wheel as he glanced over at Erin and raised his eyebrows in suspicion. She responded with a subtle nod as Indigo went on talking. "No, Mr. Frank didn't give it to her, he gave Mr. Sonny a cigar box and the ring was in it. It was right after Judge Baxter died. I was in the kitchen with momma squeezing oranges and they wuz sitting there at the table drinking coffee and going through them things in that cigar box. I remember Mr. Sonny pulled the ring out and held it up to the light. He says to me, 'Indigo, you ever seen anything this purty,' and then he put it back in the box."

"So, what else was in that cigar box," asked Brad, looking at Indigo in the rear view mirror.

"A bunch of stuff, I remember a two dollar bill 'cause Mr. Sonny gave it to me…and two pictures and some other things. A few weeks after Miz Baxter died; Mr. Sonny threw that cigar box in the trash can. I fished it out of there and I still got it. It's one of those old timey kind of cigar boxes, when they was made out of wood."

"Can you show me that box?" asked Brad, watching waves of heat shimmering on the asphalt road ahead.

"I sure can, when the time is right," she answered. "First you owe me two pints of gin." About that time they passed by a pile of junk sitting on the side of the road. *"STOP BOY!"* shouted Indigo from the backseat. "Stop *this* car!! Back this *thing* up!!"

Erin braced herself against the dash as he slammed on the brakes and screeched to a stop, "What the hell is it? Did I miss the turn?"

"No," replied Indigo, looking out the rear window. "Look back yonder at what somebody done throw'd away on the road. Hush up and back up so I can check it out while it's still fresh."

Brad shoved the gear shift in reverse and mumbled, "I don't believe this. We're stopping so you can rummage through junk!"

"Hush up, boy," she scolded. "Just give me a minute." She got out of the car and proceeded to dig through the junk pile like she was shopping in a store. Brad and Erin waited patiently in the car watching her. Erin opened her door to let in some fresh air.

"Brad," said Erin, in a low voice, "do you think that ring is the same one that belonged to Ethel Allen?"

"It's a sure bet. Indigo described the cigar box just like in the police report, even the two dollar bill. Frank Turner had access to the evidence...and he took that box and gave it to Baxter. It all adds up, it's a perfect trail to Sonny Baxter...and those pictures she was talking about...I'll bet they're pictures of Ethel Allen and Bill Kelly."

Indigo returned to the car with an old radio, a waffle iron, and a table lamp with a large, stained shade. "Look at this," she said, loading her finds into the backseat. "People throw out all sorts of things; I can fix this stuff up."

Brad started the car. "Just get in," he ordered, "we gotta get going and no more stopping at junk piles until we see the Baxter place."

"I got this thing for you, boy," said Indigo, holding the waffle iron over the back of the seat so Brad could see it. "You can fix it up!"

Brad kept his eyes on the road, "You keep it, I don't want it!"

"I want you to have it," she insisted, as Erin began giggling under her breath knowing Brad was getting a little perturbed.

"The damn thing's broke," he said, trying to watch the road ahead, "that's why they threw it away."

"You can fix it!"

"I said I don't want it."

Erin chimed in, still snickering, "Brad, you can fix it and make waffles in your motel room."

"Don't you start," he replied, slipping on his sunglasses.

"Okay, then I'll keep it," said Indigo, "but don't you come around wanting to use it when I gets it fixed!"

The road soon narrowed to a rural dirt road bordered by a rusty barbed wire fence beyond which were thick hammocks of palmetto and pine trees. "Turn in right there," directed Indigo, pointing to an old broken down wooden gate. They turned in and followed the ruts of an overgrown road which ended in a cleared area next to the foundation of an old house.

"This is it," said Indigo, as Brad stopped the car. "This is what's left of the old Baxter place." She opened the door to get out and pointed to the foundation. "That's where the old house was at. Lord, it's been a long time since I've been out here." She was talking about the remains of the old Baxter house. They were on the original Baxter homestead. J.C. Baxter, a cattleman and lawyer, purchased the two hundred acre spread in 1898 when land was dirt cheap. In 1917, he opened a law practice in Cocoa and moved his family into a two-story house on the river. In 1920 he became a judge and used his influence to control local politics. He kept the old homestead as a secluded retreat for his inner circle of friends. He always referred to it as a "hunting camp," although local gossip spoke of secret shenanigans that went on there, from Ku Klux Klan meetings to gangsters using the place as a hideaway during Prohibition. Some folks swore that Al Capone used the place as a way station on his winter trips to Miami. No proof had ever been offered to backup any of the stories, which, for the most part, had simply evolved because of Baxter's secrecy and dubious reputation. In 1932, Judge Baxter's only son, Sonny Baxter, took over the family's property, cattle business, and the law practice. As a young lawyer, Sonny Baxter was infamous for defending bootleggers of illegal whiskey. In 1978, Sonny Baxter sold the property to the state as part of a wildlife preserve. The only evidence of the old house was the overgrown foundation and concrete steps leading to nowhere.

Erin and Brad got out of the car and followed Indigo as she pointed to an overgrown pile of wooden boards. "That used to be where me and momma lived when I was a little girl. My, my, it was a long time ago, but I remember it like it was yesterday."

Brad walked over to the remains of the old shack and pulled back some of the brush. He reached down in the weeds and picked up an old rusty coffee pot. "I bet this thing is old," he said, holding it up.

Indigo reached for it. *"That's momma's old coffee pot!"*

"Then you should have it," he said, handing it to her. "It can be a keepsake, a memory of your momma."

"So, does this look like the place in your dream?" asked Erin.

"A little bit...it had a grassy area like this," he replied, glancing around where the old house once stood. "I really can't say, but it does kinda feel like the place in my dream."

"Here's a bunch of old jars," said Erin, poking a stick around the bushes. She reached down and picked one up.

"That looks like one of momma's canning jars," said Indigo, stepping closer for a look. "Momma could make the best guava jelly. Y'all do know what guavas are, don't you?"

"Guavas? Yes ma'am, I know what they are," answered Brad, recalling what the coroner's report had said about guava seeds being found stuck to the stocking around Ethel's neck and how clay was found under her nails. "Where'd your momma get guavas from?"

Indigo picked up a stick and pointed toward a small dilapidated barn, "Down there behind the barn used to be a whole grove of guava trees near the clay pit. We had to beat the wild hogs to them. Them ol' hogs loved guavas. I was always afraid of them 'cause they had big ol' tusks and they'd rip you open with them things!"

Brad's eyes widened. "Erin, did you hear that? Guava trees growing by a clay pit!"

"I know what you're thinking," she said. "Indigo, I recall you saying they used to burn crosses around here. Did you mean that Sonny Baxter and his friends were the Ku Klux Klan?"

"Oh, yes," she replied. "Mr. Sonny was the grand lizard."

"I think that's the grand wizard," corrected Brad, picking up an old can and tossing it into the bushes.

"I think you're both wrong," said Erin, brushing an ant off her ankle. "The head KKK dude was called the grand dragon."

Brad shifted the talk to the small weather-worn barn that was not much bigger than a garage. He had seen a similar old barn in his unusual dream, but this one was completely covered with vines. "Indigo, what was that old barn used for?" Leafy-green vines were creeping out of the rafters where the wind had ripped off sections of the rusty-red tin roof.

"Mr. Sonny kept hay stored in there for his cows," she answered. "It's the only thing still standing. If it weren't for all them cow-itch vines growing on it, it'd fall down."

"So why is it the only building still standing?"

"Don't ask me," said Indigo, fanning her hand at a wasp. "I guess Mr. Sonny just wanted to keep it to store hay in."

"There's a big lock on the door. Why would he lock up hay?"

"I dunno, maybe he had some tools in there too."

Brad made his way through the weeds toward the barn using a stick to beat the bushes to scare away any snakes. He pulled away some of the vines and tried to open the doors. A rusted iron padlock still held the doors firm but he could pull them apart just enough to peek inside. "It's filled with old hay and vines." He searched the bushes for something to pry the lock off. He found a brick and began striking the lock until he knocked it off.

"Brad, be careful of snakes!" warned Erin, as he struggled to pull open the doors. A large field rat scampered out and vanished under some boards. Erin jumped back, "Oh, my gosh! Did you see that big rat! That thing was big as my cat!"

He finally opened the doors and looked in. "I don't see anything except a big pile of old, rotten hay." He lightly sneezed, "It smells musty too."

Standing at the door he stabbed at the hay with a stick to see if he could run out another rat. He hit something hard, like metal. He began clearing away the hay to see what was under it. "Hey, check this out---I think there's something under here!" He quickly brushed away the moldy hay exposing the rusted rear end of a 1932 Ford coupe. Erin and Indigo waded through the weeds to see what he had found. He continued to uncover the rear of the car until he exposed an old license plate. It was a very rusty, barely readable, 1934 license tag. He could tell that it had once been black with white letters. He examined the faded numbers and was able to make them out to be 4-3-9. He pulled a small notebook from his shirt pocket and flipped through it looking for the tag number of Bill Kelly's car. "Erin...it's the car!" he exclaimed, pointing to the numbers in his notebook. "The license is 439...*it's Kelly's car!* I can't *believe* it. I found Bill Kelly's car! It's probably been here since...*since 1934...in this old barn!*"

Indigo moved in for a closer look. "What the devil is it doing in Mr. Sonny's barn?" She rubbed her hand over the license plate.

"Brad...can you see inside it?" Erin asked, hoping he would not find a skeleton sitting in it.

He brushed hay from the car's rear window so he could peak in, "Nothing inside, it looks empty. It's in pretty bad shape. Erin, would you please go to my car and bring me my cell phone."

"For what?"

"I'm calling Jessie Sims, I think we've just found the smoking gun...if not, then it's still evidence and it's on the Baxter property." He continued clearing the moldy hay from the old car until Erin returned with his phone. He dialed Detective Sims' number.

"Criminal investigations, Jessie Sims speaking."

"Hello, Detective Sims, this is Brad Kirby."

"Mr. Kirby, what can I do for you? How's your mystery going?"

"Good, thank you, very good. Remember what you said about finding a smoking gun?"

"Yes...Are you going to tell me that you found a body?"

"Not a body...but the next best thing. I found Bill Kelly's car!"

"Where? Did you make a positive identification?"

Brad switched the phone to his other ear, "I'm at the old Baxter place. I'm one hundred percent sure it's his car. The tag number matches and it's a 1932 Ford. There's no doubt...and it's a good bet that Kelly's body is buried around here somewhere."

"Okay...look, don't touch anything," directed Sims. "It's going to take me a little time to get authorization to move on this. I'll need to get some of our forensic folks together and go out there. In the meantime, I'm going to send a deputy out there to secure the place. Can you hang around until he gets there?"

"Sure...I'll be here." Brad put his phone away and gave a thumbs up to Erin and Indigo, "YES!! Detective Sims is interested! We have to wait for a deputy to get here, and then I want to go see Sonny Baxter. Indigo can you take me to see him?"

"What for?" she asked. "That old buzzard ain't worth my energy!"

As they started walking toward Brad's car, Erin interjected, "Brad, don't you think you're jumping the gun? Don't you think you should let Jessie Sims handle the investigation?"

He opened the car door for her. "Listen, if Sonny Baxter is off his rocker maybe he's crazy enough to talk about what happened in 1934. If he knows we found the car in his barn he just might tell me what happened to Bill Kelly. Besides, at his age he might just confess to everything." He held the rear door open so Indigo could get in.

"Don't you bet on it, boy," added Indigo, scooting into the backseat next to the lamp she had salvaged from the junk pile. "I'll take you to his house but don't expect much. What you gonna see is an old man just sittin' on the porch looking at the river and waitin' for the devil to come get him."

Erin and Indigo waited patiently inside the car while Brad leaned against the front fender watching the road for the sheriff's deputy to arrive. After about forty-five minutes, which seemed like an hour, he saw a green and white car with a rack of blue lights coming up the rutted road from the gate. He straightened up and shaded his eyes from the morning sun, "I think I see the deputy coming." Erin and Indigo turned to look out the rear window.

The car pulled to a stop and a young deputy got out. Brad greeted him and explained about the old car in the hay barn and its importance to a 1934 homicide. The deputy took a roll of yellow plastic tape from his car and, with Brad's help, strung it around the barn area. "I don't know if this tape really helps anything," he said. "It's just a standard procedure."

"What do they call this tape?" Brad asked, holding one end of the tape pulling the slack out of it as the deputy tied it off to a fence post.

"Durn if I know," replied the deputy. "I just call it crime tape."

"Well, it sure makes the place look like a real crime scene," Brad beamed, feeling good knowing his research was about to reopen an investigation into a seventy year old murder mystery. About that time another deputy sheriff drove up. He turned to the first deputy and said, "Since you've got enough help, we're heading back to town.

Detective Sims has my number if she needs me. Tell her I had to take care of some business and I'll be back this afternoon."

He walked at a fast pace to his car and slid in behind the wheel. He put the key in the ignition and glanced in the rear view mirror at Indigo. "Buckle-up, we're off to see Mr. Baxter to let him know Bill Kelly's car is in his old hay barn…as if he doesn't already know it."

"I still think you should let the police handle this…." Erin argued, shutting her door as Brad began turning around. "*Look at you*…you don't even let a person shut the door before you start driving off like you're going to a fire."

"I just want to get the jump on Baxter…I want to see his face…you can read a lot in a person's face…especially if you catch them off guard." He looked in the rear view mirror, "Right, Indigo?"

"That's *right*, boy, I've been reading *yours* like a book. The eyes are windows to the soul," replied Indigo, holding on to the arm rest in the backseat, bouncing around, as Brad steered the car down the bumpy, two-rutted road to the gate.

CHAPTER 13

"Don't you forget my gin, boy!" reminded Indigo from the backseat as Brad pulled out of the gate to the Baxter place and turned east on the county road. "You gonna *owe* me three pints if you want to see Mr. Sonny 'cause that ain't as easy as you think."

"You got it, three pints for Indigo!" promised Brad, glancing out the corner of his eye at the sunlight reflecting on Erin's hair. Gripping the steering wheel with one hand, he leaned over to the passenger side to retrieve his sunglasses from the glove compartment. He gave her a devilish grin, deliberately brushing his hand against her knee. She looked at him and smiled. Slipping on his shades, he leaned over to her and whispered, "You're really looking hot today!"

"And *you're* going to run us off the road if you don't watch where you're going," she said, giving him a gentle shove. Her voice then took a serious tone, "Do you think we'll see Ethel again? I mean now that the police are getting involved."

"I guess we'll find out if we get around any mirrors," he replied, as he began slowing down for the flashing lights of a railroad crossing. They stopped to wait on a northbound Florida East Coast freight train rumbling through on its way to Jacksonville.

"I really think this is what Ethel wanted us to do," said Erin, watching the passing boxcars. "She wanted us to find her boyfriend's remains. I don't think it was so much about her as it was about him, you know what I mean?"

"You're saying she couldn't rest in peace until he was found. Maybe, of course, he still hasn't been found."

"We're getting real close to finding him," she replied. "I get a strange feeling; call it my woman's intuition, but I think we were within a few feet of him, somewhere around that old barn."

Indigo was quietly listening from the backseat. As they watched the train, she leaned forward, and said, "I knows y'all is talking 'bout that dead girl. I guess y'all know you're messing with the past...know what I'm saying?" She adjusted her red head scarf and settled back in silence.

After the train had passed, they crossed the tracks and made a left on U.S.1 heading toward Cocoa. About ten miles later Indigo directed Brad to make a right on Riverside Drive. They followed the winding, tree-shaded road along the Indian River until they came to the Baxter house, one of the oldest in the area. A recent shower of rain had left a thin steamy haze causing somewhat of an eerie effect. The white, two-story house presented a stately appearance with its four tall columns and wide porch across the front. The lawn was immaculately landscaped with a green carpet of grass spotted with colorful flower beds. Leading up to the porch was a flagstone path bordered by beds of yellow and orange marigolds. As Brad pulled into the driveway, Indigo directed their eyes to an old white-haired gentleman slumped in a rocker on the porch, "See him? You can see him now. There he is...that's Mr. Sonny sittin' there on the porch, just like I told y'all he would be...just staring at the river."

"He looks like he's asleep," said Erin, glancing at Brad. "I guess you realize I don't feel comfortable with seeing this old man."

"Aw, don't worry, let me handle it," he said, taking the key out of the ignition. He reached down for the door handle and opened his door. "Okay, here we go."

Indigo led the way up the path to the house. When they got to the steps, Brad and Erin waited as Indigo went up on the porch. A nurse came out of the door with a pillow for the old man. She immediately recognized Indigo. "Indigo! What brings you around? Did you come to visit Senator Baxter?"

"That old goat don't need no visitin'," muttered Indigo. She gestured to Brad and Erin. "I gots two folks who wants to see him."

Baxter had bushy white eyebrows and his head was bald on top with shaggy white hair around the sides. On his lap was a small plaid quilt. He slowly raised his head and studied Indigo through his thick spectacles which sat low on his beak-like nose. "Indigo...is that Indigo?"

"It be me, Mr. Sonny. I brought some folks to see you." She motioned for Brad and Erin to come up on the porch. "They knows about *something* hidden in your old barn."

His eyes grew wild, "Did somebody feed the cows? What about my cows. Did they take my cows?" He glanced back and forth in a crazy manner like he was in another time dimension.

"Hush up you old fool...you ain't gots no cows. Now let these nice folks see you." She stepped aside and propped herself against the porch banister next to one of the tall columns as Brad and Erin walked up on the porch.

Baxter squinted to bring them into focus. His eyes acted as if they were drilling a hole through them. For a moment he sat silent and then he tightened his hands on the arms of the rocker. He gasped, "*It's YOU!!* No...no, it can't be...*it's you*...get them away! They've come to get me! *Nurse get them out of here!*" He grabbed his chest, slumping over as if having a cardiac arrest. Brad and Erin stood there wondering what was happening.

The nurse rushed forward, "What in hell have you done? *Senator* can you hear me? Quick, somebody help me sit him up, he's having a seizure!" She sat him back in his chair and examined him.

"He just collapsed," explained Erin, as Brad frantically dialed 911 on his cell phone. "Is he breathing?"

"Barely, his pulse is going crazy," exclaimed the nurse, nervously checking his wrist and neck.

"My cell phone isn't working," complained Brad, hitting the phone hard against his palm as if the jolt would fix it.

"Stay with him, I'll use the house phone...I need to get him to the hospital, now," said the nurse, darting inside, the screen door slamming behind her. A moment later she came back out to the porch. "The ambulance is on the way."

Erin moved out of the way to where Indigo was standing. Indigo tapped her on the shoulder, "He knows..."

"Knows what...?"

"About *you*...and that boy there." A wide grin stretched across her face. "I told y'all when the time is right you'd know. Child, I'm the old timekeeper...I knows how these things work."

"Indigo, what in the *world* are you talking about?" demanded Erin. "What do you mean he *knows* about us? I've never seen that old man in my life and neither has Brad. How would he know what Brad is doing? Are you saying Baxter has spies?"

"I ain't talking 'bout no spies, girl…" muttered Indigo, just before being interrupted by the siren of an ambulance rolling up to the front of the house. She looked around. "Here come the ambulance men to haul him away to the hospital…if the devil don't take him first."

After the paramedics stabilized the old senator, they wheeled him out to the ambulance and headed for the medical center. Brad and Erin felt obligated to jump in their car and follow. Indigo showed little emotion for the old senator, "Boy, don't you get tied up with that old coot and forget about those three pints of gin you owe me."

At the hospital, Brad paced the waiting room while Erin sat on a couch next to Indigo who was flipping through an outdated magazine about deep sea diving. "I used to want to be a scuba diver," remarked Indigo, but I never learned to swim. She held the magazine close to her eyes, carefully studying it.

"Did you see how wild that old man's eyes were when he looked at us? said Erin, unwrapping a pack of chewing gum. She offered a stick of gum to Indigo. "I mean it was like he saw a ghost."

"You were looking at evil," added Indigo, taking a stick of gum.

"I think he believed we were there to take him away," said Brad. "I just want to find out if he's going to be okay since we were there when he keeled over."

"I sure hope he'll be alright," replied Erin. "I know he's out of his gourd, but I'd hate to think we caused him to die or something. He'd haunt us forever. Indigo said he knows about us investigating Ethel's murder."

Indigo lowered her magazine and peered over her wire rimmed glasses, "I *said* he *knows* 'bout you two. He might not know what you be looking for…he just knows about you." She went back to reading the magazine.

Brad looked at his watch, then put it to his ear, "My watch has stopped. Erin what time do you have?"

Indigo, without looking up, said, "What'd I tell y'all about those time pieces. They don't never keep real time."

Erin glanced at her wrist, "Hmmm, mine's stopped too, there's a clock." She pointed to a clock on the wall. It was almost 4 o'clock. Brad set his watch, "I didn't realize it was that late, we need to get back out to the Baxter place before it gets too late."

A nurse came through the swinging doors and announced, "He's going to be alright, however, he will have to stay in intensive care for a few days." She started to walk away, and then turned back to Erin, "Miss Allen, he kept calling your name…"

Erin looked up, puzzled, "Ah, I'm not Miss Allen. He's talking about a girl who died a long time ago."

"Oh, I'm sorry; I just assumed he was talking about you. It's probably the medication he's on, sometimes it causes hallucinations." The nurse then left the waiting room.

"See there," said Brad, "he mentioned Ethel's name. I think he's at least sane enough to suspect we're on to him."

"Yeah, but he *thought* I was Ethel," remarked Erin. "That's kinda freaky if you ask me. I wish I could see a picture of her."

"You will," said Brad, "as soon as Indigo lets me look in that cigar box, but right now we need to get back out to the Baxter farm and see what's going on. I don't want Detective Sims to give up on me."

A few minutes later they were driving south on U.S.1 when Brad's cell phone began ringing. "Hey, my phone's working again!" At first he couldn't find it, until Erin traced the ringing to a used milkshake cup on the floor. She handed him the cup with the ringing phone inside, and said, "Seriously, you need to clean this filthy car."

He quickly slipped the sticky phone out of the cup and put it to his ear, "Hello, hello…this is Brad Kirby." He switched the phone to his other ear.

"Mr. Kirby, Jessie Sims here. I'm at the old Baxter homestead, I was wondering if I could ask you to take a drive out here…"

Brad cut in, "I'm on my way now. Did you check out the old car?"

"Yes, we did, we pulled it out of the old barn and it appears you were right. We've got more than one smoking gun here."

"How's that? Did you find something else?"

"We've uncovered some human remains," she answered.

"Holy cow crap!" he exclaimed. He cupped the phone with his palm and turned to Erin, "They've found a skeleton!!"

"Hello...Mr. Kirby, are you still there? Hello..."

He fumbled with his phone, "Yes, Yes, I'm still here...I was a little stunned by you finding bones...do you think it's Bill Kelly?"

"That's why I need you here," she explained. "I've got something to show you...something we found with the remains...you might be able to help me. Anyway, it's two o'clock, so you should be here by two-thirty. We'll talk about everything when you get here."

He said goodbye and handed his cell phone to Erin. "Can you believe it? They've *found* a body. It *has* to be Kelly." He checked his watch, "This damn watch...now it's working again."

"Mine too," said Erin, checking the clock on the dash. It was a little after two o'clock in the afternoon. "That stupid hospital clock was two hours ahead." She heard Indigo chuckle from the backseat.

Twenty minutes later they drove through the broken down gate of the Baxter farm and followed the dirt road to the barn. Sitting in front of the little barn was the old Ford coupe still partially covered with hay. Parked in a nearby clearing were four sheriff cars and a white van with the rear doors open. A half dozen uniformed deputies were milling about the scene while three plain clothes officers seemed to be examining the front of the old car. As Brad pulled to a stop, he pointed to a woman in civilian clothes, and said, "That's Jessie Sims." She saw him drive up and waved.

As they got out of the car, Sims walked toward them with something in her hand. "Mr. Kirby, here's the situation, after we removed that old car out of the barn we examined it but the only thing we found was this old Prince Albert tobacco can." She held up a plastic bag with the can in it. "Then beneath where the car was sitting we found several sheets of rusty roofing tin. It was under the tin where we found a shallow grave, covered by only a foot of dirt, containing skeletal material. We're still in the process of recovering these remains, but what's interesting is what we found with the bones. "Look at this," she said, her hand dangling a very old pocket watch at the end of a rusty chain. She turned the watch over in her palm and rubbed the dirt off an engraving on the back which read:

Happy Birthday Bill
July 17, 1934
Love Always, Ethel

"*Holy Moses...It's Bill Kelly's watch!*" exclaimed Brad. "And Ethel's name is on it. She gave it to him. Man, this is awesome stuff. Then we've just identified the body. It's Bill Kelly!"

"Only unofficially," cautioned Sims. "It will still require a coroner's examination and there's forensic analysis of the evidence that will be needed to make it an official identification."

"Still, this is big time stuff," he said.

"That's not all..." added Sims, taking the Prince Albert can out of the plastic bag and laying it on the hood of Brad's car. "Look at what was inside this can." Using tweezers, she carefully extracted a folded paper. It was stained and faded, and obviously very old. "I think being in the can probably helped preserve this little clue. Now don't touch it, but I do want you to read it." She used her manicured nails to carefully unfold the paper. "I knew my nails were good for something," she laughed. "This little piece of paper is a receipt."

Brad and Indigo huddled in close for a good look as Erin read it aloud, "Melbourne Watch and Jewelry. Sold to Bill Kelly...A Ruby Ring, Size 6. Price $75. Paid in full...I can't make the date out...except the year is 1934. Wow, that's Ethel's ruby ring!"

"So Bill Kelly bought the ruby ring for Ethel," said Brad. "According to the engraving on the old watch, it was his birthstone."

"A symbol of everlasting love," added Erin. "Let's check something. Indigo would you take your ring off for a moment?" Indigo twisted the ruby ring off her finger and handed it to her.

"Anybody got a magnifying glass?" asked Erin, holding the ring.

"Here...this might help," said Detective Sims handing her a small folding magnifying glass.

Looking through the magnifying glass, Erin turned the ring at various angles to the sun so she could examine the inside.

"See anything?" asked Brad.

"Ah...Yes. Looks like...ah...it's a little worn down, but there it is, a teeny tiny number six. Right there, see it?" She handed the magnifying glass to Brad, "It has to be the same ruby ring."

Detective Sims moved in to look. "Where'd that ring come from?"

Brad handed the ring back to Indigo. "It came from Frank Turner, the original investigator of the case. After Judge Baxter abruptly closed the investigation, Turner gave the evidence and ring to Sonny

Baxter. Indigo was Baxter's housekeeper. You see how all the dots are connecting?"

"That's quite a trail of events," remarked the detective. "And it sure looks like it leads to Baxter's front door."

Preferring to keep quiet about visiting Baxter, or mentioning that he was in the hospital, Brad asked, "Do you think you have enough to close the case now?"

"I suppose we're going to find out. It will take a few days for us to process everything which will include all of your research notes and what we've gathered here," replied Sims. "Mr. Kirby, looks like your cold case has really warmed up. I guess this will give you plenty to write about in your magazine."

"Well, the main thing is clearing Bill Kelly as the murder suspect," he answered, quietly thinking to himself about the five thousand dollar bonus he could claim from his publisher for solving an old homicide.

"I'm glad you helped find his body," added Erin. "Now Bill and Ethel can rest in peace side by side." She put her arm around Brad's waist. "I think that's what Ethel was trying to tell us she wanted. She just needed help with finding him." Brad held his breath in hopes she would not start talking about their unexplained encounters.

"Sounds like there's a *ghost* story to this..." quipped Detective Sims, half laughing, brushing a spider web off her sleeve.

"Maybe it's more like...well, like a love story," smiled Erin, exchanging a wink with Brad. She didn't mention seeing Ethel in the mirror. It was as close as Detective Jessie Sims would ever get to the supernatural limits of the old mystery.

"Well, some things are still best left alone," muttered Indigo, taking Brad by the elbow. "Boy, ain't it time we was going? You still needs to go get my gin. I figure you owe me 'bout four pints now."

"That's three pints," corrected Brad. "But it's been worth every pint. I might even buy myself a bottle of champagne."

CHAPTER 14

A late afternoon shower had left a thin layer of steamy fog on the road as they drove back to Cocoa. Erin watched the passing telephone poles while Indigo catnapped in the backseat. They rode along in silence having exhausted anything worth talking about, except for an occasional comment about something on the roadside. A flock of buzzards scattered to the wind as the car passed by the remains of an armadillo carcass. One bird, reluctant to leave his dinner, almost hit the windshield. *"Watch out!"* Erin yelped, as Brad quickly swerved to avoid the feathered creature. She turned around to look back, and said, "Vultures have always reminded me of undertakers; they're all black and make their living off the dead."

Near the city limits of Rockledge, Brad turned into a roadside package store to keep his promise to Indigo. He went into the store and returned with a paper sack. "I got four bottles of gin. Does that make us even?" She nodded, looking in the sack. Her face beamed a smile. "You're okay, boy, we is even with the spirits now!"

As he pulled out onto the highway, Erin said, "I thought you were going to get yourself a bottle of champagne. We could've gone to my place and celebrated your success in solving the mystery."

He thought to himself, now she tells me. I could have gone to her apartment. He slowed the car, ready to turn-around. "You want me to go back and get a bottle?"

"No, we need to get Indigo home," she said, turning to Indigo. "It's been a long day and she's getting tired, right, Indigo?"

"You can say that again," answered Indigo. "Y'all done dragged me from pillar to post today and I gots to get home to feed my cats."

As they drove past Ashley's Tavern, Erin glanced at Brad, "However, I don't work tonight if you want to come over later."

"Sure." His answer seemed short like something was on his mind. He slowed down and made a right on Mango Trail which would take them to the alley leading to Indigo's house. "I think we should check on Sonny Baxter, just to see how he's doing."

"You won't be able to see him," said Indigo, starting to gather up the items she had salvaged from the junk pile earlier that morning.

"She's right," added Erin. "He's in ICU and they're not going to let you in." Erin was ready to call it a day too. "I'm getting tired."

"It won't take ten minutes," he insisted, as they pulled up in front of Indigo's house. "I only plan to ask about his condition."

After dropping Indigo off, Brad headed for the hospital, still promising Erin it would only take a few minutes. He parked the car and she followed him through the hospital entrance to the elevator and up to the second floor to the ICU waiting room. There was a red telephone on a table with a sign instructing visitors to call the ICU desk for permission to see a patient. He lifted the phone and said, "I'm here to see Mr. Baxter."

"Are you a relative?" asked a nurse on the other end.

"I'm a friend...I just want to know how he's doing."

"You said Baxter?"

"Yes ma'am, Sonny Baxter, he came in this afternoon."

"I don't see an ICU patient by that name. Perhaps he's in another room. Let me check with admissions. Can you hold just a moment?"

"Sure," he said, turning to Erin sitting on a couch leafing through a magazine. "He's not in ICU, so he must be doing better." He waited a few seconds until the nurse came back on the line.

"Sir, I can't find a patient by the name of Baxter. Are you sure he was admitted this afternoon?"

"I'm *positive* he came in this afternoon."

"Well, I don't know what to tell you. No one by that name has been admitted. I checked back several days and still found no Baxter. Perhaps he was admitted to another hospital. Have you tried Parrish Medical Center?"

"No, it was this hospital."

"Well, I'm sorry, but he's not here."

He thanked her and hung up the phone. He stood there in silence facing the wall rubbing his hand through his hair. A dumbfounded expression covered his face as he turned to Erin, "This is crazy."

She put down the magazine. "What's crazy, Sonny Baxter?"

"He was never admitted to the hospital. He ain't here. He's *never* been here. They have no patients by that name."

"What do you mean? He was in here this afternoon."

"Just what I'm saying, he was never here. Come on let's get out of here and go to his house. This is crazy, either the damn hospital has lost a patient or something really weird is going on."

They hurried out of the hospital and ran across the parking lot to Brad's car. The setting sun was casting an orange hue against the trees and buildings as Brad squealed out of the parking lot and headed south on Riverside Drive to Sonny Baxter's house. He pulled to a quick stop in front of the house and told Erin to wait in the car. He ran up to the house and pressed the door bell with his thumb. He could hear it ring inside. A young woman came to the screen door but did not open it. Through the screen, she said, "Yes?"

"Excuse me," he said, rubbing the back of his head. "I hope I'm not disturbing you, my name is Brad Kirby, and I...well I came by to see how Sonny Baxter is doing."

The woman looked confused, "Senator Baxter? Are you a friend?"

"Yes, well actually I'm an old acquaintance." He noticed the furniture on the porch was different. He didn't see the rocker that Baxter had been sitting in. He remembered the porch floor had been painted green before, now it was light grey. Even the trim around the door was different. Only the house number was the same.

The woman unhooked the screen door and came halfway out of it, "I'm sorry, I guess you don't know...*he's deceased.*"

"Dead? When did he die?" He started rubbing his head again.

"About ten years ago. He was up in age, you know. My husband and I bought this place in 1998 and it still has a lot of the Baxter furnishings in it. I'm sorry that you didn't know."

"Ah, no, that's okay. You say ten years ago?"

"Yes, I think he died in 1995. Would you like to come in? My husband would be happy to show you some of the Senator's things."

"That's okay, thanks anyway. It's getting a little late." He turned and hurried down the walk to his car. He got in behind the wheel and just sat there slumped in his seat. For several seconds he didn't say a word, it was like he was in a daze. Erin pushed his shoulder with her hand, "Hey, what's the matter?"

He straightened up as if regaining consciousness, turned, and said, "Sonny Baxter has been dead for ten years. There's somebody else living in his house. He's dead!"

Erin hesitated for a moment. She looked at the house, then at Brad, *"Been dead ten years?* What do you mean he's been dead ten years? We saw him sitting there on the porch today."

"No we didn't. I don't know what we saw but it wasn't Sonny Baxter. Now what in the hell is going on?"

"Brad, this is *getting* weird. Indigo took us to see him."

"She took us to *see* him, Erin. The key word is 'see.' She never said he was alive. When I think about it, no one ever said he was *alive*, I just assumed he was alive. I think we saw some kind of manifestation of Sonny Baxter, but it damn sure wasn't him."

"You mean like we were dealing with a spirit?"

"I'll be damned if I can explain it," he said, looking at his watch. "It's almost seven o'clock. I'm getting hungry, let's go grab a sub sandwich or something…then I'll take you home."

He started the car and as he pulled away from the curb Erin was reminded of something. "Brad, *your watch!* You just looked at your watch. Remember in the waiting room how our watches stopped?"

"That's right, and we set them by the clock in the waiting room only to find out later they were two hours ahead. I thought that was strange, especially with both our watches stopping."

"We were two hours off in real time. I've heard of lost time, but this was like we were in a different time zone. Then, all of a sudden we were driving back to the Baxter farm. I can't remember from the time we left the hospital until we were halfway to the Baxter farm."

"I can't either," he replied. "And remember my cell phone wouldn't work. What's with that? I tell you, there's something weird going on. It's like we've solved one mystery and another one starts."

They stopped at a small sandwich shop and ordered two tuna subs with cheese, and two sodas then went over and sat down at a small wobbly table next to the front window to eat. Brad chomped into his sub and looked outside at the car headlights on the highway. Across the street he could see a neon sign for the Classic Tanning Salon with several of the letters burned out, which in bright blue neon, read, "ASS TANNING SALON." He snickered under his breath and teased

Erin, "Hey, there's a tanning salon for you." She gave a quick glance at the sign, then swiftly kicked him under the table. "Looks more like your place," she quipped, drawing a sip from her soda. "It's got your name on the sign." She looked at him and laughed.

They finished their meal in silence. Occasionally, they would glance at a customer at the counter or at the cars going by outside, or that burned-out sign across the highway. Brad took his empty soda cup to the counter and got a refill. As he sat back down, he said, "This Sonny Baxter thing is totally creepy, I mean it's like it never happened but we know it did."

"Like a dream..." said Erin, stirring the ice in her cup with a straw. She licked her straw, and said, "Like some kind of hallucination."

"Exactly, like hallucinating," he replied, finishing off his soda. He wadded up his napkin and stuck it in the empty cup. "But how can two people have the same hallucination at the same time?"

"I don't know. Maybe Indigo had something to do with it. I mean she is always talking about time and all that stuff about being the timekeeper. Maybe she...like...manipulated time or something...like put us into a different dimension. I mean we both saw the same things, Sonny Baxter, the ambulance, the hospital...and both of our watches stopped, what caused all that stuff?"

"Yeah, Indigo, we need to ask her what's going on."

"She won't tell us anything," said Erin. "She speaks in riddles and has more secrets than you can stir with a stick. She'll just say something like, 'you'll know when the time is right'."

"Well, the time is *right* now," he replied. "I'm getting fed up with stupid mysteries." He stood up and gathered their cups and napkins and put them in the waste container. "It's almost eight, let's get out of here."

They went outside and got into the car. Brad hesitated for a moment, and then started the motor. As he was backing out, he said, "What are we going to do to figure this out? We sure can't go asking anybody or they'll think we're nuts. I've heard about people who say they've been abducted by space aliens and I don't want to end up in that category. Hell, it's bad enough seeing weird images in a mirror." As he pulled out of the sub shop parking lot and made a right toward

121

U.S.1, he mumbled, "I've gone stone nuts. That's it…I've gone nuts! I came to this town as a sane man, now I've lost my marbles."

"If that's the case, then we're both nuts," she smiled, gently massaging his shoulder with her hand. "Maybe we'll end up in Chattahoochee together."

"What's that?"

"Chattahoochee? That's where the state mental hospital is at…where they send crazy people," she explained with a laugh. "I have an idea; maybe we need to talk with a parapsychologist."

"So you think I need a psychologist. So you think I'm nuts too---"

"I *said* a PARA-psychologist," she replied. "They study ghosts and psychic phenomena. Like J. B. Rhine. He was the first person to seriously research extra-sensory perception. Ever hear of the Rhine Research Center? It's named after him, and they've done a lot of scientific research into paranormal things, like ESP and stuff."

"So where's this research center at?"

"Duke University."

"What? That's in North Carolina! I'm not going to North Carolina. Is there one of these psychologists in Brevard County? Do they have, like a branch office or something?"

"Cassadaga, Florida," she said. "It's about fifty miles from here. All the residents are mediums and spiritualists. Remember Diana…my neighbor? She knows a man there who is a parapsychologist."

"I've heard of that place. A friend of mine, who writes for *Sun Travel* magazine did a story about that town. Okay, I'm for anything that might explain this…this mystery. It still don't mean I believe in the supernatural, well, except for what we saw in the mirrors. Oh, lord," he moaned, "I've gone over the edge…I know it."

"Don't worry, I still like you even if you are insane," she giggled "Let me see if Diana will go with us to Cassadaga and, if you want, we can take a trip up there in the morning."

They pulled into the parking lot of Spanish Oaks apartments and parked next to Erin's car. "Don't tell anybody about this…ah, *Sonny Baxter* thing," said Brad, almost pleading. "I don't want anybody thinking we're crazy, especially since we can't even explain it." He got out of the car and went around and opened the passenger door.

Erin put the strap of her purse over her shoulder and stepped out, "I'm not telling anybody except Diana. She understands these things and can keep a secret." She put her arms around him in a reassuring hug and cuddled her head against his chest. Then without saying anything, he lifted her chin and placed a light kiss on her lips. Suddenly a voice came out of the shadows near the trash dumpster, "Hey! Hey! You two! No public displays of affection in the parking lot!!"

They quickly let go of each other---innocently dropping their arms they looked around. It was Diana tossing a bulging black plastic garbage bag into the dumpster. *"Gawd, Diana!"* exclaimed Erin. "You practically *scared* the crap out of us! What're you doing out here in the dark?"

"I was taking my garbage for a walk," she laughed, casually strolling over to the car. "So...*where* have you *two* been all day?"

"You're not going to believe it," said Erin. "It's a long story, I'll tell you all about it when we get inside...first, how'd you like to go with us to Cassadaga tomorrow?"

"Sure, if I can be back by three when the boys get home."

"No problem," said Brad, "I'll see you guys in the morning." As the two women started up the stairs, he said goodnight and got into his car. He was ready to get to his motel and take a hot shower. It had been a long, mind baffling day for him and Erin. They had solved one mystery only to find themselves in another encounter with the unknown. It would not realize it would *not* be the last of their encounters with the paranormal?

CHAPTER 15

The next morning, after filling his tank at the Kwik Mart store next to the Sea Rest Motel, Brad picked up Erin and Diana and by 8:45 they were northbound on Interstate 95. Cassadaga was seventy miles from Cocoa, about halfway between Orlando and Daytona Beach. Erin was trying to plot the best route using an old road map she had found under the seat. "This thing is in shreds," she complained, holding up five pieces of the map. "Don't you have a better map?"

"I never use a map unless I'm going out of state," said Brad, accelerating around a string of slow moving tour buses from New Jersey. "I'll just hit the Beeline expressway into Orlando and we'll take Interstate 4 north until we see an exit sign for Cassadaga."

"That's the long way," said Erin, trying to fit the map together. "We'll get stuck in all that tourist traffic. You need to check the map." He moved over to the right lane as a big tractor-trailer truck roared by belching black smoke from its stacks. "I don't need a map."

Diana leaned forward from the backseat, "Okay, you two. In the first place, every woman *knows* that guys don't read maps and they never ask for directions. The fastest way is to stay on I-95 and take State Road 44 west. It will take us right to Cassadaga. I drive it once or twice a month and I always go that way."

"Okay, then we'll do that," he said, as they passed by the interstate exit to Kennedy Space Center. Erin shoved the pieces of map under the seat and settled back for the hour and fifteen minute trip. Diana passed a small booklet over the seat to her, "Here's a directory for Cassadaga. It has some information about the town and its history."

"Oh, thanks," said Erin, opening the booklet which was filled with information about Spiritualism and a brief history of the town. It told how Cassadaga was founded by George Colby in 1895 as a spiritualist camp and how the peaceful hamlet is one of the nation's strangest towns because its residents are mediums. According to history, it was during a séance in Lake Mills, Iowa, that George Colby, a trance medium from New York, was told by an Indian spirit guide, named Seneca, to travel to Florida and establish a center for spiritualists. When Colby arrived in 1875, this part of Florida was a wilderness of palmetto scrub cut with a few sand wagon roads. He followed the directions of his spirit guide to several beautiful hills surrounding a group of crystal clear lakes. At this spot on December 18, 1884, Colby established the *Southern Cassadaga Spiritualist Camp Meeting Association*. Originally intended as a winter haven for spiritualists, the camp evolved into present day Cassadaga complete with a post office, bookstore, hotel, parks, shops, and the George Colby Memorial Temple.

As they entered the town of Cassadaga on Stevens Street, they passed between the historic gate pillars separating the spiritual community from the outside physical world. On the left was a large hotel and on the right a meditation garden with a fountain. They immediately sensed a strange serenity as if they were entering the very soul of the little village. "It seems so peaceful," remarked Erin, as they drove slowly past quaint residences, each with a sign offering various psychic services. Diana directed Brad to make a right on Seneca Street and to pull up in front of a small frame cottage. A small sign tacked to a white picket fence identified the place as the residence of Dr. Benjamin Warren, Medium, Healer and Parapsychologist. Brad shifted the car into park and asked Diana, "How well do you know this guy?"

"Very well," she said, opening the car door. "He's done a few readings for me, but his real interest is studying psychic phenomena. I think you'll find him rather interesting." She caught a quick glimpse of a face peering out from between the curtains of a corner window. "Now, I must warn you, he's a little bit weird too."

"Yeah, I bet he is," said Brad, removing the keys from the ignition. "Of course, I'm beyond calling anybody weird these days." On the other side of the picket fence, the yellow and brown faces of tall sunflowers followed the midmorning sun. He got out and stretched his arms. He could hear a tinkling melody being played in the warm breeze by wind chimes swinging in a camphor tree.

The hinges of the gate squeaked as they opened it and walked past the sunflowers to the house. Attached to the door frame was a little bell with a small cord. Diana rang the bell as they waited on the steps. They could hear approaching footsteps inside the house. Suddenly the door opened and a gentleman stuck his head out. He was tall, at least six feet, with longish hair and a dark mustache. "Well...well...what a pleasant surprise," he said, recognizing Diana with a friendly smile. "Come in, come in, I see you have some friends with you." He wore black slacks with a black dress coat covering a black pullover turtleneck, which gave the appearance of a warlock, or perhaps, an undertaker. His left hand held the door open and on his index finger was a large silver ring studded with a black onyx guarded by engraved gargoyles.

"Dr. Warren, how are you?" asked Diana, as she stepped inside the door followed by Brad and Erin. The house was dark inside, except for the glow of a dozen or more incense candles sitting on tables and bookcases. The whole place smelled of exotic aromas like in one of those import stores at the Mall.

"I feel just fine," he said, shaking hands with Brad and Erin. "Come on back here to my parlor." He turned to Brad and Erin, "I call it my parlor, actually it's my office, but parlor seems to fit my spiritualist image better." He laughed, as he guided the trio through his darkened dwelling to a back room. "And how have you been?" he asked Diana. "Did everything work ?"

"Yes, thank you. Everything has been cool and stress free lately." She did not elaborate about her last visit with him. Instead, she switched the conversation to, "My friend Erin here...and her friend, Brad...need your advice about some...well...weird experiences they've had."

He offered everyone a seat before sitting down in a high backed leather chair behind a big mahogany desk. On the wall behind him was a framed painting of three UFOs flying through space. He sat quietly studying his three visitors for a moment, then cut his eyes across the desk at Brad, "So you and your young lady friend have had a recent spirit encounter. I can tell you're a little skeptical about these things, even though your experiences have brought you closer in a relationship...it's not a bad thing. I can see you're divided by distance, you're from Miami and she's from Cocoa." As if reading their minds, he then turned to Erin. "And you just had a birthday this past July...how was it?" He waited for her to answer.

"I guess it was okay," she responded, convinced he was a genuine psychic. "How'd you know these things about us...like my birthday?"

"Easy, my dear, it's called cold reading. In the first place you're wearing your birthstone on your necklace. I could see the Dade County license plate on your car from my corner window...Miami is in Dade County. It's an easy assumption the car belongs to this young man because he was driving it. You're a friend of Diana...I know she's from Cocoa, so it's a good guess you are too. The rest is just a matter of observing body language." He eased back in his chair and put his hands behind his head and grinned. "It's all general observations that can be done by you...or anybody else."

"But how'd you know about our...ah...seeing a ghost?" asked Brad. "Or that I'm a little skeptical...how'd you know all that?"

Dr. Warren leaned forward and propped his elbows on the desk, pointing his fingers like pistols at Brad. "Your arms are folded in a defensive manner across your chest and the girls are doing all the talking. Your facial expressions are a dead giveaway too. It's all about reading body language my friend...as for knowing about your spiritual encounters, ha, that's easy, people come to Cassadaga because they either want to contact a spirit or they think they've encountered one."

"So, you're just fooling us," said Brad, with a slight grin, "...then this stuff isn't real...is it?"

"I was giving you a quick lesson in how charlatans use cold readings to dupe you out of your money. Every medium in Cassadaga is certified, believe it or not...what we do is *real*. The first thing you must learn about unexplained phenomena is that three-quarters of it is phony, hoaxes...or whatever. It's the other twenty-five percent that is intriguing." He settled back in his chair and slowly closed his eyes. "Now, if you're ready to deal with that mysterious twenty-five percent...then tell me your story."

For the next thirty-five minutes Brad and Erin went on about the murder investigation, their encounters with images in the mirrors, and the mysterious encounter with the dead Sonny Baxter. They did their best to include every detail from Indigo Blue to the strange time differences. It was enough to fill a book and when finished, they sat silent looking across the desk at the strange Dr. Warren. For the past half hour, he had not said a word and appeared to be in a trance. "I think he's either asleep...or dead," remarked Brad, rising slightly to get a better look at him. "Hello, are you asleep?" He leaned closer, "Did you hear what we were saying?"

Dr. Warren continued sitting with his eyes shut for a few more seconds, then suddenly opened them in a glaring stare. Brad jumped back as Dr. Warren leaned forward on his desk, and said, "I heard it all. Is that it?"

"Well..." began Brad, reluctantly. "There *was* a situation with a salt shaker that...ah...moved on a table when I was in Ashley's one night."

Erin's eyes widened with surprise. "What salt shaker moved? You never told me anything about a salt shaker moving."

"You never asked," he replied, with an innocent grin. "It was that night when I changed tables. I didn't say anything to you 'cause I didn't want to sound like a wacko."

"Well, Mr. Wacko," she said, "since we've had all these weird unexplainable experiences do you still feel like a wacko?"

"Part of me wants to deny it...the other part of me is convinced something is going on that we can't explain," he replied, crossing his legs and nervously rubbing his knee with his hand. "Shoot...I don't know what the hell to think anymore. I'd just like to know what's real and how much is wacko stuff...which is the only reason I'm here."

Dr. Warren gestured to the UFO painting behind him, "We're always trying to understand these things by looking in the direction of the larger parts of the Universe, like galaxies, planets, and so forth. The secrets to paranormal physics are found in the smaller unseen world. It boggles the mind to realize how infinitely small the Universe is. I'm talking about below sub-atomic level...down to the very molecular structures that bind everything together. I'm speaking of quantum physics beyond the range of electronic microscopes. That's where you'll find the true secrets."

"If you can't see it...then how do you know about it?" Brad asked.

"You don't necessarily need a microscope to study such activity. There are many methods for measuring or observing non-visible physics in the laboratory...from complicated equations to simple devices such as electromagnetic field meters to various biofeedback instruments that can measure alpha brain waves. It's really the technical side of metaphysics."

"You sound more like a scientist than a medium," observed Erin, trying to stay focused on what he was talking about.

"Actually, I'm both," he explained, moving his hands as if they helped him to speak. "I was born gifted...a medium...and this inspired me to study physics in college. I was a physicist in the aerospace industry for nearly twenty-five years before I retired." He pointed to several framed university diplomas on the wall. "But, I've always been a medium too."

"So, how does our spirit encounters fit in to all this physics stuff? asked Brad. "And the weird stuff with Sonny Baxter...a *dead* man."

"We can divide your experiences into two parts, an encounter with an apparition of a dead girl in the mirrors, and something we call SPE to explain your time differentiation and perceived encounter with this man who did not physically exist."

"SPE? What's that mean?" asked Diana, taking it all in.

"*Spontaneous Psychic Experience*," he said, as if it was a common term. "But first let's get back to the image you saw in the mirrors. It's possible the manifestation was not actually in the mirror...a couple of things can occur in these situations...it may have been in your mind..."

"You mean...we didn't *really* see a ghost?" asked Brad, confused.

"Quite the contrary, you did indeed encounter a spirit," Dr. Warren explained. "The mirror was the means by which the dead girl's spirit communicated with your mind. Spirit activity often occurs around mirrors because they can reflect electromagnetic energy...the energy needed for materialization. Other than photographs, a mirror is the only way we can see our true physical image, and under the right conditions, to look internally at our own psyche. Most mediums see with their minds...just like you did. I note from the description of your encounters, the dead girl manifested in such a manner that you could identify her."

"Like making sure I saw the ring…" said Brad, glancing at Erin.

"Or the blood I saw in the mirror," she added, with a slight shiver.

"Exactly," he said. "SPE, you can't control it---under certain conditions it just happens to certain people. You were fine-tuned as percipients by a strong desire to believe. Your combined psychic energies worked in conjunction to make it possible for her to communicate through your subconscious minds. Psychic activity occurs at various levels, from basic intuition to transcending the limits of space and time. In your encounter with the dead senator there were a number of psychic factors at work which created something like a mutual dream state…where artificial time is suspended, or pushed aside for real time. It was probably caused by that old woman…what'd you say her name was?"

"Indigo Blue," answered Brad. "She calls herself the timekeeper and is always talking about my watch not keeping time."

"Yes, timekeeper!" said Dr. Warren. "That's exactly how she acted in your case. No doubt she possesses a superior psychic gift by which she can manipulate time in some fashion."

"…And caused us both to be delusional?" said Brad, wrinkling his brow. "So, when we saw Sonny Baxter it was all just a dream?"

"No, she suspended physical time while opening a conduit in your subconscious minds to a past event…a channel between the physical and a non-physical time dimensions. But in this event he was alive. Can you understand what I'm saying?"

"Okay, so we didn't see Senator Baxter's ghost…just a vision of him in the past. You mean kinda like a dream? said Erin, trying to grasp an understanding of his explanation.

"That's pretty close without getting knee deep physics. In general, I refer to it as AMP, meaning *Anomalous Mental Phenomena*. Think of your mind as a biological television set. The brain has two parts and at the subatomic level billions of tiny particles are zipping about at the speed of light receiving and sending information. In physics we call these tiny particles 'neutrinos.' In metaphysics we label it extra sensory perception. There's a lot we still do not understand about these things, but fifty years ago nobody could visualize *email* either. It's my guess your experience resulted from a simultaneous cerebral connection between your subconscious and another time dimension."

"You mean like...we went back in time?" asked Erin, shifting in her chair and crossing her legs. "So where were our physical bodies?"

Dr. Warren made a quick pencil sketch on a writing pad showing two stick figures connected to various time dimensions. He held it up and pointed to it with a pencil as he talked. "Let me explain it this way. We are taught to think in terms of past, present, and future. In reality, the present doesn't exist; it's only where the past and future meet. What I just said is now in the past...and what I'm about to say is in the future. It only takes a tiny rip in the fabric of time to venture forward or backward. Your experience was a case of simultaneous retro-cognition and precognition. You were able to see people in the past and they were able to see you, which for them, was like looking at the future. It's the strange paradoxical world of quantum mechanics where everything in the Universe is connected...to *include* our consciousness. It's only my theory, but you were probably in a trance-state, perhaps sitting in your car...it all happened in a much shorter time than you think." He pushed the writing pad aside while his right hand fidgeted with a pencil. He seemed ready to summarize everything. "All of the experiences you have described seem to have a single contributing basis...the deceased girl. For some reason her spirit is earthbound...unable to cross over to the other side."

"You mean...Ethel Allen?" said Brad.

"Yes. She's been the energy behind each of your encounters. Apparently, she has a very strong message to get across to you and I sense it has to do with unfinished business on the earth plane."

"In other words," said Diana, getting into the discussion, "she wanted Brad and Erin's help to do something for her."

"Precisely," answered Dr. Warren. "Isn't this crazy spirit business fascinating? If I were you, I would sit down together and do a séance to see if you can open a channel with the deceased girl instead of her trying to contact you. It might even help you to understand and accept your unusual experiences a little better."

"Do you really think we could do a séance?" asked Erin, glancing at Brad, detecting a slight frown on his face.

"Yeah...like I'm *no* medium," said Brad.

"You don't have to be a medium, besides you'll never know until you give it try," said Dr. Warren. "Considering your experiences, I'd say you'd have a better chance than most. But if anyone in the group is not into doing it, then it probably won't be successful."

"Then that lets me out," remarked Brad. "Next these two will have me pushing one of those doohickeys around on an Ouija board."

"Don't mess with Ouija boards," warned Dr. Warren. "Leave that to experienced folks...you could open the door to some bad stuff."

"Will the spirit appear if we contact her in a séance?" asked Erin.

"Materialization is rare and seldom occurs without the presence of a medium," he explained. "However, raps and knocks emanating from a table are very common as well as physical sensations felt by people in a session, or even hear the entity's voice speak to you."

"Then I wanna to do a séance," said Diana. "I think it would be exciting. Let's do it tonight and see what happens."

"Okay, late tonight in my apartment," agreed Erin, ignoring Brad's reluctance to participate. "If Brad wants to be a stick-in-the-mud, then he can stay in his motel room by himself. Besides...two of us can do it."

Brad quickly had a second thought. He wasn't going to trade being with Erin to spend a boring night alone in a motel room. "Oh, okay, count me in. I still don't put much stock in doing a séance...I don't think it will work, but to satisfy you two girls...I'll try it."

Dr. Warren stood up and walked around to the front of his desk, "You've got to be a little more positive...keep an open mind."

They thanked him for his wisdom and consultation as he courteously ushered them through his dimly lit living room to the front door. He stood on the steps and watched as they walked to the car. The big faced sunflowers were still gazing at the sun as it slowly moved into the early afternoon. Dr. Warren waved as they pulled out. Erin and Diana waved back and then rolled up the windows. Erin turned to Diana in the backseat. "Wasn't he a fascinating man?"

"I told you he was interesting," she replied, checking her makeup in a compact mirror. "What'd you think about him, Brad?"

"I'll say this much," said Brad, slowing down to make a left turn on Stevens Street. "He was one weird dude...however, it seems like we're asking one unexplained phenomenon to explain another unexplained phenomenon and I still don't understand any of it."

CHAPTER 16

That evening as Erin opened the door to let her cat out she startled Diana who was about to ring the doorbell. "Oh! You scared me," Diana laughed, clutching a bottle of wine against her chest.

Erin held the door open, "Hi, come on in. Brad's not here yet. Oh, great, you've brought a bottle of wine! What kind is it?"

"It's from *Franciscan*, my favorite a California winery...it's a *Merlot* wine," she answered, as Erin closed the door behind her.

"Isn't that a little expensive?"

"Hey, every good séance needs a good wine," she laughed, following Erin to the kitchen. She sat the bottle on the counter. "I figured we'd need something to activate our sixth sense."

Erin checked the clock on the kitchen wall, it was five till nine. The clock was a battery operated novelty clock shaped like a cartoon cat with a tail that wagged back and forth as the seconds ticked away. Diana helped Erin clear off the small, square kitchen table. Erin placed a scented candle in the center. It was one of those short, stubby candles in a glass holder. Diana struck a match and lit the candle. Soon the entire apartment was filled with an exotic aroma of sandalwood. Satisfied with the spiritual mood, Erin went into the living room to pull the shades. Outside, twilight had turned to darkness and in the distance; a full moon was rising slowly above the Indian River. She looked out the window at the street lamps casting circles of warm amber light on the sidewalk below and was about to draw the shades when she saw the headlights of Brad's car pull into the parking lot. "Brad just drove in." She could hear him jogging up the stairs as she walked over and opened the front door. He gave her a tight hug with a quick kiss on the cheek, "You smell sweet...I'm not late am I?"

"Don't fret, we wouldn't think of doing a séance without you," she smiled, closing the door. "Diana's in the kitchen with her Franciscan..."

He interrupted, "A *monk?* Diana brought a *monk* to our séance?"

She could never tell when he was serious. "It's a bottle of *Merlot*, silly. Franciscan winery makes it." They went into the kitchen.

"And how is Brad tonight?" smiled Diana, holding up the foil capped bottle to show him. "Something to stimulate our minds."

"Hi. So that's a Franciscan. Is it good?"

"It's a little more classy than the draft beer you drink," said Erin.

"Stick with us, we'll make a wine connoisseur out of you," laughed Diana, taking a corkscrew out of a kitchen drawer. She handed the bottle and corkscrew to Brad. "Here, this is your first lesson. Remove the cork." While Brad busied himself with the cork, Erin sat a bowl of party mix and three stemmed glasses on the table.

Erin sat down at the table next to Diana as Brad started to pour the wine. "Pour easy, no more than three quarters full," instructed Erin. "Remember, I'm a bartender. You got to leave room to swirl it around so the wine can breathe. To enjoy a good wine requires three senses---sight, smell, and taste...or, if you're a psychic, you can just use your *sixth* sense."

As he poured each glass he gave the bottle a fancy upward twist like a French waiter. "When I was in college, I had a part time job as a waiter in a restaurant...but, I didn't know one wine from another, I just poured it." He sat the bottle down and held his glass up by the stem, "Here's to us and our delusions, may we find comfort in our insanity." The women raised their glasses then took a slow sip savoring the velvety richness of the fruit flavors. "Whoa, that's pretty good stuff," he smacked, wiping his lip with the edge of his hand. "It beats that cheap gin that Indigo serves to her spirits."

"Really," said Erin. "But we ain't serving our wine to spirits like she does. You know how Indigo says liquor keeps a ghost from bothering you. Well, we want to attract 'em...not scare 'em away."

Diana swirled the wine in her glass, "This particular wine reminds me of a fireside romance I once had at a ski lodge."

"Oh, so that's the reason you like it," said Erin, running her finger around the rim of her glass. "What happened to the romance?"

"It was short and sweet. But the memory still lingers in my mind."

"You mean memories of how you met your ex-husband?"

"Heavens no…memories of the one who got away," she laughed, sitting her glass aside. "Now let's get down to conjuring up the dearly departed. First thing we have to do is get serious, if that's possible."

"Maybe we can contact Sonny Baxter's ghost," said Brad. "I sure would like to hear his side of the story."

"I'd like him to explain how we saw him…then found out he was dead," said Erin, taking a final drink from her glass. "On second thought I don't want to talk to him. He's mean. I think we need to call for Ethel's spirit to communicate with us."

Brad replenished their glasses with the last round, "Do either one of you know what you're doing?"

Erin got up and went into the living room and pulled a paperback book from a bookcase. "Here," she said, thumbing to a marked page. "This book explains how mediums do a séance."

Brad stuck the cork in the empty wine bottle and sat it over on the counter, "What's that…another one of your ghost books?"

She held the book up so he could see the cover. "It's about psychic experiments. It's called *Discovering Your Psychic Powers*."

"Oh, a *real* technical manual on ghosts," he said, mockingly, as Diana began clearing everything from the table except for the candle.

"Just listen and stop joking," said Erin, sitting down directly across the table from Brad, who developed a silly grin on his face as she began explaining how to conduct a séance. "All we have to do is lightly lay our fingers on the table…and silently *concentrate*. If we make contact, it might come as a knocking or rapping sound."

"I hope you two don't really expect a ghost to materialize," said Brad. "I'll admit that strange things can happen, I just don't believe you can conjure up a spirit by sitting around a table with your hands on it. If that was the case everybody would be doing it."

"There you go with your negative thinking again," scolded Erin. "Remember what Doctor Warren said about being positive…if you can't think positive then it isn't going to work."

"Okay…I'll give it a go," he said, "I'm not expecting much."

Erin sat up straight in her chair. "Alright, everybody place your hands on the table top and just concentrate."

"What about the light? Diana asked. "We need darkness."

"Oh yeah, I almost forgot," said Erin, jumping up to switch off the light. The candle in the center of the table emitted an eerie amber glow as she sat back down. "Okay, everybody sit up straight in your chairs and put your finger tips on the table and close your eyes. Now in your mind concentrate on calling for Ethel to enter our physical world from the spiritual realm. Ask her to communicate with us."

"What if she calls me on my cell phone?" tittered Brad.

"Shut up, Brad!!"

"Okay," he snickered under his breath, feeling a little silly.

They sat in total silence around the table with their eyes closed and finger tips barely touching the top. Brad cracked his left eyelid to sneak a peek at the two women; both appeared to be seriously engaged in deep concentration. For five long minutes they sat there in the candlelight and nothing happened. Then a dull rapping was heard, it seemed to be coming from the table. At first they weren't sure of the sound, thinking it might be their imagination. It was like someone was knocking on the table.

"Diana..." whispered Erin, in a very low tone. "Did you hear it?"

"I know...I heard it too," she murmured. Brad remained silent and appeared to be absorbed in the session. Then the table emitted a succession of raps sending vibrations through their finger tips. "I can feel it," whispered Diana. "Let's ask if it's the spirit of Ethel."

"Are you Ethel?" asked Erin cautiously. "If you're Ethel, rap three times." The table immediately emitted three loud raps. A shiver ran down Erin's spine as she jerked her fingers back, "Oh my God! It's Ethel!"

"What do we do now?" asked Diana. "Ask her another question." Brad was almost in a trance, still sitting with his eyes closed as if he was channeling the spirit into the table.

"Ethel, how're you feeling?" asked Erin, trying to think of something to ask a ghost. "Signal with two raps if you're okay." Immediately there were two hard raps. Then all of a sudden Erin opened her eyes and shouted, "Brad *stop* it! Diana, *Brad's* doing it! He's screwing around kicking the table leg with his shoe!!!"

"Brad, come on, *get serious*," said Diana. "I *thought* there was something wrong when you kept sitting there so damn quiet."

He was laughing so hard that tears ran from his eyes. "I almost lost it," he cackled, "when Erin asked the spirit *how she was feeling*. I almost said she's *dead*, how do you think she feels." He continued wrapped in laughter until Erin gave him a swift kick under the table on his shin. "Ouch," he yelped. "Okay, I'm sorry. I promise to be serious from now on…man that was funny. You should have seen your faces!" He sat up straight and put his fingers on the table again.

"Ahem," Erin cleared her throat. "Alright, everybody be quiet and let's try again." Once again, they placed their fingers on the table.

For several minutes they sat in the glow of the candle, quietly beckoning a spirit to make contact. The minutes stretched into five and then into fifteen. Brad sat patiently in his chair trying his best to participate in the session. The candle in the center had burned down to half its size. The cat clock on the wall wagged away the minutes as nothing seemed to be happening. They were about to give up when a loud tap came from the table. *"Stop it Brad!"* warned Erin, opening one eye to check on him.

"That wasn't me," he whispered, keeping his fingers on the table as he peeked at both women. Again the tapping sound was heard. There were two taps followed by three more. "There it is again, I swear it's not me, really!!"

"It's not me either," said Diana, her eyes opened to check on the other two. "It's coming from *inside* the table top."

"Are you a spirit?" asked Erin, turning her ear to the table top. The response came in two louder taps sending a quiver through their finger tips. All three sat there wide-eyed looking at each other. At that point the sound stopped. The flame of the candle wavered as if blown by a breeze. "Look at that!" Erin pointed at the candle. "There's no breeze and the flame is moving around like crazy!!"

"Maybe it's the air conditioning vent," said Brad, standing up to hold his hand to the ceiling vent. "Nope, no air coming out of that."

"…And all the windows are shut too," said Erin.

"It's not a breeze," said Diana, watching the flame, "because it's blowing from all sides; see how it switches back and forth?" Then all of a sudden the candle went out leaving them in total darkness.

"Oh my gawd!" exclaimed Erin. "Whatever it was blew out the candle." She jumped up and flipped on the kitchen light. "I don't care

what anybody says, it had to be a spirit!" Brad was glancing around trying to find an answer to explain it. He bent over and looked under the table.

"I think we were on the brink of really talking with a spirit when we lost our concentration," said Diana. "This is getting a little eerie." She had hardly finished her sentence when she jumped up from her chair. "*Something* just yanked my hair! I swear...*something* pulled my hair!" She stood there with her hand against her hair, looking around.

A split second later, Brad quickly swiveled around in his chair grabbing his left shoulder, "I *felt* that....I felt it! I did, I'm not fooling this time, it tapped me on the shoulder!" He looked around at the living room, then looked up at the ceiling and at the kitchen window, but saw nothing. It was like an unseen prankster was present.

"I felt a cold, tingling, sensation down my face," remarked Erin, noticing an uncanny drop in the room temperature. "It's freezing in here. Does it seem cold to y'all?" She rubbed her arms with her hands and got up to check the thermostat on the wall. "The AC is set at 73 in here." She turned the thermostat setting up to 80 degrees.

"It's colder than any 73," said Diana, "It feels more like 50 degrees. It's as cold as a tomb...oh my lord why'd I have to say that...now I've freaked myself out for sure."

Brad held his hand to the air conditioning vent again. "This don't make sense for it to be this cold if the AC is set at 73. You can't blame this on me. This is just plain weird." He glanced at Erin's cat clock on the kitchen wall, "It's almost midnight too."

Diana stood up and slid her chair under the table. "Okay guys, this is enough for me. I'm starting to get a little freaked out with this stuff. I hate to be a party pooper but it's getting late."

The room began warming up as Erin followed her to the door. "Now I'm not so sure this séance was a good idea," remarked Erin, as she switched on the outside light and opened the door. "Brad, walk Diana across to her apartment."

"That's okay, just keep your door open until I unlock mine," she said. "Just don't close your door until I'm inside." Brad and Erin said goodnight and waited until Diana was in her apartment. Once she was inside, they closed the door and went back into the kitchen.

Brad went over to the small square window above the kitchen sink and peered out into the night. A scattering of rain could be seen falling in the street lights. "It looks like it's starting to rain."

Erin was loading some things into the dishwasher. "I hope it won't be like that night when I got trapped in the motel with you. I've had all the strange stuff I can take for one night."

"Naw, this is just a late night drizzle."

She shut the dishwasher and turned it on, then turned to Brad, who was still at the sink watching the rain drops hit the glass panes of the window. "Do you reckon whatever caused that weirdness during the séance is still lingering around in my apartment?"

"I doubt it, nothing has happened since Diana left." He pushed away from the counter and stretched. "But, who knows, nothing would surprise me. I guess I oughta be getting back to the motel. If anything really terrifying happens just give me a call." He was trying to frighten her, hoping she would suggest that he spend the night.

"Wait...you're leaving? What if this...this, whatever it was, starts up again? Besides it's late, why don't you just stay here tonight?"

That's exactly what he wanted to hear. He decided to test his luck by taking it one step further, just to see how far he could get with her. "Is your bed big enough for two?"

"The couch sleeps just fine...I'll fix it up for you."

"I don't have any pajamas..."

"I can take care of that too," she said. Next to the kitchen was a small laundry room with combination washer and drier. She opened the drier and took out a pair of her pink jogging pants. She tossed them across the kitchen to him and said, "Here, you can sleep in these...one size fits all."

He tried to catch the pants as they landed against his chest. "Would it be alright if I take a shower?"

"Good lord...is there *anything* else you want? She went into the living room and picked up the remote and turned on the television. He was standing halfway between the living room and the kitchen holding the pink jogging pants with a devilish grin on his face.

"Yes, now that you ask...." he teased, "Wanna fool around?"

"No, I *want* you to go take your shower." She gave him a playful shove toward the hallway. "You know where the bathroom is. There

139

are towels in the cabinet under the sink and don't use all the hot water because I would like to take a shower too."

"If you want to take one too, I know how we could save water."

"That ain't gonna happen," she smiled, knowing what he meant. "Go take your shower and *don't* get water all over my floor!"

"What if there's a ghost in there, will you come in and get it out?"

"Knowing you it'd probably be the devil," she replied.

He finally stopped joking around and made it to the bathroom. Erin returned to the kitchen to finish up. After emptying the dishwasher, she went over to the clothes drier and filled a wicker basket with fresh laundry. She switched off the kitchen light and headed to her bedroom with the laundry basket. She was about to enter her bedroom when Brad came out of the bathroom in a cloud of steam rubbing his hair with a bath towel. A light sheen of moisture accentuated the muscular firmness of his bare chest and flat stomach. He pulled the drawstring tight on the pink jogging pants. "These silly things don't fit me very well." The girlish-looking pants extended from just below his navel to a few inches below his knees.

She sat the laundry basket inside the bedroom door, and with her hands on her hips, turned to check him out. "Wow, fancy pants!" she snickered. "You look like you're wearing high-water britches."

"Stop *gawking* at my shins," he said with a sly grin, reaching inside the bathroom door to hang the towel on the rack.

She started for the bathroom with a robe draped over her arm. "Now go in the living room and watch TV so I can take my shower. I'll get you a pillow and some sheets when I finish. She went into the bathroom and closed the door. He stood there facing the door for a moment, then went into the living room and sat down on the couch. He picked up the remote and clicked through the channels stopping on a late night show on PBS. He tried watching the program but his ears kept tuning into the sound of the shower running in the bathroom. A few minutes later he noticed the shower had stopped and a whirring sound was emanating from the bathroom. He got up from the couch and sauntered quietly down the carpeted hallway and tapped his knuckle on the bathroom door. "Are you okay in there? What's that strange sound?"

The whirring sound stopped. "What? I didn't hear you," she answered, her voice muffled by the closed bathroom door.

"I said, what's that strange sound?" He knew it was a hairdryer but was just fooling around trying to annoy her. "Is there a ghost in there? Do you need me to come in and help you?"

"It's my blow dryer, Mr. Nosey," she replied. "I'm drying my hair; get back to the living room. I'll be out in a second." She clicked on the dryer again and went back to drying her hair as he chuckled his way back to the living room.

The living room was dark except for the light of a late night show on public television. He was sitting on the couch half bored with the TV when she came out of the bathroom. He cut his eyes down the hall as she opened the linen closet. She was wearing a white terry cloth robe pulled tight at the waist with a sash. As she stood on the tip toes of her bare feet to reach a stack of folded sheets on the top shelf, the upper part of her robe fell open. He swallowed and his eyes widened like a peeping tom. A thought raced across his mind that beneath the robe, she was nude; at least it was what his imagination was telling him. He quickly shifted his eyes to the TV as she came into the living room. She was clutching a large pillow and two sets of bed sheets against her breasts. He pretended to be innocently engaged with the program on television.

"What are you watching?"

"Television, uh…it's a PBS thing on snook fishing."

"I didn't know you liked fishing."

"I don't, I'm thinking about trying it."

"Well, if you'll get up, I'll fix the couch for you," she said, silhouetted against the flickering glow of the TV. He started to get up, and then hesitated when he saw the sash on her robe had come untied and was dangling at her side. As she sat the sheets and pillow on the coffee table in front of him, the left side of her robe fell open exposing a teasing glimpse of her soft feminine outline. His eyes rapidly followed her alluring curves down a naked thigh to her bare feet. It was an arousing vision, though slightly blurred in the dim light. He sat there mesmerized with a half open smile on his face. She quickly closed her robe concealing her intimacy as if wrapping a gift to be opened at a special time. Without saying a word, she conveyed an enticing smile with her eyes. He did not need extrasensory perception to sense the subtle invitation in the expression on her face. His eyes locked with hers as he reached out for her hand and in slow motion, eased her gently down to the couch. He shifted his body and stretched out beside her. Her lips nuzzled his neck as she felt his hands slip inside her robe and around to her back. He inhaled as he drew her close against his bare chest. She could feel his heart beating with desire against her breasts as she moved her soft mouth along the shadow of his shaven jaw. His mouth was warm as it pressed against her lips sending a current of passion throughout her body. She held her breath...exhaling slowly in a whisper, "Say it Brad...I want to hear you say it...*tell me you love me*."

He withdrew his left hand from her robe and stroked her auburn hair as he gazed into her sparkling green eyes, "I do *love* you Erin. I really do." It was what she needed to confirm the mysterious mixed-up feelings she had been having about him. Her eyes filled with moisture sending a tear glistening slowly down her left cheek. She wiped it away with her little finger. "God, *I love you* so much," she said, burying her face in his neck as he embraced her and placed a kiss in her hair. Softly, he lifted her chin with his hand...staring into her eyes, as his mouth came down to meet hers in a kiss so tender and lasting it seemed to penetrate her very soul. By a strange quirk of fate they had been brought together in a spiritual bond. At the moment they were not in the mood to question fate. She reached over to the coffee table for the remote control and switched off the television. As the room went dark, she let the remote fall to the floor and then she stretched out beside him. As his arms moved passionately around her, she whispered, "Don't you wish time would stand still so this moment could last forever?"

CHAPTER 17

The next morning as Erin made coffee, Brad called his editor in Miami and went over the details of the murder mystery. During the phone discussion he brought up the legend of Ashley's Tavern and how it related to the case. However, he was careful not to say anything about his personal encounters with the unknown. He was caught by surprise when his editor said, "Hell, write the legend as a side bar to the main story, it'll spice up the feature. Readers love this odd ball stuff...write it in."

Before hanging up he decided to push things by asking for two more weeks to work on the story. Actually, he was wishing for more time to spend with Erin. He squinted as he waited for a reply. "No dice..." said his editor, bluntly, "you've done a great job, but this thing has already stretched into three weeks...we just can't afford it." He hesitated for a second, "Tell ya what, Kirby, how about a couple of weeks of working leave?"

"Working leave?"

He could hear his boss's swivel chair squeak over the phone. "Two weeks with vacation pay while you do whatever it is that you need to do...and *no expense account either*. Then I want you in Miami so we can get this thing ready for layout before it gets stale."

"Okay, it's a deal," responded Brad, figuring he could survive very well since he would be getting the five grand bonus from the publisher in addition to his regular salary for writing the story.

He was about to hang up when his editor said, "Kirby, I bet you've done found a girl up there haven't you?" His boss always seemed to have some sort of psychic ability.

"You amaze me, Boss," he answered, "yeah, I ran into an old girlfriend up here...but that's not the reason I need more time. I'll be in touch. Bye." He put the phone down and looked over at Erin pouring a cup of coffee. "I got two more weeks out of him. The bad thing is he took me off my expense account."

"Meaning no more motel," she replied, sitting down at the table with her coffee. "Okay, no big deal. You can stay here."

"You mean it? I mean…I don't want to barge in on you or anything like that." He went over to the coffee maker to get a cup of coffee. He looked around the kitchen counter. "You got any creamer?"

"Look in the fridge, it's on the door. Did I hear you tell your boss you met an old girlfriend?" she kidded, sipping her coffee. "When am I going to meet this *old girlfriend* of yours?"

He looked up from the open refrigerator door with a silly grin on his face. "I was talking about you. I had to tell him something…the man is like a psychic. It's like he always knows what I'm up to." He closed the refrigerator and took his coffee over to the table. "I'm sure glad he didn't ask what I was doing last night." A devilish grin ran across his face as he sat down and began stirring his coffee.

Erin blushed, "I suppose you're referring to the séance."

"Oh, was that *what* you call it?" he teased, reaching across the table stroking her hand. "I do love you…it's strange but I really do."

"Strange? Like how?"

"Strange because of how fast everything has happened." He blew the steam off his hot coffee and cautiously sipped it. "When I first met you at the library it seemed like we had absolutely nothing in common…then all of a sudden here we are. I mean if I had not gone to the library that day…at the right time, we would have never met. Yet, I feel like we've been together a lot longer than a few weeks."

"I know what you mean," she said, holding her cup between her palms, with elbows on the table. "I've never believed that malarkey about love at first sight, and don't laugh, but I got a tingling feeling the first time I saw you." Her eyes glistened as she looked across the table at him.

"You did? *Really?*"

"Really, I did. I tried to deal with it because I figured you didn't feel the same way and you'd just leave town and that would be the end of it. Hey, I was really mixed-up inside over you. You were so caught up dealing with that murder mystery that I figured you wasn't interested in me."

"I thought you really looked hot...I mean like cute... remember when we met for lunch at that sidewalk café...?"

She sipped her coffee. "You mean the Harvest Moon?"

"Yeah, that's when it hit me...I really wanted to get to know you better. To be near you or whatever...I was a little confused too. I'll admit I wasn't sure about how to deal with it. I couldn't get you off my mind after we went to the movies that night. Jeez...I'm starting to sound like a stupid soap opera." He glanced at the ceiling, rubbing his face with his hand.

"No, don't stop now!" she giggled. "I like it, keep going!"

"Yeah, I know you're getting a kick out of me saying this stuff," he grinned. "Really, I've never felt like this about a girl before...I'm not just shooting you a line either, I'm really serious. Last night was a special moment. I guess it means you're special to me. "

"Brad, that's so sweet..." She had found a soft spot in him. He had changed in so many ways since the first day they met. He felt open with her. Whether he had been changed by their spiritual encounters or solving the old murder case, or pure fate, it didn't really matter. She knew he was talking from his heart. She sat her coffee down and went around the table and put her arms around him. She kissed him on the ear, "I *love* you."

———

Later that morning, around 10 a.m., Brad checked out of the Sea Rest Motel and was on his way back to Erin's apartment when he saw Indigo Blue pushing a shopping cart on Florida Avenue. It was the first time he had seen her since finding out Sonny Baxter was dead. He had some burning questions which needed answers. He pulled over to the curb and rolled down the passenger window, "Hey, Indigo, what's up?"

She stopped and turned, "Well, hello boy, what's you be doing? Have them police done figured out 'bout that dead girl yet?"

"They're still working on it." He slid over to the window as she came up to the car. "Indigo, tell me about our visit to see Sonny Baxter. Did you know he was dead?"

"Sure, I know'd he was dead."

"Then how'd we see him sitting on his porch…and at the hospital? He was never admitted to the hospital…then I found out somebody else is living in his house. So what'd we see, a *ghost?*"

"Oh he's a spirit alright, a earthbound one," she grinned, leaning on the car window. "You told me you wanted to *see* him. I just fixed it so you could see him. I don't 'spect you to know about these things, but you is slowly learning. That old man was evil, he ain't like other spirits. He is trapped in time, somewhere between life and the spirit world. What y'all saw wasn't his spirit…it was a piece of time. I done told you I be the old timekeeper. I just conjured up a piece of time from when he got a stroke and had to go to the hospital. That's the vision you got to see…just like you wuz there. Mr. Sonny didn't last too long after that."

"You mean we went back in time…?"

"Only in your mind's eye," she said. "Like my video movie player, I can runs it forward or runs it backwards or I can stop it." In a way, Indigo's rambling rhetoric matched Dr. Warren's weird explanation. On the other hand, Brad thought neither one of them made any sense. He felt like he was dealing with a phenomenon no one could ever explain, at least so he could comprehend it. Just to be polite, he said, "I guess I understand."

"Listen to me, boy. Like I done told you before, when the time is right you goin' to know. Just don't go tampering with things that ought to be left alone." She pushed herself back from the window and looked down the street. "I got to be going now. Tell that pretty girl, Erin, Indigo said hello."

"Yes ma'am, I will…I'll tell her," he said. "I'll see you later Indigo, you take care of yourself." With that, Indigo sauntered over to her shopping cart as he pulled away from the curb.

His attempt to gain an understanding of his strange encounter with Sonny Baxter had only left him more confused. Indigo still held many secrets and it seemed like she was dishing them out in bits and pieces. He still wondered why she kept calling herself the old timekeeper. Out of all the eccentric folks he had met in this town, Indigo Blue had to be the most mysterious.

Erin had just returned from jogging and was stretching-out her legs against the curb when Brad pulled into the Spanish Oaks parking lot. She was wearing silky blue shorts, a tank top, and a terry cloth headband. A trickle of perspiration ran down her temple as her eyes sent him a sultry smile. "Did you get checked out of your motel?"

He opened the rear door of the car to take out his luggage. "Sure did, and I'm glad to get out of that place too." He followed her up the stairs. "I saw Indigo pushing her cart on Florida Avenue...I stopped to talk with her."

"Oh, what'd she have to say?" Erin unlocked her door and held it open so he could lug his belongings inside. Her big fluffy cat followed him in and began meowing to be fed.

"She said to tell you hello," he replied, sitting his things down on the living room carpet as the cat leaped upon the sofa. "I asked her about the Sonny Baxter weirdness...she basically said the same thing as Dr. Warren. I swear, Erin, I'm more confused than ever. You know how Indigo talks all that crazy stuff about being the old timekeeper...well, I don't know what it is, but I get a strong feeling she isn't telling us everything."

"I've always had that feeling about Indigo," said Erin, pulling off her headband. "She's as sweet as can be, yet can be extremely mystifying"

As Erin headed down the hallway to take a shower, Brad's cell phone began ringing. "Hello," he answered, moving into the kitchen. It was Detective Jessie Sims from the Sheriff's Department calling about the case He leaned against the sink looking out the kitchen window as he listened to what she had to say.

"We have summarized the case the best we can based on evidence recovered at the scene and your research," she informed him. "If you'd like to drop by my office this afternoon, I'd be happy to recap our findings for you and since we're classifying it as a closed case I can give you a copy of the report for your story."

"Sure, that sounds great. I'll see you about two." He put his phone away and went down the hallway and knocked on the bathroom door. "Hey, I was just on the phone with Jessie Sims; she's wrapped up the investigation and wants me to come by this afternoon. Wanna go with me to see her?"

Erin opened the door with a towel wrapped around her. "Yes, after all I've been through with this old mystery, you bet I want to go but I have to be back at five to go to work. Just let me get dressed and put my face on. While I get ready you can feed my cat." She disappeared into her bedroom and shut the door leaving him standing in the hallway raking his hand through his hair. Figuring it would take her some time to get ready, he went back to the kitchen and put some food into the cat's bowl and made himself a peanut butter sandwich.

———

Detective Jessie Sims was just returning from lunch when she saw Brad and Erin arrive at the Criminal Investigations building. She waited at the entrance as they came up the sidewalk. "Hello, Mr. Kirby...good to see you, Miss Albright," she said, holding the door for them. As usual, she was dressed in trendy civilian attire hardly fitting the image of a cop. "I think you'll find our conclusions brief but interesting...*and*...with a couple of new details."

They walked down the hall to her office where she offered them a seat as she went over and sat down at her desk. She shuffled through a stack of papers sitting next to a potted plant on her desk, pulled out a manila folder and opened it. "You can see, there's not much to the report, it's pretty much cut and dried. Kelly was killed by one or more knife wounds, three to his abdomen and one in the upper region of his chest. This is indicated in the forensic examination by marks to the skeletal remains. Although we had no dental records or DNA to help with identification, other evidence, specifically the artifacts associated with the remains, leads us to a reasonable conclusion the remains are those of Bill Kelly. Since the victim and his vehicle were found concealed on the former Baxter property it implicates both Sonny Baxter and his father, Judge Baxter. They are the primary suspects. Now in looking at your research, I would have to conclude that Frank Turner was definitely an accomplice. If this was a recent crime, I wouldn't hesitate to arrest all three. *Unfortunately*, our suspects are all *dead*. I learned that Senator Baxter has been deceased for several years. I didn't know if you knew that."

"Yes, as a matter of fact we just found out the other day from the people who own his old house," replied Brad, mindful not to let anything slip out about their weird encounter with the dead senator. "Can you speculate on the motive, and any connections between the homicides of Bill Kelly and Ethel?"

Detective Sims reached across and picked a dead leaf from the potted plant sitting on her desk. "I think the motive was simple," she said, throwing the dead leaf into a waste basket. "First of all, you were correct about Kelly working with federal agents, and so was Sheriff Jacobs. Through my FBI source in Washington I got this short piece of history." She handed him a fax document from the Justice Department archives. "It's a list of revenue agents in Florida between 1925 and 1930. The department keeps a pretty good history...especially things related to Prohibition and the gangster era. It's only a list of names, however, it shows that before Jake Jacobs was elected sheriff, he and Kelly were listed as federal revenue agents working out of the Jacksonville field office."

Brad showed the list to Erin, and said, "So, when Jacobs became sheriff he already had a tight relationship with the Feds and no doubt was willing to help out in local surveillance." He got up from his chair and handed the paper back to Detective Sims.

"And that's where the mysterious *Scarlet Biddy* comes in," she replied. "You mentioned it to me during our first visit...at the time, I had no idea what it was until my FBI contact searched a list of federal operations against illegal whiskey dealers. Again, Sheriff Jacob's name popped up in the old records. Apparently, he was providing support to a local federal operation called *Scarlet Biddy*."

"Scarlet Biddy..." said Erin, "Sounds like a little red chicken."

"Funny you should say that," laughed Detective Sims, "because in 1932 the Department of Justice used the code name *Red Rooster* for a covert effort aimed at stamping out the illegal whiskey business. Several federal law enforcement agencies merged into a central bureau to carryout surveillance and raids at state and county levels. Scarlet Biddy was the code name for a local operation along Florida's east coast to watch whiskey being smuggled in from the Bahamas."

"That's *why* Scarlet Biddy was mentioned in that letter I found in the sheriff's papers," remarked Brad. "Then Bill Kelly was undercover working on the inside of a crime ring providing information to the Feds."

"...And somebody found out," added the Detective. "Thus we have a motive for his murder...and indirectly that of his girlfriend."

"...So Ethel was most likely murdered at the same time."

"Ethel was simply in the wrong place at the wrong time," surmised Detective Sims. "They had to silence her, which in turn helped the perpetrators to distract from what really happened."

"How's that?" asked Brad, leaning forward in his chair.

"Think about it. By hiding Kelly's vehicle and body at the Baxter place and dumping her body in the river...some fifteen miles away, they diverted attention away from the crime scene and set Kelly up as the prime suspect."

"...And the sheriff couldn't say much," added Brad, settling back in his chair, "or he would have blown the cover on the Scarlet Biddy operation. Frank Turner was probably planted in the sheriff's office by Judge Baxter to keep tabs on what the Feds were doing. Did any of the federal agencies ever look into what happened to Kelly?"

"Interestingly enough they did," replied Sims. "The report is on microfilm in Washington from which I obtained this copy." She handed him a three page document. "Read this...you'll see that in October 1934, a confidential inquiry was made into the circumstances surrounding Kelly's disappearance, as they did in all cases of missing or slain agents. It was kept hushed up and never leaked to the press, but with a shortage of agents...and of course, no trace of a body or the missing vehicle...their investigation didn't get very far. They made no connection to Ethel's homicide, it's not even mentioned, probably because Frank Turner suppressed the investigation until Judge Baxter finally terminated it. We now know from your research into her murder, that Turner never investigated one iota of anything...he just automatically branded Kelly as the only suspect."

"Yeah, he made the victim into the perpetrator," remarked Brad, "...and the crooks went on breaking the law untouched."

"That's about the size of it," said Detective Sims, shaking her head. "However, Sheriff Jacobs remained a thorn in their side until he was shot a year later, which I *believe* was a scheme to put Frank Turner in temporary control of the sheriff's office. Evidently, this was a well organized ring of big time numbers runners, liquor smugglers, bootleggers, and who knows what else. They needed to keep the heat off their backs. I imagine this whole criminal enterprise was active until Judge Baxter died. After that his son, Sonny Baxter, tried to get a foothold in politics by running for state senate. It's a shame how much they got away with, not one was ever brought to justice. We would hope it wouldn't happen today…but it does."

"Maybe they only thought they got away with their crimes," remarked Erin, exchanging a glance with Brad. "I guess they never expected the ghosts from the past would come back to haunt them in the future."

"I suppose that's one way of looking at it," smiled Detective Sims, still unaware of the supernatural encounters which had guided the case to a conclusion. She opened her desk drawer and took out a blue folder and gave it to Brad. "Mr. Kirby, in appreciation for the work you've done, I made a copy of the report for you. Good luck with your story…don't forget to send me a copy of *Dead End Magazine* when it comes out."

"I certainly will, that's a promise," said Brad, as he stood up to shake the detective's hand. Erin stood up and took his hand.

Detective Sims started to walk them to the door. "Oh, I'm almost forgetting something," she said, clapping her hands together. "It almost skipped my mind…we are releasing Bill Kelly's remains on Wednesday and the county has made arrangements to have him buried next to Ethel in the Crooked Mile Road Cemetery. I'll call you later with the details once they figure out the time for the burial."

"That would be wonderful," said Erin. "It would be nice if we could get a few friends together and maybe have a little service for him just to show our respects since he probably has no living descendants in the area."

Brad held the door for Erin and then turned back to Detective Sims and smiled, "I guess we can finally say that this old case is closed."

She nodded with a big smile, "That's correct, Mr. Kirby…this case is not only solved and closed, it's now history."

CHAPTER 18

Brad spent the next few days at Erin's kitchen table busy on his laptop computer transforming weeks of notes into a workable outline for his story. What began with an old newspaper clipping about an unsolved murder had evolved into far more than he had ever imagined. He was writing about a double homicide connected by a love affair and a secret federal operation, and lives forever changed by a ring of corruption and haunted by a local ghost legend. It's a tabloid writer's dream, he thought, pecking away at his keyboard, plus winning the publisher's bonus for helping solve a case didn't hurt either. In his mind he knew there were really two stories, the one he was busy typing and the untold one about him and Erin and the unexplained quirkiness which had brought them together.

His white dress shirt was unbuttoned with the sleeves rolled up just above the wrists. He stopped typing for a moment and stretched back in his chair scratching his chest through his T-shirt. The table was scattered with yellow writing pads, crumpled notes and copies of old newspaper articles. The silly looking cat clock on the kitchen wall was pointing to noon when he heard Erin come in the front door. She was carrying two grocery sacks in her arms. "It's just me," she called out, kicking the door shut with her foot. She went into the kitchen and sat the grocery sacks on the counter. "How's your story going?" she asked, taking a loaf of bread from one of the sacks and putting it into the bread box.

"Alright, I guess," he replied, "...it's just a lot of material to go through and organize." Getting up from the table he went over to help her with the groceries. "I've been staring at that screen so long my eyes are getting fuzzy. I need to get away from that keyboard for awhile." He rubbed his eyes and stretched.

"I can understand why," she said, opening the refrigerator to put away a few things. "You've been working two solid days. Hand me the milk, I need to get it in the fridge before it spoils. It's really humid outside today."

He reached in the sack and pulled out a carton of milk. "This is almost like being married, I mean not like I've been married or anything, but this must be what it's like."

She glanced around from the open refrigerator as he handed the carton of milk to her. "And what inspired you to come up that?"

"I dunno," he replied, looking in the grocery bag and lifting out a square carton. "What's this?"

"My soy milk energizer, it goes in the fridge. So you don't know why you think this is like being married? Putting groceries away sure doesn't make me think of being married...I do it all the time anyway."

"Yeah, but *not* with me helping you."

She stood up with one hand on the top of the refrigerator door and the other on her hip and with a sparkle in her green eyes, said, "And so if this was a marriage, I suppose you'd always be helping me put the groceries away? Is that what you're saying?"

He handed her a head of lettuce wrapped in cellophane. "Yes, I suppose I would...if that's what it would take."

She wasn't exactly sure what he was getting at, but had a pretty good idea of the direction he was taking her. "Hand me that package of tomatoes and those carrots."

"Salad reminds me of being married too," he said, watching as she arranged things inside the refrigerator.

She finished putting the vegetables away, then closed the refrigerator door and rested her back against it. "Salad *reminds* you of marriage?" she laughed. "Is that some kind of writer's analogy?"

"Separately, vegetables are just vegetables," he said, trying to think of which way to take his silly sounding analogy. "But when they...well...like come together, they make a salad. Providing nobody adds any cucumbers, I hate cucumbers in salad."

"Then we have one thing in common," she said in a soft sensuous tone as her eyes turned serious. "I don't care for cucumbers in my salad either." He placed his hands on her shoulders pressing her easy against the refrigerator and kissed her. As he brushed back her auburn hair with his nose he caught the sweet aroma of her perfume. He moved his mouth to her ear, and mumbled, "I just ran out of analogies. Wanna make a salad?"

"Without cucumbers?" she giggled, wrinkling her nose, as her arms found their way around his waist. She locked her fingers behind him in a hug. "Are you proposing to make a salad or *something* else?

"I was just thinking about something..." he said, softly nibbling her ear lobe and down the left side of her neck causing her to shiver.

"Thinking about what?"

"About how funny it would be if we got married," he said, as his lips teased her mouth. "I bet it would shock everybody."

"I bet it would too," she answered, with almost breathless words.

He pulled his face back and gazed intently into her eyes as he drew her body close to his. He cleared his throat, "Ahem, ah...you know I *love* you, Erin...will you *marry* me?"

Without hesitation her arms immediately tightened around him in a confirming hug. Her eyes moistened. *"Yes...yes! Of course I will!"* she answered, planting a full kiss to his mouth so passionately strong he could not speak. He could only mutter something that sounded like, "great." For the next few seconds they embraced each other in romantic silence against the kitchen counter, causing an apple to roll off and fall to the floor.

Then the door bell rang. They let go of each other as Erin said, "I think I better get the door." He pulled her back into one more kiss. The door bell rang again. "Leave it," he said, "it's probably somebody peddling religion."

"I better see who it is..." she said, breaking away to answer the door while he leaned against the kitchen counter. He could hear her open the door and say, *"Oh...Diana! It's you!"* Brad quickly slicked back his hair, and buttoned-up his white dress shirt and stuffed the tails into his slacks.

"Yep, it's me," Diana replied, a little perplexed at Erin's exuberance. "Your neighbor, the one from next door who borrowed your laundry detergent...I'm returning it." She held up a bright orange-colored, plastic container of liquid detergent with special stain remover.

"Oh...that's *really* wonderful...I mean, like there was no hurry. You wanna use it again? It's wonderful detergent..."

"What's with the crazy excitement?" asked Diana, thinking Erin was acting a little strange. "Your eyes are red...have you been crying?"

"No...*Yes*...well, *maybe*...come on in," she replied. "Brad's in the kitchen by the fridge...he made me cry."

"What...?" Diana glanced at the kitchen table with Brad's laptop computer sitting on it and scattered with his research notes. She saw him standing cross-legged by the sink with his arms folded across his chest. "Hi!" he replied sheepishly, with a big Cheshire cat smile covering his face.

"Hello, Brad. So why'd you make Erin cry?" Something seemed out of the ordinary. "And why are you grinning like a possum?" He immediately straightened his smile, unfolded his arms and slipped his hand in his pocket.

"It was about salad..." he began, "I mean it was about vegetables."

"Brad doesn't like cucumbers in his salad," injected Erin.

"And you *squalled* about that?"

"No, I *mean* it was a happy cry, because I don't like them either and a salad is like...well you know...like a marriage."

Diana, a little puzzled, glanced at Brad, he was grinning again. "What the hell are you talking about? Salad, cucumbers...and Mister Cool is standing there with a ridiculous grin on his face. Okay, what's going on? Are you two high on something?"

"Brad asked me to *marry* him!!"

"What??" Diana dropped the container of laundry detergent on the floor. It hit with a thud. *"You're kidding!* You're *NOT* kidding! That's wonderful." She grabbed Erin's hands and they jumped up and down in the kitchen screaming like school girls on a playground. Brad's grin got wider. Diana went over and gave him a hug. "I'm so happy for you both. Hey, I'm *jealous* too," she laughingly frowned, "I had my eye on this guy too. Shucks, I lose again. But isn't this a little quick? I mean, like you guys just met a few weeks ago."

"I know it sounds kinda sudden," said Erin. "But the whole thing is totally strange. I mean the way, well, the way we came together...it's like fate or something."

"Well, it doesn't matter," Diana said, hugging both of them again. "As long as you're in love that's all that counts...it makes me feel so happy for you." About that time Brad's cell phone started ringing. As usual, he had to follow the sound to find it. This time it was in his coat hanging on the back of a kitchen chair. He put the phone to his ear. It was Detective Jessie Sims calling from the Sheriff Department.

"Hello, Mr. Kirby. I promised to give you an update on the status of Bill Kelly's remains. Arrangements have been made for interment next to Ethel tomorrow afternoon at three. I know this is short notice, however, I just found out about it. I thought you and Miss Albright might want to have a little service or something."

"Yes, I think that would be nice. We'll try to get a couple of friends together and arrange for some flowers. I'll talk to Erin about it. I appreciate you calling me, thanks."

As he hung up the phone Erin asked, "Talk to me about what?"

"That was Sims, she said they are burying Bill Kelly's remains tomorrow and thought we might like to have a little service."

"That's not much time; we've got to get moving. We need to call some people...we need to do something for him... *flowers*...we need flowers. We *can't* have a funeral without flowers!"

"Leave the flowers to me," said Diana, "I'll sweet talk my cousin out of a couple floral sprays...or something."

"Your cousin...?" said Brad.

"She runs Old Village Florist and she owes me a favor too."

"Great," said Erin. "I'll start calling some people and tonight I'll pass the word at work...OH!! We're forgetting about Indigo! She doesn't have a telephone. We need to let her know."

"No problem," said Brad, "I'll drive by her house." He slipped on his coat and gave Erin a kiss, and followed Diana to the door. He turned to Erin, "If you're not here when I get back, I'll see you at Ashley's tonight, and make sure Roberta knows about the funeral."

When Brad drove up in front of Indigo's house he made a quick count of the grocery carts parked in her yard. None were missing, which meant she had to be home. He walked up on the porch and knocked on the solid wood door. While he waited for an answer, a half dozen cats on the porch kept their eyes on him.

"Who that be?" came a voice from inside the house.

"Indigo, it's me, Brad." About that time the door opened with a squeak and he could smell the aroma of turnip greens cooking. The smell reminded him of his grandmother's kitchen.

"Hello boy, you come visitin'?" she grinned, holding the door open. "Don't just stand out there on the porch, come on in here." Inside, the little house was dark and crowded with all kinds of items Indigo had salvaged from junk piles all over town. There were several bookshelves crammed with magazines, jars of unknown things, and an animal skull of some kind. A picture of Dr. Martin Luther King hung on the wall next to a picture of the Space Shuttle. "Let me fix you a bowl of turnips," she offered, starting off to the kitchen. "I got some good smoked neck bones in them and they've been cooking all day long."

"No thanks," he said, sitting down in a big overstuffed chair covered with a patchwork quilt.

"Shush up," she ordered, "I'm fixing you a bowl of greens. Now you just sit there and *talk* with me."

"Yes ma'am..." he answered, knowing not to argue with her. Of course the smell of the turnips did bring back special memories to him. He looked over at a window. A cat was sitting on the outside ledge looking in at him. Not only did she have half the grocery carts in town, she also had all the stray cats. "The reason I dropped by..." he began, "is because they are burying Bill Kelly's remains tomorrow afternoon and we figured you'd like to attend a little funeral we're planning. It's not going to be anything fancy, just a little memorial service."

Indigo came back out from the kitchen with two bowls of steaming turnip greens and handed one to Brad. "Here, eat this, it's just like your granny used to make."

He took the bowl wondering how she knew about his grandmother. He stuck his fork in the bowl, wrapped up some greens on it, and shoved them into his mouth. "How'd you know about my grandmother cooking turnips?"

"That's what was in your mind when you smelled my greens cooking. Smells always bring back memories," she replied, taking a healthy bite of greens. "Never you mind what I knows. So, they's goin' to bury that boy's bones tomorrow. That'll rest their spirits."

"We hope so," said Brad, stuffing another fork of greens into his mouth. "Indigo, these are really good turnip greens."

"How's that pretty girl, Erin, doing? You behaving with her?"

"Oh! Yes ma'am," he replied, taking in his fourth fork of greens. "She's doing fine. I asked her to marry me today."

"I know'd that was coming," she said. "I could see it. The time was right. You see, when the time's right, anything can happen. I know'd y'all was goin' to marry a long time ago." Brad no longer wondered about Indigo's mysterious rhetoric, he was close to believing anything she said, regardless of how bizarre it sounded.

When they finished eating the bowls of greens, Indigo took Brad's bowl into the kitchen. "You sit there while I put these bowls in the sink. I want to get something for you to take to that girl." A minute later she came back into the room and went over to a book shelf and picked up a little package wrapped in newspaper and tied with cotton string. "I fixed this up the other day 'cause I know'd you was coming by to see me." She walked over and handed it to him.

"What is it?" he said, looking at the two-by-two inch package.

"None of your business..." she said. "It ain't for you, it's for that girl. Now don't you go opening it up or you will fall dead in your tracks." She knew if she scared him he would be less likely to open the package.

He slipped the package into his coat pocket. "I'll give it to her tonight. What about showing me that cigar box with the pictures in it? You said you would show it to me."

"I can't do that right now," she replied, sitting down in her chair.

"Why?"

"Because I gots to dig it up. It's buried out yonder by my banana trees and I ain't digging it up right now."

"You said there were two pictures in the box. Can you tell me if they are Bill and Ethel?," he asked, getting up, ready to leave.

"That be them," answered Indigo. "I've know'd what those two looked like for a long time."

Brad was surprised that she finally admitted she had photographs of Bill and Ethel. "Then the time is right for me to see them," he said, using Indigo's own words.

"You is right, boy," she replied, getting up to walk him to the front door. *"The time is right.* After all you did to fix things for them, the time is right. I'll bring them two pictures to the cemetery tomorrow and you can have them, but I'm keeping the cigar box."

"Thanks, Indigo. You've been a good friend." He gave her a hug as she patted his back like he was a son. "Do you want me and Erin to pick you up tomorrow?"

"Don't you worry about ol' Indigo," she answered with a mysterious look in her eye. "I'll be there, I have my ways." He knew not to question her ways. He said goodbye and walked to his car as she watched from the porch.

———

After leaving Indigo's house, Brad went back to the apartment and took a shower. It was five-thirty and Erin had already left for work. He put on a clean shirt and fed the cat and headed out the door for Ashley's. It was six o'clock by the time he walked through the door of the tavern. The bar crowd was light, mostly the regulars, he walked around to his usual stool to find Diana and Roberta sitting together. As expected, Roberta was looking like a real lady. "Hi Sweet Cakes, what's new?" said Roberta, as Brad took a seat beside him.

"Hi, Roberta, you're looking good tonight," he said. "But don't get any ideas, I'm spoken for."

"You're always spoiling my fun," said Roberta. "Let me buy you a drink. Roger, bring Brad a beer!"

Diana looked around Roberta from her stool, and said to Brad, "Did you see Indigo? Is she going to the funeral?"

"Yeah, she'll be there, I don't know how, she just said she had her ways," he replied, as Roger slid a draft beer in front of him. "I told her we would pick her up if she needed a ride."

"She'll be there…" said Roberta. "Nobody knows how she gets around but she does. I even saw her over at the beach one time."

It was a lazy night with more talking than drinking. Erin took a few minutes to come over and chat, "How's Indigo?"

"She's okay, she fed me a bowl of turnip greens," replied Brad, reaching to get handful of peanuts from a bowl on the bar.

"Turnip greens?"

"Yeah, they were good too. Oh, and that cigar box, there are two photographs in it, one of Bill and one of Ethel, and she is going to give them to us tomorrow."

"Awesome, cool, then I can see what Ethel looks like," said Erin.

"And I'll have two photographs to use in my story," he added.

Erin turned to Diana who was just finishing a martini, "What's the word on the flowers?"

Diana was nibbling an olive stuck on the end of a toothpick from her martini. "It's all set, I talked to my cousin and she's sending three standup arrangements and two floral sprays. It was some arrangements leftover from a recent funeral that was canceled."

Brad leaned around Roberta, "Somebody canceled a funeral? What happened, did the corpse come back to life?"

Diana laughed, "It's a long story, anyway…we'll have plenty of flowers at no charge."

"Oh, Erin, I almost forgot," said Brad, reaching into his coat pocket. "Indigo told me to give this to you." He handed her the little package wrapped in newspaper.

"What is it?"

"I don't know. She told me not to open it or I would die."

"Oh, she just told you that, Indigo wouldn't hurt a fly," she said, while everyone anxiously watched her open the package. Inside the package was a small white box. Erin removed the lid, and exclaimed, "Oh my God, Brad look!" It was the ruby ring. "She shouldn't have, I can't take her ring."

"Erin, it's beautiful," said Diana. "Hey, she wants you to have it."

"Here, let me put it on your finger," said Brad, taking the ring. "After all, I didn't have a ring to give you. It can be your engagement ring and it's your birthstone too. Remember what you said about a ruby symbolizing everlasting love?" He slipped it on her finger and kissed her cheek.

She held her hand out admiring the ring. "It fits perfectly. Gosh, I feel totally strange wearing Ethel's ring."

"I think both Ethel and Indigo really want you to wear it," said Brad. "Indigo claimed she knew we would get married. Of course, she might have just pretended she knew about us getting married."

"Oh, she knew," said Roberta, "I told you she was psychic."

"Well this calls for a toast to Brad and Erin," announced Diana. "Roger, bring me another martini...put an onion in it this time." Roger served up drinks to everyone, including himself. Diana, slightly tipsy, climbed off her stool and held her glass high. "Here's to Brad and Erin...and to Bill and Ethel, a ruby ring, and to everlasting love."

CHAPTER 19

It was a beautiful sunny afternoon on Merritt Island. Near the entrance to Crooked Mile Road Cemetery, a gentle breeze whispered through the outstretched limbs of century old oaks beneath which were parked several cars. Halfway down the road running through the center of the cemetery, a dozen local friends had gathered near a cluster of old tombstones at the final resting place of Bill Kelly. The freshly exposed soil capping his grave was covered by colorful sprays of flowers and ferns and two large wreaths. Bill and Ethel were now side-by-side, finally together in everlasting peace. You could almost feel their presence during the brief, but solemn service conducted by Dr. Benjamin Warren, a reverend of the Universalist church.

Brad held Erin's hand as she looked down at the colorful flowers covering the grave. The last time she was at this spot, she had experienced a dizziness and unexplained visions, but now she felt nothing but peace for Ethel and Bill. She felt no sadness at all because it was a blissful reunion of two lovers who had been separated far too long. Her eyes moistened with happiness, sending a single tear down her cheek. Diana handed her a Kleenex. Around the grave was a circle of friends who had taken a moment out of their day to pay their respects to Bill Kelly. Erin nudged Brad and pointed out a guy in an orange jump suit. Brad turned to look. It was Owen, the skeptical ghost hunter from the spook hunters group he had met at Ashley's one night. Next to Owen was Adele from the Harvest Moon café. It looked like everyone had showed up. Roger the bar manager, had taken time off to attend and was decked-out in an outdated pin-stripe suit that he had not worn since he married his first wife twenty years ago. Even Herbert Hoover was there with his squirrel, Sweet Baby, perched on his shoulder, and standing next to him was Roberta, the only one attired in a black funeral dress and veil. Mrs. Davis from the records depository was there too. She had followed the case ever since Brad arrived in town, and next to her was Detective Jessie Sims who had helped bring closure to the mystery. Christine had managed to drag her husband Vincent to the funeral, and standing next to them was Indigo Blue, clad in a dress that matched her name. It was a mystery how Indigo got there, after all, the only wheels she had were on her grocery carts. Sometimes Indigo seemed to materialize out of nowhere, of course, if anyone dared pry into her mysterious ways she would just tell them,, "some things are best left alone."

The service took no more than fifteen minutes. One by one, the small group began walking back to their cars, some stopping to look at a tombstone. Roger had family members buried in the cemetery and on his way to his car, he stopped to show Roberta the burial plot of his uncle. Detective Sims paused to say a few words to Brad before she left. Indigo waited patiently until most of the crowd had left the grave site...then she walked up to Brad and Erin. "I gots something for you two," she said, handing a small paper bag to Erin.

Erin gave her a hug. "What is it?" she asked, taking the bag.

"Open it...it's two Kodak pictures," said Indigo, looking down at the two graves, "...of that girl and boy that's buried right there."

"The old photographs from the cigar box...?" asked Brad, stepping over as Erin looked in the bag.

"Ain't that what you been wanting?" answered Indigo. "I told you when the time was right you'd know. I been knowing all along, 'course I couldn't tell y'all 'cause y'all couldn't handle it. Now that y'all done put that boy's bones to rest...it's time for you to have these pictures. It be the only way you goin' to understand."

Erin pulled the two photographs out of the bag. Her green eyes grew large as she stared at them. "OH, *MY GOD!!*...BRAD!!" she exclaimed, in an almost state of shock. Her mouth gapped open. She could not speak as she handed the two pictures to him. He quickly looked at the two photos and immediately saw what she had seen.

"Erin, there's no way...!!" He could not believe his eyes. The photographs of Bill and Ethel were the identical images of Brad and Erin. "It's a hoax! I don't believe this, Erin...*they look just like us*...that's simply *not possible!!*"

"Yeah, how could they look like us?" she said, glancing around. "Indigo, how can they...Indigo? Where did she go...?" Indigo Blue was nowhere to be seen.

"She...she was just standing here a minute ago..." said Brad, looking across the cemetery to where the cars were parked. "She *couldn't* have left that fast." His eyes glanced back and forth, but there was no one in sight. "And where did everyone else go?"

Erin's eyes searched across the rows of tombstones, now even the cars were gone. "Everybody was sure in a hurry to leave, I don't even see Diana, she left without saying goodbye. Maybe Indigo got a ride with somebody."

"There's no way," he replied, mystified. "She didn't have time to make it to where the cars were parked. What'd she do...*vanish?*"

"I think it's time we were going too," Erin said, with an intense feeling that something out of the ordinary was going on. The late afternoon sun was casting long shadows over the graves as a strange wind blew through the leaves of the trees.

"Yeah, it's getting late," he replied, putting his arm around her waist and pulling her in close. Taking one last look at the flowers covering Bill's grave; they turned and slowly walked away to the road running through the center of the cemetery. After a short distance they paused and looked back once more, but this time there were no graves to be seen. There were no tombstones anywhere. They stood back-to-back, their eyes moving left and right, then turned and faced each other. A bewildered expression covered Brad's face, "Now what? What *the hell* is going on? Explain to me what has happened to all the gravestones!!" Not one tombstone could be seen.

What Brad and Erin did not understand was that some things exist in a mysterious zone where space and time become twisted beyond comprehension of worldly minds. They now found themselves walking not through a cemetery, but on a dirt path through a city park shaded by tall, live oaks. In the center was a playground where three little girls were playing hop-scotch while boys in knickers quarreled over a game of marbles. A short distance away, a lone, little black girl in a blue dress was bouncing a ball as her mother watched cautiously from a bench.

Erin turned to Brad and said, "Bill, look over there at that cute little girl with the ball." By some quirk in the dimensions of time the present was rapidly blending with the past.

Bill turned just in time to see the ball come bouncing toward Ethel. He picked it up and tossed it back to the little girl.

Her mother politely waved, "Thank you sir..."

Ethel waved back. "This reminds me of something. Sort of like a déjà vu feeling...like I've done this before...maybe it's like a premonition of some kind. I could swear I know that little girl. Have you ever had a feeling like you've done something before?"

"There's no such thing," laughed Bill, his arm tightened around her waist. "It's just that it seems like you've done it before. It's only your mind playing tricks." He was not one to believe in paranormal things like premonitions and ghosts.

As they proceeded up the winding path toward the street, they saw Sheriff Jacobs walking toward them pulled along by his big old dog, Bubba. He was chewing a cigar stub and dressed in khaki with his slouch hat slanted over one eye. A look of concern covered his face. He took the cigar from his mouth and spit. "Bill, we gotta to talk, son." He sounded serious. He tipped the brim of his hat at Ethel. "Afternoon, ma'am." She nodded back with a shy smile.

"Talk about what?" Bill asked, reaching down to rub old Bubba's neck and ears. Bubba was a friendly dog with an equally friendly tongue that was always dripping with drool. If you scratched his side he would sit down and fiddle with his hind leg.

"You've been fingered..." said the sheriff, striking a match to re-light his cigar stub, one end of which was chewed into a brown slimy mess. Puffs of blue smoke issued from his mouth. "One of Agent Stiles' tipsters got wind of a plan to rub you out. Baxter has been tipped off about the Scarlet Biddy operation. Stiles is pulling his agents off so they can cool their heels for awhile. We've got a rat."

Bill stopped petting Bubba and looked up, "Frank Turner...?"

"Yep, that would be my bet," said the sheriff, glancing warily around the park in case someone was watching them. Several yards away he saw the black lady and little girl with the ball sitting on the bench. He tipped his hat at them and continued talking. "I think

Turner either went through my desk and found something or he put a tail on me…whatever…they've got it out for you."

"So, you're thinking I should lay low for awhile," said Bill, looking at Ethel. Her green eyes reflected a nervous stare.

"I'm saying you're in a jam and need to blow town. Sonny Baxter's goons are looking for you." The sheriff turned to Ethel. "I have a fear she might be in danger too. I'd rather see both of y'all get out of the county for awhile…at least until the Feds can bust these sons of bitches…" He caught himself and apologized, "Excuse my language, ma'am…sometimes I do get carried away…especially when I'm a bit skittish."

"That's alright," she said, glancing nervously at Bill. "We can go to Wauchula to my sister's place."

"It'd be best," agreed the sheriff, "until this mess simmers down."

"Who tipped Stiles off about this?" asked Bill, curiously wondering how Baxter had found out about him working for the Feds.

Sheriff Jacobs gestured with a nod of his head, "See that colored woman sitting over yonder on that bench? She works for Stiles, you got her to thank for exposing this, otherwise you'd end up with a slug in you, which could still happen if you don't disappear for awhile."

Bill gave a discreet glance at the woman. "Who is she?"

"Georgia Blue…Judge Baxter's housekeeper," said the sheriff. "She's been the Fed's inside source since the start of Scarlet Biddy. That's why she's out here in the park…I needed to talk with her too."

"Why would she want to risk her neck tipping the Feds on Baxter?" asked Bill. "Hellfire…don't she realize what he'd do if he found out? I mean she's colored…Sonny's Klan buddies wouldn't think twice about bumping her off."

"I reckon she does," said the sheriff. "I think she's carrying a grudge. Her old man drowned about a year ago…his body washed up at the inlet. I heard she blames Sonny Baxter."

"You mean he *drowned* her husband?"

"Well, let's just say there was a Baxter connection." The sheriff adjusted his wide brim hat. "Evidently her old man was a deckhand on Billy Marshall's boat smuggling illegal hooch from Bimini for Baxter's distributors. Of course, he didn't know what was going on at first, but when he figured out he was working for big time bootleggers...he tried to quit. Well, a day or two later he washes ashore...*deader than a door nail*...not far from where Marshall's boat was docked. It was Marshall who allegedly found his body."

"Sounds like they were worried about him knowing too much," remarked Bill, sprinkling Prince Albert tobacco into a cigarette paper. He rolled the paper into a cigarette, sealed it with a swipe of his tongue and lit it. He took a drag and exhaled, "I reckon they intended to keep him quiet."

"Of course you couldn't prove it one way or the other," said the sheriff. "Worse than that, it's going to happen to you too, if you don't stop jawing and get a move on."

Bill took out his pocket watch and checked the time. Ethel had given him the watch for his last birthday. "Okay, it's near 'bout five o'clock. I need to get Ethel to work. She needs to pick up her pay. We'll leave tonight right after she gets off work."

The sheriff knew she worked at Jack's and felt uneasy about them waiting so late to leave town. "Y'all watch your backs 'cause Sonny's thugs hang around that juke joint...every last one of them pack heat. I'm going to send Newt out there...just to keep an eye on things until y'all leave."

"We'll be okay," said Bill, flicking ashes off his cigarette.

"You carrying a gun?" asked the sheriff.

"My thirty-two," he said, pulling up his pants leg exposing a snub-nosed pistol in a holster strapped to his leg. He dropped his cigarette butt on the ground and stepped on it with his shoe.

"You got any dough?" asked the sheriff.

"Not much..."

The sheriff reached in his pocket and handed him a ten dollar bill. "Here, take this sawbuck. I'll send you more later...right now y'all get on out of here." He gave Bill a stiff pat on the shoulder and walked off in the direction of the black woman sitting on the bench. Bill took Ethel by the arm and made haste for his car that was parked on the street next to the sheriff's truck.

He opened the door to his 1932 Ford coupe so Ethel could get in, then went around and climbed in behind the steering wheel. He pressed the starter with his foot until the motor started. Ethel rolled down the window, and said, "Take me by Mrs. Kimmel's...I'll pack my things, then you can take me to work. I don't want to leave my suitcase in your car so I'll ask her to keep it until we can pick it up after I get off tonight." She pulled a half empty pack of Lucky Strikes from her purse and lit one.

"Bring your suitcase with you," he said, rounding a corner on the winding unpaved road running next to the river toward Rockledge. It had not been grated since the last rain and was like a washboard. The Ford coupe vibrated as the tires rolled over the rippled surface. "Damn road's going to bust the springs out from under this jalopy..." he complained, trying to ride the edge of the road to miss the bumps.

"I'm packing everything I own in that suitcase," she said, her voice shaking as the car as the car hit every bump. "Th-th-there's t-t-too many thieves hanging around J-Ja-Jack's place. I'd just feel better if we picked it up later on our way." Two miles later, the road began smoothing out.

Bill pulled up in front of the Kimmel boarding house and parked. He got out and walked up to the porch with Ethel and sat down in a rocker while she went inside to pack. When she came back out, Mrs. Kimmel stepped out on the porch drying her hands on a towel. She looked at Bill, and said, "Hello." Then turning to Ethel, said, "Your suitcase will be right here in the front room. If I ain't up when you come back tonight, just reach inside the door and get it. Y'all be careful driving to Wauchula...that's a long dark road at night. There ain't nothing between here and there except swamps, if you breakdown on that road it'll take hours before somebody will come along to help."

"Don't worry we'll be careful," replied Ethel, giving her elderly landlady an affectionate hug. Mrs. Kimmel stood in the door watching as they walked out to the curb and got into Bill's car. Ethel had not told her the real reason for suddenly leaving town. It was better that way.

CHAPTER 20

It was a warm night and the dirt parking lot in front of Jack's Tavern was dusty and dark except for a street light attached to a telephone pole. Bill turned in off the highway and slowly passed the rear of five or six parked cars carefully checking out each one.

"Do you know any of these cars? Do you see Baxter's car?" Ethel asked, with a look of worry in her eyes. "Maybe this wasn't such a good idea. I can make it without my pay...we should have gone ahead to Wauchula." She was jittery and having second thoughts about going to work, but she really needed to at least pick up her pay.

"Aw, there ain't no need to worry, I don't think we're goin' to have any trouble, none of these heaps belong to any of Baxter's people," replied Bill, steering his Ford coupe into a spot beneath the street light near the front door. The sweet smell of jasmine drifted through the night from a vine growing on a nearby telephone pole. He shut off the engine and glanced up at several moths flittering around the street light. Then he noticed a car half hidden in the shadows at the south end of the tavern. "Stay put..." he said, trying to conceal his nervousness from Ethel. "That may be Newt in that car. Let me make sure before you get out." He put on his hat, took a deep breath, and opened his door. He could see the silhouette of a man sitting behind the wheel and the faint glow of a cigarette. Bill pulled up the leg of his pants to check the loaded snub-nosed pistol strapped to his calf. He hoped he would not need it.

Shifting her eyes toward the car sitting in the shadows, Ethel whispered loudly, "Bill, be careful..." An intense expression of worry covered her face as she watched him cautiously approach the driver's side of the car. She knew that he could be gunned down if it was one of Baxter's people. She crossed her fingers hoping it would not be one of Baxter's thugs. She closed her eyes...fearful of what could happen. Then she heard Bill call to the man in the car.

"Hey, Newt! Is that you...?" He was hoping it was Newton Simmons, the sheriff's youngest and most trustworthy deputy and the only deputy who knew about the sheriff's involvement with Federal agents. Sheriff Jacobs could not risk exposing the operation to the other deputies because he knew his chief deputy, Frank Turner, was funneling inside information to Judge Baxter.

"Yeah, it's me," said Newt, flipping his lit cigarette out of the window. "I'm supposed to sit here and keep an eye on things." He was wearing his deputy uniform but wasn't in one of the sheriff's marked cars.

Bill slapped at a mosquito and then leaned his right hand against the roof of the car, "Is this your jalopy?"

"Yeah, it's mine. I really wanted me a roadster but I couldn't pass up the deal on this one...it used to be old man Slater's car. When he died Mrs. Slater put it up for sale...I got it for three-fifty."

Bill stood back, folded his arms and looked the four door sedan over. "Not bad for three-fifty. So what are you doing in your own heap instead of one of the sheriff's cars?"

Newt swatted at a mosquito buzzing around inside the car. "Sheriff Jacobs said it was best if I didn't sit out here in one of the marked cars. Besides I get to fill up my tank at the county pump."

"Well, I don't think we're going to have any trouble tonight," said Bill, glancing around at the dimly lit parking lot. "None of those cars belong to Baxter. You ain't seen nobody have you?"

"Nope, I ain't seen hide nor hair of anybody since I got here about an hour ago, but the sheriff told me to stay until y'all leave. He's the boss and I gotta do whatever he tells me."

"Okay, but you're going to have a long wait, 'cause Ethel don't get off work until midnight. I'm going inside and tip a few beers...you want me to bring you a cold one out?"

"I'd get in trouble...I'm on duty...but you can bring me a bottle of R.C. and a pickled egg..." Newt answered, watching the headlights of a car going by on the highway. "...Make that two pickled eggs, I ain't had no supper yet and my belly's starting to growl."

"Okay. Let me get my girl inside so she can start work then I'll be back out in a bit." Bill started to walk away, then turned back and said, "Ah, Newt, so if you see Baxter's boys, what are you supposed to do? You're by yourself and there could be a carload of them."

"Beats me," he shrugged, striking a match to light another cigarette. His face reflected the glow of the match until he shook it out. "I guess if they show up I'll just go inside and let you know...then I'll call the sheriff."

"Well...keep an eye out," said Bill, as he turned and walked back over to his car. Several cars went by on the highway but none turned into the parking lot. He escorted Ethel into the tavern. Even though everything seemed safe, he knew how ruthless Baxter's gangsters could be and he wasn't going to take any chances.

Inside the tavern, a cloud of cigarette smoke hung low over the bar and the whole place smelled like stale beer. The unstable wood flooring was littered with cigarette butts and had several dark spots where people had spilled their drinks. A dozen working men dressed in coveralls, were at the bar trying to out-talk each other over bottles of beer. Ethel went behind the bar and put on an apron as Bill climbed on a stool next to an inebriated fellow who had emptied eight bottles. He glared at Bill. "Waz zure name?" he asked, his words were slurred and raspy. "My name ish Frog...and zure on my schtool and by gawd...I'm goin' to kick your ash!"

"Yeah? You ain't kicking nothing...you're soused to the gills," responded Bill, trying to ignore him. The drunk belched loudly then laid his head on the wet bar and appeared to go to sleep. Ethel came over and slid a cold beer in front of Bill and glanced at the drunk. "Hmmm, looks like Frog is smashed again."

Bill propped his elbows on the bar, tipped his bottle and took a short swig. He wiped his mouth on his shirt sleeve, "You know him?"

"Frog...yeah, he's a regular that's in here almost every night. He comes in drunk then drinks four or five beers...what he don't spill...then wallers all over the counter until he sobers up."

"A real smashed frog," chuckled Bill, taking out his pocket watch to check the time. "Give me an R.C. and a couple of those pickled eggs. I told Newt I'd bring him out something to eat." Ethel went over to the ice box and pulled out a bottle of R.C. and wiped it off on her apron. Then with a long fork, speared two pickled eggs in a big jar on the counter and wrapped them in a napkin. She sat the R.C. and eggs in front of Bill. "You don't look too worried," she said. "What if them thugs come in here looking for you?"

Bill stood up from his stool and picked up the R.C. and eggs. "They ain't going to try anything inside, it's what they might do outside that I'm concerned about…just the same, as soon as you get off work we're leaving here." She began removing the empty bottles from the counter and watched as he started for the front door.

Outside the same cars were parked under the street light. Bill's eyes cautiously searched the shadows but only saw Newt's car. He walked over and handed the R.C. and eggs to Newt. "Any sign of Baxter's boys yet?"

"Yep," he said, turning up the R.C. bottle and taking a long swallow. He wiped his chin and burped. "Sonny Baxter drove through here just before you came out. It looked like there was two, maybe three, inside the car. I'm purty sure they spotted your roadster 'cause they stopped right behind it and looked at it… then they drove off real slow and headed south."

Bill leaned against the car. "Then they know I'm here, which means they'll be back." He had hardly finished his words when a pair of headlights pulled in at the far end of the parking lot. Instinctively, he crouched down, quickly making his way around the back of Newt's sedan to the other side. He climbed in the backseat and hunkered down in the darkness. "Can you tell who it is?" he asked, nervously trying to get the pistol out of his leg holster. Newt was keeping a low profile behind the wheel but could see the car as it drove slowly through the parking lot.

"It looks like them…" cautioned Newt, hoping they would not stop to check his car. "I think they'll probably keep cruising through here until they catch you outside."

With his right hand gripping his pistol, Bill peered warily over the back of the seat. "Yeah…no doubt about it, that's Sonny Baxter's Buick." They kept low until the car drove through and pulled onto the highway and then headed south. Bill straightened up in the backseat rubbing his forehead. "That was a little too close. They'll be back. I don't feel good about this…it ain't safe here. Me and you ain't no match for them. I'm going inside and get Ethel. We've gotta get out of here while gettin's good." He opened the door and got out of the car. He put his foot on the running board, pulled up his pants leg and slipped his pistol into the leg holster. "Hang tight until I get Ethel. Crank up your car and park it right in front of the door. If something happens have the motor running in case we have to make a fast run." He then hurried inside to get Ethel. She was at the opposite end of the bar waiting on a bar patron. He wiggled his finger for her to come over. She could sense something was wrong. "Listen, we have to go now! Baxter has been driving in and out of the parking lot and he knows we're here."

"Is he by himself?" she asked, sounding worried.

"He's got a carload...two or three others. It's not safe here."

She started untying her apron. "Okay, give me a minute. Let me square it away with Jack and see if he'll give me my pay," she said, throwing her apron under the counter. "Wait over there by the door."

Bill went over and stood by the door which had a small square window through which he could see Newt's car idling in front of the tavern. After a minute or two Ethel came up behind him. "I'm ready, let's get out of here." They pushed the door open and walked out into the night. There was no sign of Baxter. Bill waved at Newt, and headed directly for his car. Ethel got in as Bill climbed behind the wheel and started the motor. He quickly shifted into reverse and backed out. Newt waited for them to pull out of the parking lot just in case Baxter got in behind them.

"Did you get your pay?" Bill asked, shifting from first to second gear as he pulled onto the highway.

"Ah, yes...thirty dollars," answered Ethel, at this point she had other things on her mind. "What if they go back to the parking lot and not see your car?"

Bill jammed the floor shift into third gear and let out on the clutch. "When they don't see my car they'll come looking for us...mark my words on that...I know this bunch of thugs. With luck we'll make it to Mrs. Kimmel's so you can get your belongings." For the first time he was openly showing his fear. He concentrated on the dark highway, glancing occasionally in the rear view mirror knowing he would be a dead man if Baxter ever caught him. In his mind he hated to think what would happen to Ethel if she was caught with him. His grip tightened on the steering wheel as he pressed the gas pedal to the floor sending the speedometer to almost fifty miles per hour. "One of these days they'll make cars that will do a hundred...I sure wish I had one right now!" He tried to lighten the tension. Keeping his eyes on the road, he asked, "You still like the ring?" He had given her a ring when he asked her to marry him. He only hoped they would live long enough to enjoy a wedding.

"I love it, and it's your birthstone...that's very special," she said, holding her hand up to look at the ring. The stone reflected the headlights of a car behind them. She quickly turned around and looked out the back window. "Bill...there's a car behind us...I think it's *following* us."

He looked in the rear view mirror. "It could be Newt...just keep an eye on it," he said, slowing down to make a left on a side street that would take them to the boarding house.

Ethel kept an eye on the car behind them. "Bill, that car turned...it's still *following* us."

"Then it has to be Newt," he said, as they neared the driveway to the boarding house. He wheeled into the driveway and shut off his headlamps and motor, then cranked down his window to look for the car. He could see it about a half block down the street. It had pulled over to the curb and shut off its headlights. "I don't think that's Newt. If it was he would have stopped behind us. Don't get out yet...sit tight for a second." The street was dark except for the faint glow of a corner street light. Every shadow seemed to move. Bill's eyes strained trying to see through the darkness.

"Could it be Baxter?" Ethel's voice reflected her apprehension. All of a sudden, as she shifted around to look out the rear window, the passenger side door jerked open and a man's arm grabbed her around the throat. She felt the cold steel of a knife blade under her chin. She threw her head back trying to keep her neck from feeling the blade.

"Easy, sister...*don't wiggle,*" growled a rough voice, *"Move and I'll cut your goddamn head off!"* Ethel sat still, frozen with fright.

Bill immediately recognized Frank Turner's voice and started to lunge for his arm when someone reached through the driver's window and struck him in the back of the head with a lead-filled sock. He slumped over against the steering wheel as blood began oozing from the back of his head. The man who had hit him was Billy Marshall. "You've *killed* him!" cried Ethel, as Turner held the knife firmly against her throat. "Get your mitts off me..." she struggled, reaching out for Bill's limp body. She could see a crimson trail of blood trickling down the side of his face.

"Shut your yap!!" shouted Turner, back-handing her across the face. It hurt and left her momentarily stunned. Her eyes welled with tears and she began to cry. She tried to reach out for Bill but Turner jerked her back and stuffed a rag into her mouth. He pulled her out of the coupe and dragged her to the end of the driveway where a black, four-door sedan was idling with its headlights off. The car's exhaust fumes permeated the humid night air.

Ethel recognized the car. It was the same car that had been parked down the street and Sonny Baxter was behind the wheel. He rolled down his window and flipped out a cigar butt. "My, my, she's a fiesty bearcat..." he said, with a sinister grin. "Throw her in the backseat." Turner opened the rear door, forcing her inside, then climbed in, keeping his arm bent around her neck. Baxter shifted the car into low and drove off down the street.

Meanwhile...after tying Bill's feet and hands with a rope, Marshall had shoved Bill's limp body into the passenger side of the coupe. Marshall slid into the driver's side and was about to start the motor when somebody turned on the porch light of the boarding house. Mrs. Kimmel heard the commotion and came out on the porch to see what was going on. Marshall slammed the floor shift into reverse and quickly backed out of the driveway. He wheeled around in a cloud of exhaust, then, with a grinding noise, shifted to first and straightened the car out. He floored the gas pedal and sped off down the street toward the river. He could see Baxter's tail lights a few blocks ahead of him.

The bumps on the rough road caused Bill to regain consciousness. He sat up moaning...trying to figure out what was happening. He tugged at the ropes binding his wrists. "What'd you saps do with Ethel?" he asked, his vision still blurred. "Where you taking me?"

Marshall kept his hands on the wheel and stared straight ahead. "Your girlfriend is okay, she's up ahead in Sonny's Buick...I'm taking you for a joy ride in your own car." He let out a cackling laugh like a mad man. "The only damn thing you need to know is that Sonny Baxter don't cotton well to rats who snitch on him. *Now shut your face!"*

"Yeah...real tough guys, huh," mocked Bill, the back of his head still throbbed with pain. "I imagine by now the sheriff knows about your scheme 'cause Newt Simmons saw you tough guys cruising through Jack's tonight." He could feel his pistol still in the holster strapped to his leg but at the moment his hands were bound tight and it wasn't doing him much good.

"*Newt...*" laughed Marshall, steering around a hole in the road, "Hellfire, that dumb palooka is already home in bed. Ain't nobody gonna help you now. If you know what's good for you, you'll shut your pie hole and enjoy the ride...*unless* you want me to hog tie you." Marshall had the gas pedal to the floor and was closing in fast in the dust-trail behind Sonny Baxter's Buick. He rolled down the window and spit into the night air then laughed, "Yessireee! We're taking you and your girlfriend to a big time party tonight...all the way out yonder to the Baxter farm...that's a mighty far piece from nowhere." He glanced over at Bill propped against the passenger door and grinned, "Yes sir, a *mighty* long way from nowhere! Of course, I don't think y'all will have to worry about walking back."

———

The Baxter farm sat in a remote part of west Brevard County yet to be reached by electricity. It was a large spread bordered by the St. Johns River to the west and a good fifteen miles from the next nearest house. It was a perfect place to hide a crime, whether it was illegal whiskey or perhaps, even murder. No one would ever risk trespassing on the property of the county judge. The old two story house where Sonny Baxter was raised was still standing and now used as a hunting lodge, which in reality was an innocent sounding name for the headquarters for Baxter's illegal whiskey ring. Sonny and his father, Judge J.C. Baxter, had made a small fortune by distributing illegal, untaxed whiskey to speakeasies during Prohibition. In recent years they had extended their criminal enterprise beyond bathtub gin and moonshine to smuggling whiskey from the Bahamas Islands. This had drawn the attention of the U.S. Treasury Department and eventually led to Sheriff Jacobs and Bill Kelly working with federal agents in the clandestine *Scarlet Biddy* operation. As a federal informant posing as an illegal whiskey distributor, Bill Kelly had worked his way into the heart of the Baxter crime ring and was the main leak to the Feds. Baxter was feeling the heat and desperately needed to plug this leak or he would soon be facing a long stretch in the penitentiary.

Sonny Baxter pulled his black Buick up next to the old house and cut the headlights off. Crickets were chirping, and the entire place was dark except for the glow of Baxter's cigar. He got out of the car, adjusted his eyes to the darkness, and then glanced at Frank Turner holding Ethel in the backseat. "Keep the dame inside the car, Frank…if she makes a sound, punch her face." The dust had hardly settled in the night air when Billy Marshall roared up in Bill Kelly's coupe. He parked in front of a small hay barn between the two-story house and a little clapboard shack where Georgia Blue lived with her little girl. Georgia usually kept house for Judge and Mrs. Baxter in town, but on special occasions, like during hunting season, would stay in the little shack when she was needed to do the cooking. Both Judge Baxter and his son were totally unaware that Georgia Blue had been passing inside information to the Feds.

Sonny Baxter went over to the coupe as Marshall switched off the motor. "How's our stool pigeon Kelly doing?"

"I think he's got a sore head," Marshall replied, lighting a cigarette, "but he's still alive and he's got a smart mouth."

"No problem, we can fix that smart mouth," grinned Baxter, taking the cigar from his mouth and thumping off the ashes. He then turned toward his Buick, "Frank, bring the dame over here and y'all take her and her boyfriend down yonder behind the barn to the clay pit. It's blacker than a skillet out here…I'm going to find some kerosene so we can build a fire and see what we're doing." Turner and Marshall forced Bill and Ethel down a dark path to the clay pit while Baxter walked over to the little shack and knocked on the door. Through the window pane he saw someone light an oil lamp. The door creaked opened and Georgia Blue, holding an oil lamp, stuck her head out, "Mr. Sonny, I *thought* that was you I heard out there...what you be needing at this hour?" Her dark eyes reflected like glass marbles in the flickering light of the oil lamp.

He leaned his hand against the door frame, "Georgia, fill me a mason jar full of kerosene, we want to build us a bonfire down yonder in the clay pit." Without saying anything, she just turned and walked back toward her kitchen. He waited on the porch and could see the face of her little girl peering curiously through a pane of glass in the front window. After a minute or two, Georgia returned to the door with a greasy, quart jar of kerosene. "Don't you boys be catching anything on fire down there," she cautioned, handing it to him. Then she shut the door and latched it from the inside. Her little girl was still watching through the window as Baxter walked around the corner of the shack and past the little hay barn.

Baxter walked down a narrow path to the clay pit with the jar of kerosene, where Frank Turner had been stacking wood to build a fire. Marshall was close by keeping a gun on Bill and Ethel.

"Go ahead, untie them two," ordered Baxter, pouring half the jar of the kerosene on the wood. He sat the half-filled jar on the red clay soil, and then struck a match to the wood pile. He stood back and waited as a blazing fire soon formed a circle of light in the clay pit. "Now we can see," said Baxter, walking over to Bill Kelly. Baxter stood with arms folded and looked down at him. "You made a serious mistake, boy. One thing my daddy don't like is a *damn* rat. I don't like rats either." Bill was sitting on the ground rubbing the raw marks on his wrists caused by the rope. He could smell the aroma of kerosene and guavas. Behind him were several guava trees and the ground was scattered with fruit, some half eaten by wild hogs.

The fire was now in a full crackling blaze sending glowing sparks mixed with blue smoke drifting upward to vanish in the darkness. Bill knew he had to sneak the pistol out of his leg holster. He could see Marshall and Turner silhouetted in the flickering light of the fire. He knew they both had guns.

Baxter picked up the half full jar of kerosene and poured it over Ethel's head. "Stand up!" he ordered, "...or *I'll light you up* like a Roman candle!" Gripping her arm he yanked her up from the ground. Her hair and blouse were soaked with kerosene. She was too scared to cry and her eyes were burning from the kerosene. "You done got yourself in a real fix and you can blame your boyfriend over there...'cause if you wasn't with him tonight you wouldn't be here. But if you behave yourself, we might even let you help us kill him...at least you'll get to see him die..." He grabbed a handful of her hair and jerked her head back, and in a tight lipped, tough guy tone, said, "But we've got ourselves a *real* problem 'cause I can't have you squealing to the law..." At that instant, a shot rang out hitting Baxter in the left side of his butt. As he fell to the ground he could see Bill Kelly holding a pistol. "Get that *son of a bitch*...he plugged me in the ass!!" he moaned, rolling around smashing the fallen guava fruit on the ground, like an oversized, spoiled child having a tantrum.

Ethel scrambled out of the way as Marshall and Turner aimed their guns. Bill quickly swung around...firing a single round grazing Marshall's shoulder. Turner fired back striking Bill in his upper right arm causing him to drop his pistol. Marshall, holding his shoulder, ran up and kicked the pistol away. By this time Baxter was on his feet limping toward his two accomplices. "I don't *believe* you damn fools didn't search him...if I didn't need you...I'd shoot both you nitwits right here...I'm telling my daddy about this too...you can bet on it!!" He felt the seat of his pants then looked at his hand in the fire light. "Jesus, I'm bleeding like a stuck hog." He was infuriated. Waving his pistol around at Ethel, he shouted, "Fetch me that damn broad...*we're going to do them both right now!!* "

"I'll pump lead in this one..."growled Marshall, pointing a forty-five at Bill's forehead. "I owe him for shootin' my shoulder..." He had hardly finished his words when a loud voice came booming out of the blackness. "HOLD IT RIGHT THERE BOYS!! GET YOUR HANDS IN THE AIR!" It was Deputy Newt Simmons standing in the palmetto bushes with the barrel of a thirty-eight pistol pointed at them. "Drop your pieces on the ground...*and do it now!*"

"What in hell you think you're gonna do, Newt?" responded Frank Turner, refusing to drop his pistol. "You ain't got the brains of a jackass...you planning on taking all of us?" Suddenly, from behind a large oak, Sheriff Jacobs stepped out holding a shotgun aimed at all three thugs. "How 'bout me, Frank? Wanna try to take on both us? Did you *really* expect me to send Newt out here by hisself...now if y'all don't want a face full of buckshot, then you'd better throw your guns over here and get your hands up! That *means* you too, Sonny!!"

Sonny Baxter did not intend to make it easy; he faked a move to throw his gun, then squeezed the trigger sending a slug into Sheriff Jacobs, penetrating his left thigh. As the sheriff went down, Marshall and Turner opened fire on Newt, causing him to leap for cover behind a tree. Ethel was crawling in the red clay soil trying to keep a low profile as she made her way toward Bill. Her eyes still burned with kerosene as she strained to keep a cautious watch on Sonny Baxter as he limped past the bonfire toward the sheriff. The night air was mixed with odors of smoke, guavas, and kerosene.

Marshall and Turner were crouched in a gully with guns ready, waiting for Newt to stick his head out from behind the tree. "You might as well come on out Newt!" yelled Turner, slipping bullets in the cylinder of his thirty-eight. "You lose, boy, it's all over. You hear me, boy...the sheriff is finished...you're all by yourself..."

"IT AIN'T OVER YET!!" bolted a voice from the dark woods behind them. Turner and Marshall quickly shifted around in the gully to see Special Agent Stiles walking out of the guava trees flanked by four of his agents. "Federal agents!" he yelled, keeping a double-barreled shotgun focused on them. "Drop your weapons...let's see some hands in the air." The agents quickly moved in clapping handcuffs on the three thugs while Agent Stiles hurried over to check on Sheriff Jacobs. He was still alive, but unable to stand up.

Bill had propped himself up against a stump. His arm hung limp at his side and his sleeve was soaked with blood. He was drifting into unconsciousness. Ethel struggled to his side, shaking him and calling his name, over and over, *"Bill...Bill...Bill wake up!"* He felt her nudging his side. She shook him, "...Brad wake up! Brad wake up!"

He tried to focus his sleepy eyes, trying to figure out what was going on. Erin was still shaking him, "Wake up, Brad, wake up!"

"What?" he yawned, "What is it?" He pulled the sheet up around his neck and rolled over. Music started playing on the clock radio sitting on the night stand. It had been set to come on at six. The morning sun was coming through the bedroom window casting striped shadows from the Venetian blinds against the wall.

Erin pushed him again. "You were *dreaming*...and kicking the covers like a mule. Was Big Foot chasing you?" she laughed, leaning over to kiss his cheek. "Come on, time to get up...it's a work day."

He rolled over and propped up on his elbows, then raked one hand through his messed-up hair. "God, *what a dream!!* I got shot, I think it was in the arm or somewhere, and you were there...in my dream...and there were these gangster guys shooting at me! Heck, I can't even remember what it was about now. I hate it when I can't remember my dreams." He sat up on the edge of the bed.

"Hey, that's good you can't remember them," she teased, climbing out of bed. "I can imagine how crazy they'd be. You'd be trying to publish a story about them in one of your tabloids." She slipped into a shear robe and went over to the window and pulled up the Venetian blinds letting in the Miami sun. She stood at the window of their second floor apartment, rubbing her stomach and looking out at Biscayne Bay. "Time sure does fly by...it doesn't seem like I've been living in Miami for ten whole months."

"I know..." he yawned, trying to stick his feet into a pair of corduroy slippers. "Actually, it's been eleven months...and next month we'll be married a whole year." He smiled at how beautiful she looked silhouetted against the morning light of the window. Her once slim form was now swelling with motherhood.

She looked down at the parking lot below. "There's that old black lady again...down there by the dumpster."

"You mean the old bag woman...the one with the grocery cart?"

"Yes...she's down there almost every morning. I feel sorry for her, having to dig through the trash for things. Uh, oh...she's looking up at the window...I think she saw me gawking at her. It looks like she's pointing to her wrist watch..." Erin gave a friendly wave from the window. The old lady smiled and returned the wave.

Brad stretched, and with a long smiling yawn, said, "Maybe she's trying to tell you that I'm going to be late for work if I don't get moving."

Erin lowered the blinds and looked around at him, smiling. She walked over and put her arms around his neck. "Brad, now that you're the new editor, and we have a little more income, we ought to think about getting a bigger place...before the baby comes?"

He stood up and warmly embraced her. "You know, I was thinking about that too."

"You mean about getting out of this apartment…?"

"Sure. I think it's time we got our own house where the baby can have his own room and a yard to play in."

"His? So you think it's going to be a boy?" She drew back from his embrace and smiled, "I guess when I have my sonogram done next Tuesday we'll find out if you are right."

"I'm betting it's a boy…we can name him William Bradford Kirby after his great-grandfather. Of course, if it's a girl we could still give her the same name," he joked, as he pulled Erin close against his chest.

"You're teasing…you *can't* name a daughter *William*," she laughed. "Can you *imagine* a girl named *Bill?*"

"Well, I really don't care if it's a girl or boy," he said, "it's going to be our baby…and you'll make a beautiful mother." He brought her hand up to his lips and kissed it. A ray of sunlight sparkled on the ruby setting in the ring on her finger. He lifted her chin and looked into her green eyes. Taking a deep breath, he whispered, "I will always love you, Erin."

The End

"Indigo Blue once said, '*Time is not what it seems.*' Her words were now lost somewhere in time and space in that mysterious moving zone separating the past from the future. It's what we all think of as the *present*."

--*Dr. Benjamin Warren, Ph.D.*

About the Author

Charlie Carlson is a tenth generation Floridian born and raised in Seminole County, Florida. As a youngster, he spent summer evenings slapping mosquitoes on his grandmother's front porch while listening to her ghost stories. This led to his interest in the unexplained and Florida's folklore. As a folklore historian, he has written or co-authored several books and newspaper articles about Central Florida's past. He released his first book about mysteries of the Sunshine State in 1997, titled, *Strange Florida, The Unusual and Unexplained.* [Luthers Publishing, 1997]. His readers liked it and soon dubbed him, *Florida's Master of the Weird.* The success of *Strange Florida* led to the author contributing several Florida articles to a national best selling hardback titled, *Weird U.S.* In 2005, he released his own best selling regional hardback, titled, *Weird Florida, Your Travel Guide to Florida's Local Legends and Best Kept Secrets,* [Barnes and Noble, 2005].

Charlie Carlson is a past president of the Seminole County Historical Society and still serves on boards of several historical organizations and museums. As a native, he has a fondness for the state's flora and fauna. As an out-spoken environmental activist, he takes a strong stand against what he calls the greedy destruction of Florida's environment by irresponsible developers and politicians. Charlie has been featured in nine television history documentaries and has played a folklore historian on the Sci-Fi Channel in the *Curse of the Blair Witch.* He has appeared in the *Weird U.S.* television series on the History Channel and as a special guest on more than sixty radio and TV talk shows. When he is not on the road searching for strange things or hanging out with his fans, he resides on Florida's east coast south of Daytona Beach.

CHARLIE CARLSON....
FLORIDA'S MASTER OF THE WEIRD
AUTHOR OF WEIRD FLORIDA

OTHER BOOKS BY CHARLIE CARLSON

Strange Florida, The Unexplained and Unusual.
Luthers Publishing,1997.
Florida's folklore of strange phenomena and oddities.

Weird Florida,
Your Travel Guide to Florida's Local Legends and Best Kept Secrets.
Barnes and Noble Publishers, 2005.
Explores the State's weirdness, eccentric people and places.

Tux and Tales of a Wizard.
Luthers Publishing, 2004.
The true story of magician Harry Wise. America's last ghost master.

From Fort Mellon to Baghdad,
Unx-Publishing, 2002.
A Timeline of the 2nd Dragoons from Florida to the invasion of Iraq.

The First Florida Cavalry Regiment, C.S.A.
Luthers Publishing, 1999.
A history of a Florida Confederate Civil War Regiment.

Swedish History of Seminole County, Florida.
Sanford Historical Society, 2000.
Co-authored with Christine Kinlaw-Best and Teri Patterson.

Bookertown, A Journey to the Past.
African-American Series, 2001.
A folk history of an African-American settlement.
Co-authored with Charlie Morgan.

Curious Files of Seminole County, Florida.
Unx-Publishing, 2001.
A collection of weirdness from Seminole County, Florida.

I Got My Dress-tail Wet in Soda Water Creek.
Unx-Publishing, 1998.
The story of Gladys Hawkins, a Florida Cracker girl growing up in Florida.

The History of Monroe.
Sanford Historical Society, 2000.
A history of a small Florida town.
Co-authored with Christine Kinlaw-Best